"A BEAUTIFULLY ROUNDED WORK OF ART,

as warm and wry and sensuous as the island she so clearly loves . . .
The heart of her novel lies in a funny, extraordinary other world
where men, hit by lightning, start to read everything backward and
women swallow silver dust to cure themselves of hallucinations."

—*Time*

"Wonderful . . . Astonishing . . . Dazzling . . . *The Agüero Sisters* is
indeed impressive, a book about revenge and love and hatred but
especially about courage, in all its forms: courage to antagonize a
regime, courage to be reconciled with one's own past, courage to find
the truth. . . . García is an immensely talented writer, whose work,
like that of Jessica Hagedorn, Sherman Alexie, and David Foster
Wallace, is renewing American fiction."

—*The Nation*

"Remarkable . . . Lyrical and rich in metaphor . . . García is an
enthralling storyteller. . . . *Dreaming in Cuban* announced the presence
of a new star in the American literary firmament. . . . *The Agüero
Sisters* is even better, a deeper, more profound plunge into the
mysteries of loyalty, love, and identity."

—*Newsday*

"A rich and complex novel about the entanglements of family and the
possibility of redemption that comes with knowing the story of the
past. In *The Agüero Sisters* Cristina García offers us a redemptive and
involving story that takes us across generations to the island and
back to the mainland of the heart."

—Julia Alvarez

"This book is warmly human, deeply concerned with nature (not
least our human one), and extremely well written. It deserves to be a
bestseller. I haven't been so impressed since Alejo Carpentier's *The
Lost Steps*."

—John Fowles

"Bold and very richly detailed . . . Fluid, graceful, and extremely
rewarding: a work of high seriousness and rich detail."

—*Kirkus Reviews* (starred review)

Please turn the page for more reviews. . . .

"A RICH, VELVETY WORLD ONE IS LOATH TO LEAVE."
—*Elle*

"*The Agüero Sisters* illuminates the troubled relationship between parents and children, between Cuba and the United States, and between secrets and lies, with beautifully spun elegance. Cristina García offers us a profoundly moving insight into the difficult questions of identity which haunt both individuals and nations."

—Caryl Phillips

"This is truly generous writing: García animates the worlds of naturalists and electricians and cosmeticians alike with subtley, grace, and wild unpredictability. Her two sisters are particularly enthralling—at once bigger-than-life, they speak piercingly to the Cuban moment even as they pull the reader, running, from the beginning of the book to the end."

—Gish Jen

"If her accomplished first novel, *Dreaming in Cuban,* marked García as a writer to watch, this compelling and resonant story of thwarted relationships, intense, unslaked desires, and family secrets surely confirms her promise. . . . The sinuous and absorbing plot provides recurrent bursts of surprise delivered with deceptive simplicity. . . . García gives us beautifully nuanced portraits of a riven people, separated by more than an ocean. . . . [Her] lushly vibrant prose evokes a tropical atmosphere and a seething sexuality, both steamily intensified by santero rituals and mystical phenomena."

—*Publishers Weekly* (starred and boxed review)

"Highly recommended . . . Richly imagined . . . García shapes her material beautifully, keeping the reader with her until the end."

—*Library Journal* (starred review)

"Beautifully written . . . Her prose is lush and rhythmic, so that the novel has an almost feverish air."

—*Booklist*

THE AGÜERO SISTERS

ALSO BY CRISTINA GARCÍA

Dreaming in Cuban

CRISTINA GARCÍA

The Agüero Sisters

One World
The Ballantine Publishing Group · New York

A One World Book
Published by The Ballantine Publishing Group

Library of Congress Catalog Card Number: 98-84511

ISBN: 0-345-40651-6

This edition published by arrangement with Alfred A. Knopf, Inc.

Manufactured in the United States of America

Cover photo by Geoff Spear

First Ballantine Books Edition: May 1998

10 9 8 7 6 5 4 3 2 1

For Pilar

THE AGÜERO SISTERS

PROLOGUE

❦

ZAPATA SWAMP
SEPTEMBER 8, 1948

Ignacio and Blanca Agüero took the long route to the Zapata Swamp, horseback riding in silence along the Río Hanábana through the familiar wide-open countryside of palm trees and hardwood hammocks. It was their first collecting trip together in nine years. They had visited the swamp many times before, but never in weather so oppressive. Now they were back, hunting ruddy ducks for a new museum collection in Boston.

The ducks were notoriously difficult shots and required immortal patience. They hardly flew, preferring instead to swim submerged to the tips of their beaks, which slyly peeked from the water. When the ruddies rested on the swamp's fragile skin, it was always amidst the shelter of the *malanguetas*, the great upstanding cow-lily leaves. Only the locals had any skill in shooting the ducks. Stealthily, the *guajiros* propelled their pirogues with bamboo poles and surprised the birds in their hiding places. By aiming just ahead of where the ruddies dove for cover, they always got their prey.

Years earlier, before Blanca fell ill, the Agüeros had gathered many fine specimens in the Zapata Swamp. Crab hawks, spotted rails, purple gallinules, even a peculiar local crocodile, unknown anywhere else in the world. There, too, they once spotted—but failed to catch—the *Capromys nana*, a homely rodent descended from an ancient order of mammal.

As naturalists, Ignacio and Blanca Agüero had traversed Cuba with a breadth and depth few others achieved over considerably smaller territories. They knew intimately every cleft of the island's limestone mountains, every swell of its plains and pine forests, every twist of its rivers and underground caves. Together they had spent years cataloguing the splendor of Cuba's flora and fauna, and had decried with each passing season the decline and extinction of once populous species.

The Agüeros often imagined what Cuba must have been like before the arrival of the Spaniards, whose dogs, cats, and rats multiplied prodigiously and ultimately wreaked havoc with the island's indigenous creatures. Long ago, Cuba had been a naturalist's dream. Why, then, had so much been sacrificed to successive waves of settlers and the spreading monotony of sugarcane fields?

On cloudless days like this, the light in the Zapata was so fierce that even the most experienced travelers were deceived, made to consider all manner of ruinous delusions. The swamp was known to exert a hypnotic effect on ambition, that all-welcoming peril. But the stagnant waters of the Zapata rationed its secrets sparingly. Ignacio Agüero lovingly studied his wife and understood that satisfaction came not in the pursuit of modest discoveries but in the bald act of approaching the very essence of things. *Science is primarily a yardstick waving in the dark of the unknown, approximating what it has yet to learn from what it has partly exposed.*

It was noon, and the sun was unsparing. The saw grass and bulrushes quivered in the morass. All morning, Blanca Agüero had followed her husband reluctantly, trailing the wily ruddy ducks without success. The heat weighted her lungs like mercury, slipped beneath her netted helmet, inside her hip-high boots. Damp wisps of hair clung to her forehead and cheeks. How long had it been since she'd endured such physical discomfort? Blanca Agüero restlessly stroked her shotgun, decoratively inlaid with mother-of-pearl. She hadn't used it since dawn. She set the gun against a clump of hyacinths and wiped her face with a pocket handkerchief.

Behind her, a sudden whirring arose, a soft breath at the nape of her neck. Blanca Agüero turned and spotted a brilliant apparition, vibrating inches from her helmet. A bee hummingbird with a metallic pink gorget and strange markings on its wings. A gorgeous specimen, no bigger than a wasp. An adult in full plumage, exceedingly rare. It would no doubt cause a mild sensation in certain scientific circles. She turned to alert her husband and found him staring at her, fixed as a muscle behind his double-barreled gun.

At the sound of the shot, their two horses, ordinarily even-tempered and accustomed to gunfire, snapped their restraints and bolted into the *tembladera*, sinking without a trace. Blanca Agüero collapsed with an unexpected violence, half sliding into the rippling marsh.

Ignacio Agüero waited until nightfall, watched and waited until a lone red-tailed hawk soared above them in the sky. Then he carried his wife seventeen miles to the nearest village and began to tell his lies.

PART ONE

Tropical Disturbances

ACTS OF GOD

❀

EL COBRE

DECEMBER 1990

Reina Agüero, cleaving to a telephone pole with thighs strengthened by many such climbs, is repairing a high-voltage cable outside El Cobre, a copper-mining town in eastern Cuba, when another storm blows in from the Cayman Trench. Lightning, intricate as a skeleton, shatters the afternoon hum of the Sierra Maestra, illuminating the pitted, open-cast mine in the distance. Reina Agüero wipes one hand, then another, on her regulation jumpsuit as she works her way down the splintered pole. Her tools clang reassuringly from her belt. In the evening, she will climb the coconut tree behind the government hotel and mingle its milk with a little rum. She hopes the concoction will finally permit her to sleep.

Reina Agüero's insomnia began last summer, on the thirty-seventh anniversary of El Comandante's attack on the Moncada Barracks. On the road, traveling for *la revolución,* it is especially difficult to rest. The beds are unpredictable, too soft or infested with fleas, and the days are lengthened by extra work. As a visiting master tradesman, Reina is expected not only to repair the balkiest electrical equipment in rural Cuba but also to conduct seminars for local electricians and suffer nightly ceremonies in her honor. Generally, she eats too much fresh pineapple at these events, upsetting her sensitive digestive system.

A cluster of electricians applauds as Reina descends the last few feet of the pole. The ground is saturated with weeks of unseasonable winter rains. Together she and the men slip and grapple their way down the hill toward town, a quarter of which is newly lit by her effort. Reina is drenched, and her jumpsuit clings to her still-curvaceous form. She is forty-eight years old, but her body appears many years younger. She ignores the men who linger behind her, mesmerized by the size and swing of her buttocks.

Reina is five feet eleven, a good four inches taller than most of the men with whom she works. Her mouth is large and flawless, with barely discernible corners. The most daring of her colleagues call her Compañera Amazona, a moniker she secretly relishes. Often, Reina selects the smallest, shyest electrician in a given town for her special favors, leaving him weak and inconsolable for months. After she departs, black owls are frequently sighted in the ceiba trees.

On the way back to her hotel, Reina stops in at the Basilica del Cobre. It is Gothic and gloomy and unwelcoming, like so many Catholic churches, but Reina has heard of the impressive curative powers of La Virgen de la Caridad del Cobre, the island's patron saint. Reina doubts that La Virgen, with all the tragic ailments laid at her feet, would bother about a little sleeplessness. But Reina is desperate. She's tried every soporific—herbal teas and sleeping pills, even sweet-potato plasters for her head—all to no avail.

Not even the usual rigorous lovemaking with Pepín Beltrán, her lover of twenty-four years, exhausts her sufficiently into slumber. Last week, during a dusk-to-midnight session, Pepín's face went slack as he dropped dead asleep beneath her pleasure. Afterward, she lay awake in the dark until she could perceive every crack and crevice in the ornate room. Years ago, it had been her father's study, one of eight chambers in their commodious old apartment in the Vedado section of Havana. After the revolution, the government rented out the remaining seven rooms to as many families.

Pepín blamed the anarchy of books in the study for Reina's insomnia. There are over three thousand volumes on the carved mahogany shelves, stacked on the marble floors, and on six lavishly decrepit armchairs. Many of the books were written by her father: *A Naturalist's Guide to the Pearl of the Antilles*, *Reconsidering Bats*, *The Owls of Oriente*, *In Search of* Erophylla Sezekorni, and his classic, *Cuba: Flora and Fauna*. A former china closet serves as a display case for his most cherished skins, rare birds and bats long extinct, specimens he himself stuffed with arsenical soap and that looked as fresh and alive as on the day he'd shot them.

Pepín begged Reina to clear these relics from their love nest. But Reina refused. Nothing had changed here since her father's death, forty years before.

Reina stands before La Virgen's shrine in the back of the basilica. Hundreds of candles burn to her in pleading and thanksgiving. Centuries of offerings are piled into wobbly, glittering towers: medallions and military badges from those who survived wars under her protection; crutches from devotees to whom she gave the strength to walk; ancient tiaras, chalices, Egyptian silks, and wedding rings donated by pilgrims and the miraculously healed. The brown-skinned Virgin presides over these offerings in a cream satin gown, a gold lamé cape, and her crown, poised and soothing as her Yoruban name: Oshún.

"Bless me, *Virgen*, for I have sinned," says Reina, kneeling before the saint and awkwardly crossing herself. She barely recalls the prayers she learned as a child, the rituals of the Protestant boarding school she and her sister were sent to after their mother died. "Well, I haven't sinned exactly, but I can't sleep, and there must be a reason."

A medal from the Spanish-American War catches Reina's eye. A year after Cuba's independence, her grandfather had come to the island from the hills of Galicia. Reinaldo Agüero became a *lector* in the second-largest cigar factory in Pinar del Río and was greatly admired for his erudition and his rich baritone. Reina's sister, Constancia, used to say proudly that this made them true *criollos*.

"I'm not very good at this, and you must have a lot on your mind, but I was hoping you could give me a direction of significance." Reina unsnaps a wrench from her tool belt and places it next to the medal from the Spanish-American War. "It's not much, I know. But maybe when you get a chance you could check in on me, okay?"

That night, Reina lies in bed and considers La Virgen's dark methods of grace. Reina is uncertain of her own beliefs. What she enjoys most is the freedom from a finality of vision, of a definitive version of life's meaning. If she could perceive nothing in its entirety, then why not celebrate what she could grasp with her own senses? *Vive de la vida lo sublime.* It had been her personal motto for as long as she could remember. After all, it seemed futile to chase what was forever elusive, when reality remained so largely unexplored.

Reina presses the musty hotel pillow over her nose and mouth and begins to count. One minute passes, then two. If she succeeds in rendering herself unconscious, Reina thinks, slumber might return. Six minutes pass, then seven. After eight minutes, Reina, fully conscious and supremely irritated with La Virgen de la Caridad del Cobre, removes the pillow from her face.

After her mother died, Reina's father also suffered from insomnia. But his was complete and incurable and drove him to suicide two years after his wife's death. At least, Reina thinks, most nights she manages to sleep an hour or two before dawn. Her body sighs with one long releasing breath, and that is the last thing she remembers before the faintest light awakens her, puzzled and refreshed.

Reina has thought often of her father's last night in his study, of his double-barreled twelve-gauge shotgun of Irish make, which is still in its velvet-lined case in the closet. His gun was ideal for pulling birds out of any but the highest trees. Although her father never considered himself a killer by nature, he'd been an excellent shot nonetheless, as effective on horseback as he was crouched low to the ground. Many of his specimens had found their way into the collections of the world's most prestigious museums.

The week after his death, a parcel arrived for Reina and her sister, Constancia, at their boarding school. In it was a selection of their father's lecture notes, rare stuffed bats and birds, and a dozen of his books, first editions, glossy with color plates. Constancia wanted nothing to do with any of them, but Reina carefully repacked the artifacts and slid them under her bed. Despite her suspicions, she couldn't bear to leave the work of Papá's lifetime for beetles and bookworms to devour. "The quest for truth," Ignacio Agüero had written his daughters, "is far more glorious than the quest for power." Their father had written this, and then he shot himself in the heart.

• • •

It is the fourth of December. Reina is up before dawn. In the countryside, people are already on the roads and the hillsides. This is a comfort to Reina, who hates to wake up feeling alone. As the first light filters and spreads through the darkness, colors seem to her less concentrated, as if sunlight, not its absence, diluted their strength.

During her long wakeful nights, Reina mentally inches her way from the periphery of her bed, reconstructing the world in concentric circles. Everything is at its most elemental in these circles, pure with the vital sheen of existence. Then a drift of memories overcomes her, reversing the progress of her life.

On the worst nights, Reina feels herself trapped as if on a magnetic plateau, with no fix on the blackness. She confuses the stuffed bats with the birds, and the books with the extinguished chandelier. She thinks often of her mother, hears her voice again, feels the warm press of her breast against her cheek. Reina was six years old when her mother died on the collecting expedition in the Zapata Swamp. How is it possible that she has existed without her all these years?

Reina has one more job in El Cobre before returning home to Havana for a two-week vacation. The incessant rains have flooded the copper mine. The electric water pump dragged to the site is almost prehistoric and has electrocuted two men since mid-November. Now not even the most skillful electricians will go near it.

The same group of men greets Reina in the hotel dining room, over a breakfast of rolls and fresh papaya with lime. Reina looked them over carefully the day before but deemed nobody worthy of her desire. They are all much too sure of their allure. This is a problem in Cuba. Even the most gnarled, toothless, scabrous, sclerotic, pigeon-toed, dyspeptic, pestilential men on the island believe themselves irresistible to women. Reina has often pondered this incongruity. Too much mother coddling is her theory. After the love and embraces of a Cuban *mami*, what man wouldn't think he is the center of the universe?

Electricians, in Reina's experience, are in a category apart. Adept with their hands and making sparks fly, they often look upon women as something of another electrical challenge. They are reliable but rarely inspired, which is partly why Reina enjoys reducing them to helplessness. Gratitude, she thinks, is a refreshing quality in a man. This is why Pepín Beltrán continues to be her ideal lover, despite the fact that he's married and wears orthopedic shoes. As an official in the Ministry of Agriculture, Pepín has nothing to do all day but rustle papers and daydream about her. By the time he arrives at her room every evening, with a packet of black market delicacies, he is nearly faint with anticipation. He follows Reina's body like music.

Reina admits to a certain vanity. She basks in the admiration she receives in her trade and in her bed, in the image of her image of herself. She is fond of saying she has few specialties but prides herself on doing them exceedingly well.

Nobody is allowed to carry Reina Agüero's toolbox. She insists upon this, forcibly when necessary. It weighs close to seventy pounds, but Reina carries it as if it contained no more than a pork sandwich and a carton of milk. Most days she makes do with her tool belt, but the pump at El Cobre's mine requires more electrical finesse. It is a forty-minute walk uphill in the rain.

Others from the town join the electricians on their trek to the mine. Word has spread of the lady electrician's ingenuity, and soon a colorful procession of El Cobre's truants and elaborately underemployed citizens follow Reina and her associates up the hill. Salvation or catastrophe, Reina notices, is always guaranteed to draw a crowd. The rain comes down harder. The citizens protect themselves with palm leaves and torn strips of cardboard and two black umbrellas marked PROPRIEDAD DEL ESTADO.

Topsoil slides down the hill in black rivulets. Snakes and mice and a profusion of underground creatures sweep past them as they climb. The trees are crowded with fretful birds, frogs, and lizards seeking refuge from the floods. One electrician, a flat-headed man named Agosto Piedra, steps knee-deep into a pocket of mud and unleashes a string of profanities so original it makes everyone laugh.

Reina is the first to reach the mouth of the copper mine. It is an amphitheater of decay. In the seventeenth century, slaves extracted enough ore from the mine to meet all of the country's artillery needs. A hundred years later, they turned on their masters with muskets and machetes and, eventually, through the intervention of the Bishop of Santiago and La Virgen de la Caridad del Cobre herself, were declared free citizens.

It will take something of a divine intervention to get the thick, foul-smelling water out of the mine, Reina thinks. The pump, actually two pumps clumsily linked by a series of exposed wires, is sunk in a foot of mud. Reina motions for her attendant electricians to help her push the pump to drier land, but nobody moves a muscle. Instead they look back at her, alternately embarrassed and defiant. The machine has already claimed two lives. Revolutionary dedication goes only so far.

Reina puts down her toolbox. She circles the machine once, twice, three times, before deciding on an angle. The mud sucks at her knee-high regulation boots. She takes a deep breath, settles loosely on her haunches. Then, with the speed and strength of a wrestler, she forces the power of her entire body into her right shoulder. The machine moves two feet out of the mud. She repeats the maneuver, so focused she appears in a trance, then again and again until the whole contraption sits precariously on the lip of the mine. The crowd is silent. The rain continues to roar down. Overhead, an aura vulture wheels through the air.

What happens next occurs so fast that nobody present can describe the events accurately or in sequence. One moment, Reina is removing a side panel of the water pump with her battery-operated screwdriver, and the next, thousands of birds flee the trees at once, whirling madly in the rain. The ground begins to shudder and fissure. Reina jumps on the pump as it begins to careen downhill on a wave of mud belched forth from the mine. The pump crushes everything in its path, leaving a flattened double wake of dirt and brambles that stops short before a giant mahogany tree. Reina sees the tree coming and is almost relieved. It is a healing tree, she remembers, its bark used to treat rheumatism, tetanus, and pneumonia. Like the earth, it is violently trembling.

The impact rattles Reina's spine, breaks her nose and both thumbs, and loosens a back molar. A tangle of her hair is pulled out by the roots.

Reina is pinioned forty feet high in the tree's uppermost branches. It is another kingdom entirely. Her pores absorb the green saturation of leaves, the merciful scent of the earth slowly ascending its limbs. Above her, the sky blossoms with gray velvet, with the fading light of long-departed stars. Suddenly, Reina wants her daughter to be with her, to share this air and the strange exhilaration of height. She would say: "Dulcita, all the gifts of the world are here." But Reina knows too well the uselessness of words, their power to divide and create loneliness.

Reina's body is sticky with blood and emulsions she does not recognize. Then nothing matters except an unexpected blindness, her heart's rhythm, and an exquisite sense of heat.

NEW YORK CITY

Constancia Agüero Cruz straightens the rows of teal boxes at her cosmetics counter and checks her lipstick in the magnifying mirror. In five minutes, the doors of the Manhattan department store will open. It is the week before Christmas, and the crowds have thickened to unruly proportions. There is a sense of urgency with every purchase, an ever-elusive quest for holiday perfection.

Constancia is promoting a new artichoke extract that promises to eradicate even the finest lines around the eyes. Seconds after application, the gel hardens to a crystalline sheen that sets the skin for several hours. A dab of concealer and powder, and the need for surgery is temporarily camouflaged. Constancia's sales break all company records. But she is motivated not by commissions, only by the satisfaction of staving off women's little everyday deaths.

Constancia doesn't need to sell cosmetics. Her husband,

Heberto Cruz, owns a tobacco store on Sixth Avenue, where sheikhs and politicians shop. She helps him there on Saturdays, her day off, selling antique meerschaum pipes, custom blends of tobacco, porcelain cigarette holders, and the finest hand-rolled cigars in the world (there's a cache of illegal Cuban imports in the walk-in humidor). Sales double whenever Constancia is on duty, but her heart isn't in the transactions. She considers cigars to be merely agreeable distractions, not at all in the same category as a good night cream.

Within minutes, her cosmetics counter is lined with customers. Constancia works most efficiently alone, demonstrating her products with a quiet, authoritative air. No woman is immune to the subtle anxiety she creates with her sales pitches. In the first half hour alone, she makes twelve hundred dollars in sales.

Constancia considers her own image her most effective selling tool, and so she takes great pains with her appearance. She is fifty-one years old, but her skin is soft and white. Her dark hair is arranged in a French bun, and her nails are lacquered to match her carnelian lips. Constancia is partial to Adolfo suits, which set off her petite figure, and she completes every ensemble with a short strand of pearls. Her foreign accent and precise manner intimidate clients into buying whatever she suggests.

The morning passes quickly as Constancia rings up compacts and emollients, eyeliners, lip pencils, facial defoliants. Her division supervisor announced yesterday that Constancia had won a powder-pink Cadillac convertible, the fiscal-year award for the top salesperson in North America. Constancia wondered what she would do with such a fancy car in New York City. But Heberto suggested that the company ship it straight to Miami, where they plan to move after the holidays.

Constancia is uncertain whether she wants to leave New York, but Heberto is determined to retire. He is eleven years older than she and exhausted, he says, from standing on his feet all day inhaling other people's smoke. In September, Heberto bought a condominium on Key Biscayne, overlooking the ocean, not far from his widowed father's house. There is a pool and a sandy beach and the daily theater of sunsets, but Constancia is not persuaded by such attractions. She likes her work, fears all inactivity. When silence surrounds her, the temptation to remember is too great.

During her lunch break, Constancia steps out onto Third Avenue. The air rings with the competing voices of a dozen vendors selling pretzels, chestnuts, earmuffs, knockoff watches, and wooden carvings from Senegal. Around her, women march purposefully in sneakers and fur coats. The city's sidewalks are savage to high-heeled feet, but Constancia rejects the modern ethos of comfort before style. If she doesn't look good, it hurts her a lot more than a mere pair of heels. Her daughter, Isabel, doesn't understand this. She's a potter and lives barefoot and overalled in a rural part of Oahu.

At her favorite coffee shop, the waiter brings Constancia a dish of cottage cheese, puréed peaches, and a cup of chamomile tea. The meal settles her stomach after the morning tumult. She is careful to eat only soothing foods. Like her sister in Cuba, Constancia has a fragile digestive system. Neither of her children inherited this trait. Her daughter lives on hot-plate-warmed hash poured from cans, and her son, Silvestre, eats nothing but sausage heroes from an Italian take-out place in Morningside Heights.

Constancia tastes a forkful of her cottage cheese, shudders at the thought of all that indescribable meat. She opens the newspaper to the day's horoscope. Her birthday,

March 21, is on the cusp between Pisces and Aries, a volatile combination, and she often finds it difficult to interpret the dispatches from the stars. "Expect a serious loss. Cling to what you truly want and release all that is ephemeral. A financial coup may be yours if you play the part right." Constancia is irritated by such equivocal advice. She prefers the more direct approach of the soothsayers back in Cuba.

At precisely three o'clock, the Algerian diplomat appears at Constancia's counter. She declines his dinner invitation, as she has for the past two weeks, but he is not easily dissuaded. Although Constancia is intrigued by his gentility, by the irregular pattern of hair on his brow, she cannot envision herself out with another man. She hasn't bothered to tell her husband about the diplomat. Heberto is genetically incapable of jealousy. How else could he have married Constancia when she was still sick with love for his brother?

Constancia continues a brisk pace of sales throughout the afternoon. There is an interlude just before five o'clock when the number of male customers invariably increases. It is their time of day to buy perfume: to beg forgiveness, to surprise a lover, or to sweeten the end of an affair. Constancia can always tell whether hope or guilt is fueling a purchase. For men, it is always hope or guilt, never anything in between.

On her way home, the sky darkens to a bluish gray. The weatherman predicted snow, but no snow has fallen. Constancia wants the snow to come, to envelop the city in its mending white. Along the southern edge of Central Park, the trees grow heavy with obscurity, with the weight of impending night.

Heberto is closing shop when Constancia arrives to pick him up. He is flush with satisfaction. The finance minister of Venezuela stopped in to buy ivory pipes for his mistress. Constancia examines the receipt her husband flourishes: $1,940. The minister paid for the pipes with two thousand-dollar bills and told Heberto to keep the change.

"Look how excited you are, *mi cielo*. Are you sure you're ready to retire?" Constancia asks, patting her husband's hand. She wonders what Heberto will do with himself in Florida. He has no hobbies or passions, only this steady mercantile drive.

Together they walk down Avenue of the Americas, against the tide of the crowds. They pass the skyscraper where Constancia's son works on the thirty-sixth floor. Silvestre clips newspapers for the library of a prestigious newsmagazine, sorting through sports and celebrity gossip, serial murders and monsoons. He says the fact that he's deaf makes his job easier, filters out distractions. His father, Gonzalo Cruz, is Heberto's brother. Constancia was married to him for exactly four months in 1956. Gonzalo lives in Miami now with his sixth wife, a Salvadoran teenager he met at a Kentucky Fried Chicken in Coconut Grove. This is another reason Constancia does not want to move to Florida.

Constancia is supposed to meet Silvestre at the Cloisters the first Sunday of every month, but her son hasn't shown up since August. Last time she saw him, he complained that she kissed him too hard on the mouth. Then he lifted his hand with a nervous flutter in a gesture that was pure Gonzalo. Silvestre looks so much like his father now that each time Constancia faces him in the medieval courtyard, it momentarily defeats her.

Still, she enjoys the view from the hill high above the Hudson River, the hodgepodge of European monasteries that make up the Cloisters' main structure. There are frescoes and tapestries and, in the formal gardens, dozens of plants commonly found during the Middle Ages. Constancia frequently spots crows and jays in the foliage, occasionally a chipping sparrow trilling its long monotone.

She and her husband head west on Fifty-third Street until they reach their apartment building on the edge of the river, iridescent with ribbons of oil. Constancia has grown accustomed to the river's lethargy, to the pustular smokestacks on its far banks.

In Cuba, she'd worked near the water, as a receptionist for the Cruz family's shipping line. The foyer, decorated with an oversized compass and vintage nautical gear, overlooked Havana harbor and its comforting pattern of ships. Without checking her watch or consulting her calendar, Constancia could tell the time of day and the day of the month by the particulars of the flotilla outside.

She was still in the habit of walking home along the Malecón then, humming in time with the aimless waves on the other side. She and her father had walked this stretch so often in 1949, the year after her mother died, that Constancia knew the wall's indentations inch by inch. Her father rarely spoke during their walks, but something in the shiver of his stride made Constancia fear he would jump over the wall without saying good-bye.

There is leftover carne asada for dinner, the remains of a pineapple crumb cake. Constancia serves Heberto in the kitchen, pours him a glass of milk. She cooks up a fresh batch of rice for herself and steams two zucchini until she can mash them to a pulp with her fork. Heberto studies pamphlets for a motorboat and fishing gear he plans to buy once they settle in Key Biscayne. This from a man, Constancia thinks, who doesn't even take his socks off at the beach. During their vacation in Rio de Janeiro, Heberto sat amidst

all the fleshly splendors of Ipanema reading the latest issue
of *Cigar Connoisseur*.

Constancia turns on the radio to her favorite show, *La
Hora de los Milagros*, and ponders the latest news: a rash of
Virgin sightings in and around the tourist hotels of Cozumel;
a Chilean pig rancher with unmistakable stigmata on his
palms; a long-barren woman who finally conceived a boy at
Lake George.

During the call-in portion of the program, a man from
the Bronx reports in with another miracle. He says his son
had a pet chicken named Wifredo that flew backward into a
pot of boiling water to save the boy's life. "You see," the man
explained, "my son was dying of pneumonia, and Wifredo
made the ultimate sacrifice in turning himself to soup. That
broth is a miracle! We still have some in the freezer! Come
and see for yourself!"

Heberto is impatient with Constancia's obsessions,
characterizes the *milagros* as nothing more than freakish inci-
dents grounded in perfectly logical explanations. He refutes
statistics showing that New Jersey, hazily visible through
their living room window, has the highest number of
reported miracles of any state in the nation. That doesn't
count Puerto Rico, of course, but Constancia knows it's just
a territory.

Constancia dismisses her husband's skepticism. She
knows in her heart that miracles arrive every day from the
succulent edge of disaster, defying nature, impossible to
resist. When Constancia was only five months old, her
mother disappeared without a word and didn't return for
two and a half years. Her father hired a nanny for Constancia, a mulatta from Regla, who carefully hid her disregard for science. Beatriz Ureña inducted little Constancia
into the worthier mysteries of life.

• • •

After dinner, Constancia retreats to her high-watt vanity mirror, sniffing the ruin that lies waiting for her there. She avoids most of the products she sells, devising instead her own youth-conserving therapies. She smooths warmed honey over her face and throat, letting it congeal for at least thirty minutes. Constancia read of its preservative powers in a book on ancient healings. Archaeologists discovered a jug of honey, still soft and sweet, in a prehistoric Turkish tomb. Primitive people also treated burns with honey to promote the growth of new skin.

Constancia rinses her face with mineral water and fresh pomegranate juice. She coats her skin with paraffin distilled from century-old redwoods, then smears the mixture on the soles of her feet before slipping on flannel booties. She saves the hand lotion for last: a special blend of vegetable shortening with a hint of oleander, which erases all traces of age.

The first time Constancia felt a rush of heat across her chest, she was trying on a black cashmere sweater in the dressing room at Saks. She thought she was having a heart attack, but then the heat swept up over her face and lingered there for several seconds. Her skin became damp and splotchy, rippled with chills. On an impulse, Constancia decided to steal the sweater.

After this, her periods came less frequently, until her flow diminished to just a few threads of blood. Her breasts ached every month like when she was twelve. She found herself elated one moment, despairing the next. It occurred to her that her parents had died long before they were old. How, then, could she possibly know how to grow old herself?

In Cuba, aging was not such a disgraceful affair. Most elderly women were venerated and sought after for counsel. They were surrounded by their families and often lived to see their great-grandchildren grow up. The *abuelitas* were the eyes and ears of a clan, the peacemakers, the storytellers and historians. They held each young destiny in their hands. Although this was not true in her own family, where her mother and grandmothers died young, it didn't prevent Constancia from desiring a rich old age.

Constancia lowers her bedroom blinds. Northern winds rattle the windowpanes, stir the garbage in the streets. Green stars skim the sky, shedding their forgotten light. Constancia settles under her quilt with the cross-stitch design and assesses her progression toward death. Death troubles her deeply, but not nearly as much as the prospect of an untimely transition. If only she could choose the hour and manner of her passing, plan for it properly with the caterers, she could avoid any unseemly panic. She is the first to admit she has a low threshold for disorder.

The smoke of Heberto's cigar filters into the bedroom like the thinnest of voices. It is the last thing Constancia registers before falling asleep.

A SIGUAPA STYGIAN

✦

My name is Ignacio Agüero, and I was born in the late afternoon of October 4, 1904, the same day, my mother informed me later, that the first President of the Republic, Estrada Palma, arrived in Pinar del Río for a parade and a banquet and a long night of speeches at the governor's mansion. Cuba had gained its independence two years before, and despite the Platt Amendment, which permitted the Americans to interfere in our country from the day it was born, the citizens of Pinar del Río poured into the streets to welcome the President.

A brass band played on a wooden platform decorated with ribbons and carnations, and children scampered about in their Sunday finery, clutching pinwheels and balloons. Angry cigar workers pressed through the crowd, shaking placards protesting the high foreign tariffs levied on tobacco. My father, Reinaldo Agüero, a lector who read to the cigar workers in their factory, marched among them.

Back at our whitewashed cement house, which was shaded by the crown of a graceful frangipani, my mother was readying herself for the festivities when she felt the first of my violent kicks deep inside her. She sat down at the edge of the bed and slowly rubbed her stomach, humming a Mozart sonata whose soothing effect on me she had previously noted. Instead the kicking intensified, followed by a series of rhythmic contractions. Mamá was all alone. She would miss the parade and the suckling pig and the ballroom lit with candelabras.

No sooner had she settled back on her matrimonial bed than Mamá spotted the shadow on the far wall. Straight ahead, standing guard between the open shutters of the bedroom window, was a siguapa stygian owl. My mother did not know its official name then, only that it was a bird of ill omen, earless and black and unmistakable. It was doubly bad luck to see one during the day, since they were known to fly about late at night, stealing people's souls and striking them deaf.

Hoo-hoo, hoo-hoo, it called to her as she breathed a voluminous breath that caught her very center. She grabbed the etched glass lamp on the nightstand and threw it with all her might, but it fell short of the owl's luminous eyes. Suddenly, the pain inside her spread upward and downward like two opposing tidal waves, and despite her fear or because of it, she delivered a nine-pound, four-ounce baby boy.

The owl remained still on its perch until the placenta spilled forth in a rush of blood. Then, with a dark flap of its wings, it swooped forward, plucked the sodden organ from the floor, and flew with it like a rumor out the window.

Later, my mother learned that the bird had flown low over the President's parade with her placenta, scattering the crowd and raining birthing blood. Even President Palma, trembling with fear, crossed himself twice before jumping headlong into a flowering angel's-trumpet bush, his crisp linen suit spattered with Mamá's blood.

Word of the incident quickly spread throughout Cuba. Mamá told me that for once the priests' and the santeros' interpretations were in accord: the island was headed for doom. Since then, the siguapa stygians are no longer so common in Cuba, killed over the years by superstitious country folk and the disappearance of the vast, unlit woods that once concealed them.

From the start, my mother blamed the siguapa stygian for my tin ear, although she was grateful it hadn't flown off with my hearing altogether. Both my parents were accomplished musicians, and as a child I studied the piano, the violin, the flute, and the oboe, but I never coaxed more than rudimentary sounds from any of them. This was a heartbreak for my parents, who had hoped we might one day form a trio.

Pinar del Río was a steamy backwater in those days. Its cultural amenities included a theater with a red tile roof, where my mother and father and I attended an occasional concert, and a natural sciences museum—a dusty back room in a deteriorated municipal building—that had on exhibit a rare cork palm, a species indigenous to Cuba that can be traced back 250 million years.

The Sierra de los Organos loomed to the northwest, and though the mountains were far off, they managed to stamp the town with their somber mood. Tobacco fields stretched in every direction: on the vales, on the hillsides, on the mountaintops, and on the sheer sides of the mogotes, *limestone bluffs that the workers ascended and descended by means of ropes. Although there were pineapple fields nearby and orange groves and acres of sugarcane, nothing competed with the supremacy of tobacco.*

My father, as the lector of El Cid Cigar Manufacturers Company, was revered for his intellect and his splendid renditions of the works of Cervantes, Dickens, and Victor Hugo. For two hours every morning and then again after lunch, Papá read

aloud from an assortment of newspapers, novels, political trea-
tises, and collections of poetry. While the workers occasionally
voted on what they wanted my father to read, more often than
not they left the choice to him, a testament to their utmost con-
fidence in his taste. For twenty-one years (not counting strikes,
holidays, and illnesses), Papá stood at his lectern and read to
the hundred or so workers seated below him. Most of them
smoked continuously as they listened to him, stripping and
sorting and rolling the finest tobacco in the world.

Papá had a deep, sonorous voice, cured to huskiness over
the years by the sheer volume of smoke he inhaled. Although he
nursed his throat regularly with honey and lemon, he refused to
yield to the temptations of the microphone, which, he was con-
vinced, distorted the robust timbre of his voice. In the after-
noons, when he customarily read from novels, townspeople
gathered outside the factory with their rocking chairs and
embroidery to listen to the intriguing tales that drifted through
the open windows.

My father was particularly proud of the literary name that
was imprinted on the factory's cedar boxes and its gilded cigar
rings. Once a year, an occasion for which he would dress up in
a jacket and waistcoat and his patent-leather spats, my father
read in its entirety El Cid, that great medieval epic poem,
moving even the stolid factory director to tears.

What most people did not know was that my father was
also a superb violinist. Many who heard his serenades from the
street or in the nearby square assumed that the music came
from my father's phonograph, prized by the town as evidence of
their collective sophistication. Papá did not discourage this
assumption. The violin was a link to his past, to his own father,
who had lived like a pauper in the hills of Galicia, carving fine,
sturdy fiddles that nobody bought. My father's father had
grown demented in his last years, convinced that he was
descended from the great violin makers of Cremona, which had

bestowed upon the world the successive geniuses of Nicolò Amati and Antonio Stradivari.

I have often wondered why someone of Papá's talent never sought to make a larger impression on the world, why he had so whittled down his dreams, for dreams he must have had to abandon Spain. It seems to me now that Papá had exhausted his lifetime's supply of adventure on his one voyage across the Atlantic. The hardships of that trip must have sated him, cured him completely of any further scheming. By the time he'd arrived in Cuba, my father wanted nothing more than to reclaim the stability he'd so recklessly left behind.

During brief nostalgic lapses, Papá re-created his favorite dishes from Spain. He made his own sausages, complaining that the local chorizos slept on his palate, and he taught himself to bake perfect empanadas, plump with spiced ground beef. When he cooked codfish and white-bean stew, his eyes watered in happy relief. One winter, he planted a dwarf olive tree in our backyard, but despite his painstaking care, the sapling never bore fruit. My mother, seeing how homesick Papá was for the verdant hills of Galicia, often encouraged him to return for a visit. But Papá shook his head and said, "My fate was decided a long time ago."

That is not to say that my father was a melancholy man; not at all. Most days he awoke with a heightened sense of purpose. His readings engrossed him enormously, and as he strode to work, his throat rumbled with anticipation over what the morning newspapers might bring.

It was my mother who was the moodier of the two. Her name was Soledad, and she knew better than anyone the meaning of solitude: that the beginning already implies the end, and that at the end we understand only the vague dimensions of our ignorance. As you get older, you question the utility of your life.

Years later, I learned that Mamá had had a child out of wedlock long before I was born, a little girl named Olivia, who'd drowned when the Guamá River overflowed one rainy September. I remember my mother was always saddest in September, and to this day it seems to me the bleakest of months.

CONDITIONS OF SURVIVAL

❖

SANTIAGO DE CUBA

JANUARY 1991

The talk at Céspedes Hospital is of blindness. Thousands of Cubans are losing their sight in Santiago de Cuba. There is speculation that a *yanqui* virus or infected fish is to blame, though this last theory is quickly dismissed because fish is impossible to obtain. The blindness, they say, begins with a pain like a bad mosquito bite in the eye.

Reina Agüero watches as the blind patients stumble down the corridors, their arms waving like frontal antennae, cursing the revolution and El Comandante himself. Ten years ago, Reina wouldn't have put up with their blaspheming. Now she doesn't even flinch.

Others still talk of the earthquake that shook the province in December. Eleven people died from the mud slides and fires and the collapse of El Cobre's mine. The weather since has been unpredictable, freezing one day, summer hot the next. People blame the Fosa de Batle, seven thousand meters deep in the Windward Passage. Santiago de Cuba faces it head-on. When too many drowned men stir in the ocean trench, misfortune is certain to spread.

As a child, Reina learned about the island's geological tensions from her father, about the ancient foundations of rocks carved by erosion into arid plains. She learned that Cuba, in all probability, was connected to Haiti and the Yucatán long ago. That the depth of its limestone sustains an unheard-of variety of mollusks. That its system of subterranean drainage prevents lakes and ponds from forming. Rivers, yes. Lakes and ponds, no. Except in the great Zapata Swamp, Cuba's waters are never still.

The Tana, the Najasa, the Jatibonico del Sur, the Toa, the Damují, the Saramaguacá. Dozens of sleepy rivers, with their whimsical names, crisscross the island. Reina wants to float in these rivers, quench the incessant burning. Instead she lies suspended in a hospital bed. Around her, machines blink with cool assurance, red lights and green, a parade of bulging blue waves. A grimy window overlooks Santiago Bay. Thorn and scrub savanna trim the coastline for miles in both directions.

The doctors tell her that she is lucky to have survived a direct hit of lightning in that mahogany tree. Already they've scraped acres of cinereous flesh from her back, charred a foreign gray. The tools on her belt branded their silhouettes on her hips. Her hoop earrings burned holes in her neck. For weeks, her pores oozed water and blood, until Reina thought it might be better to die.

Against all medical precedents, experimental skin grafts from loved ones miraculously took. Pepín Beltrán donated a patch of his backside, Dulcita a long stretch of thigh. Other people, dead and alive, gave Reina their skin, unblistered, unsinged. On bad days, she wishes they hadn't tried.

No one will bring Reina a mirror. There's a lump of

gauze where her nose is healing, a dull pulsing where her molar remains loose. Her thumbs have lost all sensation. They say her face survived best of all, but Reina is not permitted to see it. Each time she asks, the nurses refuse her, then release a familiar tug of drugs in her veins. Reina decides she can stand anything but lies.

Nothing is allowed to touch her. The slightest breeze refines her pain. And so she is motionless all day, remembering the moment before the heat. The mass shifting of leaves, the branches violet with light, offering her to the sky. She understood then the private language of nature, the patience and debts it defines. She lost two weeks of her life to this knowledge.

When Reina awoke again, she believed the world had converted to fire. Hadn't anyone noticed but her? Everything simmered with heat. Fevers rippled like snakes through her room, rattling their tails of sparks. Her skin gave off a sweetish smoke. Electricity had replaced her voice.

Reina understands that lightning has its work to do. It's an atmospheric discharge, urgent between clouds or between clouds and the ground below. Many thousands of bolts strike the earth daily, searing their fatal messages. Yet Reina cannot accept a rational explanation. What she knows is this: that she was singled out to die but, instead, has survived.

In Cuba, Reina has heard it whispered, Changó owns the lightning, uses it to display his displeasure, his brazen force. Oyá, his first and favorite wife, also owns the fire. She stole it from Changó once when he went off to battle. Reina asks a nurse to tie two ribbons for these fractious lovers — one red, one maroon — to the foot of her bed, just in case.

It is winter. Pepín Beltrán comes from Havana for the weekend with a suitcase of her father's books and the ancient binoculars Reina requested. To the west, a Batista hawk glides high on invisible drafts. Reina lifts the binoculars, her arm muscles aching with effort, and watches the hawk circle just below the clouds, imagines its musical three-call note. An hour later, as if summoned by the mountains for tasks unknown, the hawk drifts out of sight.

"I'm thirsty," she says, still searching for the hawk, her binoculars unsteady. Her throat is parched, beyond slaking, like the thirst she endured nursing Dulcita for eighteen months.

"You must accept this as a condition of survival," Pepín says. He offers Reina a local drink made with pepper leaves, vanilla, pine needles, soapberries, and Indian root. She's surprised by its sweet smoothness, drinks it down with a long swallow. But her thirst immediately returns.

Her daughter arrives while Pepín is there. Dulce is thirty-two years old, but she wears a miniskirt and white go-go boots to show off her missing strip of thigh. Her daughter's scar reminds Reina of the purplish burns on her own mother's forearms. Blanca Mestre Agüero had started out as a chemist and bore the telltale signs of her profession's serious demands. But to Reina, her mother's scars had seemed more decorative then disfiguring, like exotic tattoos.

"Read to me," Reina pleads. She rarely asks this of her daughter. Dulcita deliberately ruins the melody of a sentence, skips words she doesn't understand. But her voice is high and girlish and reminds Reina of a happier time. Reina's father had made a habit of reading to her from a tender age: *The Meditations of Marcus Aurelius*, classics of zoogeography, nineteenth-century French and Russian literature, histories of the Greeks, the Romans, and the Mongol invaders. He allowed no naps or intermissions.

Dulcita reluctantly accepts a brown leather book from her mother, already opened to a favorite passage. Dulcita's thumb darkens the corner of the page with perspiration, picks up tiny flecks of gilt from the edge. Reina mouths the words as her daughter reads:

> *The substance of the universe is obedient and compliant; and the reason which governs it has in itself no reason for causing evil, for it has no malice, nor does it do evil to anything, nor is anything harmed by it . . .*

Abruptly, Dulcita stops reading. She has an announcement to make. She is leaving the country with a sixty-four-year-old airline reservations clerk from Spain. Reina doesn't have the strength to say what is necessary, to point out that Dulcita's actions are no more than restlessness in disguise. Her daughter has boyfriends from Sweden and France, from Brazil, Canada, Pakistan. They send her letters and trinkets and family pictures. Then send her nothing at all. Dulcita doesn't want children. Not with the Spaniard, not with anyone.

"At least he isn't married," Dulcita sneers, staring at her mother's lover.

"Do you love him?" Reina asks.

"Of course not."

"What will you do in Madrid?"

"Take up boxing." Dulcita rolls her eyes.

"*Bueno, mi amor*, you are long past the age of illusions."

Pepín Beltrán reaches for a vial of silvery powder hidden in a slit in the mattress. He taps the vial gently, sprinkles the talcum-fine powder onto Reina's tongue. He procured it from La Sequita, a famous herbalist in Guanabo, who said that by the time Reina finished it, she would be either completely healed or dead.

"It's worst after midnight," Reina tells him after Dulcita leaves. Her daughter's sharp saffron scent permeates the room.

"It always is, *querida*."

Pepín stays with Reina as the dusk extinguishes the clouds one by one, then on through the endless continent of the night. Reina stares out the window for hours, trying to make sense of the density of stars.

At dawn, Pepín carries in a tattered shopping bag he'd saved from El Encanto, a department store in the capital that had burned to the ground years ago. He reaches inside and pulls out a stark white rooster. Its pink eyes widen in the sudden light, but it does not otherwise stir.

"See how gentle he is, Reina? How perfect?" Pepín holds the rooster upside down by its legs and begins circling the room. He climbs onto a chair, then balances on the windowsill, waving the bird toward the far corners of the ceiling. The rooster remains perfectly still.

Reina follows the slick red flesh of its comb. She has heard that in Moscow they eat cocks' combs in cream sauce when there are shortages of meat.

"*Así, así,*" Pepín croons under his breath. He holds the rooster over Reina's midriff and begins a prayer she cannot understand.

Pepín insists that a persistent evil is interfering with La Sequita's cure. The rooster, he says, will trace it, absorb it, fling it back to its dank origin.

Reina is drawn by the semblance of order to Pepín's universe, to the unifying principles he calls gods. Like him, she believes that the world functions through a myriad of vital linkages, animate and inanimate, infinite and infinitesimal, a grand interdependency that survives in order to perpetuate growth and change and decay. Nothing, Reina knows, can ever be dismissed.

She studies the luster of the bird's cape, the arch of its sickle feathers. The spurs are particularly pronounced, the claws and beak strong. It could have been a fighter, a champion. Reina disapproves of cockfighting, but she cannot help admiring the rooster's attributes all the same.

"Where did you find him?" she asks, as a mysterious rushing storms her veins.

"*Concéntrate*, Reina. Close your eyes."

A moment later, it's over. The rooster squawks as it flies out the window, blazing newly black against the wild, colluding sky.

KEY BISCAYNE, FLORIDA

Constancia Agüero Cruz considers the illumined corpse of her father-in-law at the foot of the altar rail. Arturo Cruz's face is overly rouged, and his hands, enlaced with a worn wooden rosary, appear stiff and squared-tipped as piano keys. His family and friends, spent by the upheaval of his death, are gathered in the front pews. Constancia adjusts her veiled hat, smooths the sash of her black chiffon dress. Against the back wall of the chancel, a dominion of faded saints hovers with long-forgotten ecstasies.

Dusk erupts through the stained-glass windows of the church. The candles gutter as if disturbed by a draft. Constancia is startled. In the tropics, twilight is such a swift affair, one flamboyant cloak exchanged for another, with a flare and a whirl. In New York City, she recalls wistfully, the days receded gradually, sulking for hours.

"It is a season of ruin, a season of salvation." Constancia

ignores the pouchy-eyed priest, the irksome hymns prescribed for grief. Her father-in-law died from a surge of
blood that flooded his brain during a game of dominoes at
Gerardo's *carnicería*. Constancia doesn't question his passing.
There are, she knows, reasons good enough for everything
that happens.

Maldición, maldición, maldición. Constancia imagines the
words colliding along the stone floor, rattling the coffin and
the narcissistic saints. She reaches for her husband's hand. It
is cold and fleshy. Heberto has been irascible for weeks, is
worse now that his father is dead. The family was close back
in Cuba, before debt and exile drove them apart. Now Constancia fears that Heberto, too, will choose to die, like the
aborigines who paint their faces and disappear into the forest
when their time comes.

From a nearby pew, her first husband, Gonzalo Cruz,
scrapes his way to his father's coffin on his flame-tree cane.
Constancia hasn't seen him in thirty-three years. It is difficult for her to reconcile the sight of this man with the
memory of him, with the despair that corrupted her for any
other love.

Gonzalo's left leg is shorter than his right, a souvenir of
the Bay of Pigs. When Constancia knew him, there was no
limp. His legs were his best feature then, muscular and
smooth as a boy's. Still, something of his old rapacity lurks in
his wilted bearing, in his fading marauder's face. Constancia
wonders, shrewdly assessing her ex-husband, if this is what
their son will look like at sixty.

Relatives have informed her that Gonzalo Cruz is
slowly dying. His malady yellows his skin to a delicate tar-
nish, as if privileged by the sun, and he exudes a potent,
beckoning odor. From his eleventh-floor suite at the Good
Samaritan Hospital, Gonzalo holds court like a deposed dic-

tator, with every manner of refugee and sycophant. He is pleased when he is caught, as happens frequently, in flagrante delicto.

Constancia considers what her daughter told her over the phone last week. That doctors today know what will kill you by the time you are thirty-five. There are magnetic resonance imaging machines, Isabel said, that spit out cross-sections of the human torso, pinpointing the petrified specks that ultimately signal death. "We are *all*," she stressed, "radiant with disease."

Isabel is two months pregnant. She's been living on Oahu for the past year with her painter boyfriend, Austin Feck. She makes oddly shaped objects from clay, fires them in the Japanese manner. Girl or boy, married or not, Isabel and her boyfriend plan to name their baby Raku. Constancia isn't ready to be a grandmother yet, but she plots, during the countless minute deliberations of her day, how she can wrest this child, her first grandchild, from its undeserved fate.

Recently, Constancia received a catalogue of Austin's latest exhibit, *Images of Isabel.* Her daughter's face, her naked body, whole or in select close-ups, floating in a strange, distorting light. Constancia blanched to look at them, the glossy, vulnerable pinks of Isabel's private parts. Her daughter says she plans to continue modeling for Austin throughout her pregnancy, all the more now since she's stopped throwing clay. She fears that the lead in her glazes might harm their unborn child.

It's dark by the time they reach the cemetery. Constancia has never heard of a nighttime burial, but her father-in-law left a will with specific instructions. Everyone lights white tapers from a tiki torch, then slowly circles the funeral tent. Two clarinetists in black tie play a tune Constancia doesn't recognize. Arturo Cruz's longtime mistress, Jacinta

Fuentes, all ruddy bulk, with pearls the size of tamarinds, tries to leap into her lover's grave but is restrained by a circle of friends.

The following evening, Constancia's husband announces he's going fishing in Biscayne Bay. Constancia knows that Heberto will return at dawn without a single fish. One night, he'll pledge to bring home a catch of red snapper; the next, a dozen sea bass for a bouillabaisse. Heberto keeps up with the fishing reports: this school of marlin moving offshore in unfathomable numbers; a swordfish the size of a man recently caught in the Gulf Stream. Constancia imagines her husband upright in his little motorboat, addressing the sky in his earnest, formal manner. She's convinced that he doesn't even bother to drop his line.

How different Heberto is from his younger brother. The two of them lie continually, congenitally, but Heberto's lies are more innocent, a quiet, wistful habit. Gonzalo's lies were blatant and unapologetic, inaccurate as language itself. In fact, Constancia could accuse Gonzalo of only two straightforward acts during their marriage: impregnating her, then leaving her when he found out. In all these years, he has never set eyes on their son, Silvestre, deaf from the time he was four. Another casualty of that *dichosa* revolution.

It is the last day of January. Constancia folds a sheet of stationery in half and slips in a pair of hundred-dollar bills for her son. Silvestre used to reproach her for sending him cash, but he no longer acknowledges the monthly supplement. Constancia doesn't know whether he saves it or spends it or throws it away. It doesn't matter anyway. The money, she realized a long time ago, is more for her than for him.

Constancia keeps a large store of high-denomination bills hidden in the false bottom of her traveling vanity case and in a secret account at a local Nicaraguan bank. She siphoned the money from the tobacco store in the last months before it was sold. She thought it prudent to hoard the stash for unexpected plans. Surprisingly, Heberto didn't miss the cash.

The lights parade in the sliding glass doors of her balcony, aimed at the sea. The sky is muddy with low-hanging clouds. Constancia imagines the tops of the palm trees piercing the soft masses, drinking in the purity above. Tonight she is grateful for the moon's absence. Without a moon and with the sea nearby, she can lose herself in the night's imprecisions.

In the pool below, a wrinkled woman swims with a snorkel mask and fins. What could she be searching for at this hour in the concrete blue?

Constancia goes to the kitchen and heats a plate of rice, cooks a yam to bulging in the microwave. Her slacks are getting a little snug, her espadrilles too. She's gained three and a half pounds since she arrived in Florida. Her acquaintances at the yacht club tell her the extra weight becomes her. But Constancia doesn't believe these women. She knows she isn't one of them, that her life outside Miami will always mark her as a foreigner.

The problem, Constancia decided, is that the *cubañas* here can't make comfortable assumptions about her. One of them, a socialite named Rosalina Bellaire de Lavigna, asked her where she'd had her face "done." Rosalina was skeptical when Constancia vowed she hadn't undergone surgery. Another time, Constancia mentioned she'd voted Democratic (just once, for Jimmy Carter), and the room fell starkly silent. How could she possibly define herself by such unambiguous terms?

Constancia doesn't consider herself an exile in the same way as many of the Cubans here. In fact, she shuns their habit of fierce nostalgia, their trafficking in the past like exaggerating peddlers. *Her* father was a scientist, concerned with the biological exigencies of origin and barter. Evolution, Papi told her again and again, is more precise than history. Who, then, could pretend to the answers?

Of course, she wouldn't dare say this aloud in Miami and expect to survive.

Constancia moved to Key Biscayne just before the new year. She decorated her apartment all in white from a closeout furniture sale at Burdine's. She's thought of getting a job in sales—Avon has an opening for a district manager—but Heberto has persuaded her to wait until they're more settled. Constancia misses her work, but there is something more. Miami is disconcerting to her, an inescapable culture shock, the air thickly charged with expiring dreams.

The light is blinding too, a sentence to the past, to her life in Cuba. Everywhere, there is a mass of disquieting details. The deep-fried croquettes for sale on the corner. The accent of the valet who parks her car. Her seamstress's old-fashioned stitching. And the songs, slow as regret, on the afternoon radio.

At the best *bodega* in Little Havana, two dozen varieties of bananas are sold. There are pyramids of juicy mangoes, soursops, custard apples, and papayas. In a flash, they'll make her a milk shake that tastes of her past. Every Friday, Constancia loads up her pink Cadillac convertible with fresh fruit to purée and cries all the way home.

Constancia remembers the time she accompanied her father to the central market in Havana. Mamá was already dead by then. She and Papi wandered around for hours, surrendering themselves to a thousand aromas. Her father loved the poultry stalls best, squawking with barnyard fowl and the more delicate clamor of pheasants, partridges, and quail. She preferred the fish vendors' displays—giant Morro crabs, toothy parrot fish, oysters, eels, and always a few good-sized sharks—perhaps because when she was a child in Camagüey, the ocean had seemed so far away.

When Constancia was five months old, her mother abandoned their house. Then shortly after Constancia's third birthday, Mamá returned, eight months pregnant and bruised. There were terrible welts on her body, and one eye was swollen shut, but Mamá did not cry or complain. Constancia remembers wishing her mother would leave and never come back.

Constancia found a pearly black powder in her nanny's drawer. She'd seen Beatriz Ureña use it on a photograph of her last boyfriend. *"¡Fuera, diablo!"* she shouted, before setting the picture aflame. Constancia took the same powder and sprinkled it on her mother's windowsill so that it would look like soot. But despite Constancia's primitive invocations, Mamá stayed, and her half-sister, Reina, was born that June.

The baby was dark-skinned and fat and impossibly placid, with hands larger than Constancia's own. It was a formidable task to make her cry, although Constancia frequently tried. She dropped spiders in her sister's crib, forced clumps of mud in her tiny mouth. If her mother hadn't found out, Constancia wonders how long Reina might have survived.

After Mamá threatened to leave again, Papi took Constancia to stay on Abuelo Ramón's ranch in Camagüey. It was supposed to last only the summer. It endured for the next six years. Constancia remembers the still, buzzing heat of her grandfather's ranch. The monotony of expectation. The solace of sudden thunderstorms. Although Papi visited frequently and, as she got older, began taking Constancia on his collecting expeditions, she never shared a home with her parents again.

Constancia lived with Abuelo Ramón and his six unmarried sons until just before Mamá's funeral in 1948. It was then she saw her half-sister again.

Reina still lives in Havana, in the old family apartment in Vedado, the apartment from which Constancia was expelled as a child. Reina's continuance there irks Constancia. Why did her sister inherit their past—Papi's stuffed birds and bats, his books, the family's photographs—while Constancia managed to receive nothing at all?

Her sister writes to her now and then, with news of successive deprivations. Reina says it's sad to see the near-empty baskets and shelves of the markets in Cuba, the withered vegetables, the chickens too scraggly even for soup. People trade anything they can, home-roasted coffee or their ration of cigarettes for a used brassiere or a gallon of gas. She's heard of brain surgeons baking birthday cakes on weekends to earn extra cash.

No, Constancia thinks, she could not have been happy in Cuba after 1959.

Nearly thirty years ago, Constancia escaped the island on one of the Cruzes' cargo ships. By then, she had married Heberto, the proprietor's middle son, who had resolutely pursued her after her divorce from Gonzalo. She yielded to Heberto, not with passion, but with a deep sense of relief. Constancia gave birth to their daughter, Isabel, the same day the government expropriated her father-in-law's shipping company.

She and the baby were crossing the Straits of Florida when officers from the revolution came aboard to search for defectors. For an hour, Constancia hid with Isabel in a two-ton container of grapefruit, with barely enough air. Isabel grew limp with the heat and the asphyxiating citrus. Constancia tried everything to revive her; slapped her daughter hard, held her upside down like the obstetrician did when Isabel was born and short of breath, even tore open her blouse and offered her a breast suddenly dried out from fear. But Isabel didn't stir. Finally, Constancia bit her daughter so hard on the heel, she ripped out an inch of flesh.

At four in the morning, Constancia wakes up in distress. She slips on her slacks and a silk blouse and goes straight to the condominium's garage. Her pink Cadillac convertible is not in its usual parking space. Constancia checks the upper level, but her car is nowhere in sight. She borrows a bicycle from the night watchman and rides a mile to the yacht club where Heberto keeps his motorboat.

Nobody else is on the road. The muscles of her legs flex and lock, moving her forward with unaccustomed speed. Everything appears the same veiled color: the bottle palms and the blacktop road, the mini-malls with their lusterless promises, a flock of plastic flamingos in a man-made lagoon. No one stops her at the solitary guardhouse.

Heberto's little boat is rocking in its moorings, but there is no sign at all of her husband. The door to the clubhouse is locked. The children's pool is drained, its paint an unnatural blue. In the harbor, a manatee surfaces in search of fresh water.

Constancia follows a low droning sound to the storage warehouse. Her pink Cadillac convertible, its motor running, is wedged inside among anchors and ropes. The air is thick with a killing exhaust. Heberto lies naked on the backseat, unconscious, his arms tied behind his back, a dirty crew sock stuffed in his mouth. There is a bucket of orange roughy rotting in the driver's seat.

For a moment, Constancia hesitates, struck by the strange peacefulness of her husband's expression. She climbs onto Heberto, slips, climbs again, then starts pounding his chest until she resuscitates him, pounds him and pounds him until his eyelids flutter.

Dulce Fuerte

HAVANA

Sex *is the only thing* they can't ration in Havana. It's the next-best currency after dollars, and much more democratic, if you ask me. The biggest problem is competition. Then policemen. Almost everyone I know my age, male or female, turns a trick once in a while. It's the easiest thing in the world, and most of the time you can convince yourself it's just a date that went a little too far. The foreigners like us because there isn't supposed to be any AIDS in Cuba. That's probably El Comandante's most successful propaganda campaign yet. But it's just that. Propaganda.

Take a stroll with me down the Malecón, and you'll see what I'm talking about. It's a fucking safari. And anybody with a pair of brand-name sneakers or sunglasses is the big game. See those *jineteros* over there? I know them. Very ambitious. They make a living from the hustling. With their dollars and closets of tourist-shop gifts, they're the perfect go-betweens for ordinary Cuban citizens. Don't be so shocked. What the hell else are people supposed to do? Do you really think a family of five can live on one scrawny chicken a month? *¡Por favor!*

Despite what my mother suspects, I'm not a professional. I only buy what I need. I only buy what I *need*. Right now, I'm out here earning pocket money until my visa comes through for Spain.

Like I said, it takes an occasional *novio* to get by. Mamá doesn't understand this. She's immune from the day-to-day hassles because she's had that bureaucrat lackey lover of hers since the dawning of *la revolución*. Every night, Pepín brings her a feast from God knows where. Fresh steamed lobsters. Steaks thick as my thumb. Mangoes so perfectly ripe and sweet—not the stringy stuff you get with coupons— they're a kind of ecstasy. He also brings her shampoo that doesn't glue your hair together like the local brand, when you can find it. Let's just say the woman hasn't had to wait in a line since the Year of Ten Million, when the whole country went crazy cutting sugarcane.

Mamá isn't the most fervent revolutionary on the island, but she's basically tolerant of the system. She and Pepín say that young people today are spoiled and don't appreciate all we have, that we should've seen how things were before the revolution to understand deprivation. Everybody I know is sick of these arguments, sick of picking potatoes and building dormitories, only to find no meaningful work in the careers we trained for. Sick of not washing our hands after we shit because there isn't any soap. Sick of the blackouts and dry faucets. Sick of having nothing to do, period. At minimum, it can make a person permanently irritable.

You can never work hard enough here, either. Cuba is like an evil stepmother, abusive and unrewarding of effort.

More, more, and more for more nothing. Until last month, when they fired me for fraternizing with a foreigner, I was the volleyball coach at José Martí High School (we came in sixth last year at the national championships), and I earned one hundred eighteen pesos a month. *Créeme*, it's not easy staying in shape on sugar-and-lard sandwiches. At least this way, I make a few dollars. That's how it breaks down here — those with dollars and those without. Dollars mean privileges. A roll of toilet paper. A bottle of rum. Pesos mean *te jodes*. You're fucked. It's that simple.

Come here. Look at this view, this harbor, this gorgeous curve of coast. Men from all over the world tell me that Havana is the most beautiful city they've ever seen. So when will we get it back? When will it be truly ours again? *Coño*, El Caballo has four broken legs, and no one has the courage to put him out of his misery.

My father, José Luís Fuerte, was one of the original revolutionaries. He was at Moncada and in the Sierra Maestra side by side with you-know-who. Part of a museum display in Santiago de Cuba is devoted to his exploits. Mamá took me there when I was a kid. There was a blown-up photograph of him with a rifle across his back. He's smoking a too big cigar and has a beaded bracelet on his wrist. The odd thing was that he seemed very familiar to me, even though I'd never seen him before. Then I realized it was because I'd inherited his face.

All the while I was growing up and misbehaving, Mamá used to say: What would your father think if he were still alive? It used to shame me for the moment. I have a tattoo on my shoulder, three twisting vines intertwined with the name of my first boyfriend, coincidentally also named José Luís. When I was fourteen and got pregnant by him, my father was the first person I thought of. Mamá never found out, or she would've insisted I have the kid. She was sixteen when I was born and says she couldn't have imagined her life otherwise. Mamá's been after me to have a child. And for what? So she can coo over the kid before shipping him off to some boarding school in *el campo* like she did with me? Forget about it.

These days, I find myself wondering not what my father would think of me but what he would think of his revolution and his former heroes.

People know my father was José Luís Fuerte, and so it makes it difficult sometimes. They expect more from me. I used to be friends with Che Guevara's son in high school. We used to joke about our respective revolutionary burdens. Last I heard, he was a heavy-metal musician, pierced everywhere and trying to leave the country.

I thought of leaving too. At night on an inner tube with other *balseros*, from the beach at Jaimanitas or Santa Fé. A friend of mine from junior high, Lupita Núñez, tried it in 1989, but she got picked up by the Cuban coast guard and sentenced to three years in jail. Others get eaten by sharks or go insane from the thirst. The people who make it to Miami become the real heroes of the revolution. My friends and I listen to the shortwave or spend hours trying to tune in to Radio Martí to get the news. Or if we're really lucky, a TV report from south Florida.

Leaving. Leaving and dollars. That's all anybody ever talks about anymore. *¡Basta ya!*

Sometimes, late at night, I wonder how my life would've been different if Mamá had left for the United States with her sister. Tía Constancia lives in New York and has two grown children. I like to imagine how cold it gets there. I'd like to wrap myself in fur and skate endlessly on frozen lakes. Round and round I'd go, my breath a trace of vapor behind me. In Cuba, there aren't any lakes. And only the future is frozen.

When I'm not out here on the Malecón, I ride my bicycle to pass the time. Not by choice, believe me. The damn island ran out of gas, and then the government started importing these bulky black bikes from China and tried to convince everyone that it was good for their health. Well, for once they were right. People started losing weight and having more energy for sex—not that there's ever a shortage of *that* here. Now something like a million bicycles clog Havana, and total chaos reigns in the streets. It's as if cars never existed.

I like to take my bike out of the city and ride for hours in the countryside. On weekends I've gone clear across to the Viñales Valley in Pinar del Río province. There are fields of tobacco everywhere you look. Mamá tells me her father's family came from there, that they were refined people who recited poetry and played music every night. She still has the handmade violin my great-grandfather Reinaldo brought with him from Spain in 1903. Every now and then, Mamá takes the violin out of its little coffin and rubs the horsehair bow with a speck of rosin. I often think of my great-grandfather as I ride, suspended low over the earth, skimming along just fast enough to notice anything important.

My boyfriends come from everywhere. But the Canadian tourists are the easiest tricks, because they want to believe everything you tell them. Like that guy over there. Look how he can't keep his eyes off that trashy number in the hot pants. *¡Que nalgotas!* Something happens to their brains when they hit Cuba. My theory is that it's the ratio of sunlight to oxygen to ocean here. Ninety percent of their cells are dormant until they arrive and see a good-looking *habanera*. Then all hell breaks loose. Unfortunately, they're so sexually deprived, they make you work harder than anyone else on the planet.

From what I can tell, the only people making a decent living here are the *babalawos*. There's one around the corner from my building who's redone his entire house with money from *santería* initiations. Only a couple of years ago, everyone knew where to find Lisardo Cuenca if he was needed, but it was all very hushed. His house looked like any other on the street, peeling with old paint. The occasional bleating of an illegal goat or the appearance of a horde of paralytics on his doorstep was the only clue to the secret power inside.

Now you should see the place. A thirty-foot statue of San Lázaro stands on his minuscule lawn, and his house is painted white with bright-blue stripes. Seventeen matching flags surround it, and people come from all over, openly carrying pigeons, sacks of beans, and toasted corn. Cuenca's best clients are referred to him by the government: foreigners who want an authentic initiation. Cuenca charges them a fortune, too. Four thousand dollars in cash is what I've heard. The government, of course, gets its cut. Anything in the name of foreign exchange.

You know things have gotten desperate when the Party needs to buy off the *babalawos*. I don't care if a white dove came to rest on El Comandante's shoulder during his inauguration speech, or that he was clearly the gods' chosen one. I don't think anybody, god or mortal, could have imagined how bad things would get here, to what depths people would stoop for a pork leg or a rusty saw. You always hear how the revolution divided families left and right. But what's going on now is worse than anything that preceded it. I heard of one family committing their grandmother to an asylum to get her apartment in Old Havana, of a brother killing his twin over a used battery for his Chevrolet.

• • •

The Malecón's been getting rough lately with lowlifes and black marketeers. The hustlers carry knives now, work the strip in pairs. You have to be careful. They don't appreciate girls like me, who come out only occasionally and give them competition. See this scar on my stomach? Some bitch came after me with a metal nail file when her French boyfriend dared look me over. That's when I decided to try my luck at the Habana Libre Hotel. No Cuban woman worth her salt would wear the ugly sandals and calf-length skirts I see on the tourists, so that's what I put on to pass for an *extranjera*. My English is pretty convincing too, for about ninety seconds, just enough to get me a seat at the rooftop bar. That's where I met Abelardo.

At first, I thought he might be an undercover cop, on account of his exaggerated Castilian accent (one of their stupider tricks). But he started off by telling me how he lives with his widowed sister in a tiny high-rise apartment in Madrid. His left hand is partially withered, and he held it up in what little intermittent light reflected off the revolving mirrored ball, as if to say, *Are you sure you still want to talk to me?* He seemed surprised when I did.

Then he told me he had a tumor the size of a plum on his balls, but the doctors assured him it was benign. I almost lost my nerve right then, but he took my hand and told me, sincerely, I thought, that I was the most beautiful woman he'd ever seen, and the kindest, and would I give him the pleasure and honor of becoming his wife.

The old man scared the hell out of me, and it must have shown, because he pulled back, apologized profusely, and—¡*Coño!* ¡*Cojones!* ¡*Hijo de la gran puta que es tu madre!*—he began to cry. Not a little disappointed snuffling but loud, heartrending sobs. Everyone turned to stare at me. The room became utterly still. Out. Out. Get out of there. But I was glued to my seat like an idiot while Abelardo wailed on. Hotel security arrived three abreast and arrested me. *I* was arrested at the bar of a Cuban hotel because I couldn't produce a foreign passport.

The rest is too tedious to tell in detail, but here's the bottom line: I got booked for prostitution, lost my job coaching volleyball, worked two hours in a cement plant with no cement before walking out, and decided to marry Abelardo.

TREE DUCKS

❀

My father liked to boast that he'd arrived in Cuba with ten pesos in one pocket, a volume of verse by the great Romantic poets in another, and his handmade violin. For one month he played his caprices and sonatinas, collecting coins on the streets of Havana, interspersing his selections with the more mundane requests of passersby. One day, a young widow spat at him on the Paseo del Prado. Her husband had been killed in the Spanish-American War, and she could not stand to hear Papá's Castilian accent.

The desk clerk at my father's pensión recommended that he become a lector on account of his grandiloquent voice. A week later, Papá got a job in a cigar factory in the Vuelta Abajo region of Pinar del Río. His first day on the platform, perspiring with nervousness and encircled by cigar smoke and the scrutinous eyes of a hundred workers, he began to read:

*"In a village of La Mancha the name of which I have
no desire to recall, there lived not so long ago one of
those gentlemen who always have a lance in the rack,
an ancient buckler, a skinny nag, and a greyhound
for the chase . . ."*

As a boy, I often wondered how Papá had endured those
first months away from home, surrounded by strangers, a
refined misfit among coarser men, a man whose first purchase
in Cuba, after much sacrifice and diligent saving, was a gramo-
phone and a thick record of the "Witches' Dance Variations" by
Paganini.

In time, my father met Soledad Varela, a local flutist, ten
years his senior. It was a Sunday afternoon, and they were
attending a concert by a chamber music quartet from Havana.
In fact, they were the only ones in the audience. Mamá sat in
her wide-brimmed straw hat. Papá smoothed a Panama in his
lap. She liked the way his mouth moved, his unseemly mustache. He liked the way she held her silence, unafraid, weighing
her words like silver on her tongue.

It turned out they had much to say to one another, about
the muddy-sounding flute and the violin tuned half a note too
high. They continued their conversation after the concert,
beginning a three-day courtship that ended in Pinar del Río's
town hall. Mamá was thirty-one years old and by then had
refused proposals of marriage from suitors women half her age
would have coveted. But in Reinaldo Agüero of Galicia, a new-
comer not long off the boat, she had found her destiny.

From my parents' first meeting, my future was born and
the very moment I am living was predetermined. From my parents' first meeting, two more people walk the earth in search of
solace, two more people with Papá's first loneliness echoing in
their breasts.

• • •

Music is my earliest memory, earlier than sight or smell or touch, earlier than consciousness itself. My parents spent most evenings playing duets, for which they were technically, if not temperamentally, suited. Papá worshiped the magnificent "Carnaval de Venice," while Mamá preferred the stateliness of Beethoven's adagios or the more restrained brilliance of Tchaikovsky's "Danse Russe." I remember how the mood of our house was colored by the music in it, as if the notes themselves could brush the air with paint.

Although I was not musical in any conventional sense, I could, at an early age, accurately imitate the calls of every bird in the woods around Pinar del Río. Our neighbor, Secundino Robreño, used to coax me into the forest to help him secure doves for his poultry cart. I warbled with such proficiency that within moments, dozens of birds dropped from the trees to welcome his shotgun. Secundino rewarded me with sticky candies from his pockets, usually less than fresh, or a handful of spent bullets.

During one of our expeditions, I discovered the nest of a tree duck in a hollow stump north of town. Inside were four eggs and, fortunately, no mother yaguasa in sight. Secundino offered me twenty cents apiece for the eggs, a fantastic sum at the time, but I refused him and decided to raise the fledglings myself. I gathered the eggs carefully, placing one in each trouser pocket and holding the other two in my cupped hands. On the way home, balancing on the balls of my feet, I whistled the yaguasa's one-note song to soothe the unborn chicks.

In those days, people used to gather tree-duck eggs for profit. The nests could be found in clumps of regal bromelias or in the crooks of trees cushioned with thick Spanish moss. Common folk and breeders alike used to raise the yaguasas among their own domestic poultry, because they broke up barnyard quarrels and whistled at the approach of strangers.

Tree ducks, I daresay, were an avian blend of bouncer and rural guard.

My yaguasas grew to be quite elegant, with lovely long necks and the hauteur of fine geese. Of course, they were excellent watch ducks too. In fact, my mother credited them with saving my father's life during a particularly fractious strike at the cigar factory.

Early one morning, two men I did not recognize knocked on our front door. The taller one carried a tree limb studded with nails. The shorter one, unshaven, had pineapple fists. It was apparent they had come to teach my father a lesson for his leading role in the strike.

No sooner did Papá come to the door than my ducks raced from the backyard, whistling and squawking and scattering feathers. They attacked the men with the resolve of old hens, viciously pecking and scratching them until the thugs stumbled away in a daze. No one ever came to disturb our peace again.

Sadly, the once abundant yaguasas have disappeared along with the island's lowland forests. With luck, one might still spot a few in the remotest regions of the Zapata swamp. At night, they fly out to visit the palm groves of cultivated plantations and eat the palmiches, *the clustered fruit of the royal palms.*

Neither of my parents had any inclination toward ornithology, so it was all the more remarkable that they encouraged in me a preoccupation so far removed from their own interests. They indulged me with frequent trips into the countryside for my field observations. On one trip near Bailén, I spotted a pair of sandhill cranes, already quite rare when I was a boy. They were digging in the scorched earth of what was probably their former breeding grounds, digging with their bills for roots or beetle larvae in land that had been cleared to plant more sugarcane.

On another trip, to the Lomas de los Acostas, I caught my

first sight of a red-tailed hawk. It was known locally as the gavilán del monte by the peasants who lived in the huts high on the open savanna hills. "¡Gavilanes del monte! ¡Gavilanes del monte!" the women cried from ridge to ridge when they spotted the hawks. Then they turned to warn their own chickens, which scurried, terrified, into their coops.

Every spring and fall, I searched the trees for the many migrants that lingered in Cuba en route to and from South America. I collected hundreds of birds over the years, shooting them with my sling and a few well-chosen stones. Mamá complained that our house flew with feathers, but how else could I study my beloved birds? I watched their migrations and imagined flying in their immense flocks, darkening the unreachable parts of the sky. Often, they traveled at night, billions of them, at altitudes too high to be easily observed, taking their cues from the sun and the stars, wind directions, and the magnetic fields of the earth. That, I decided, was how I'd fancy traveling.

During the winter of 1914, a record number of American redstarts and black-throated blue warblers sojourned in Cuba. The trees around our house positively shook with their commotion, disturbing my father, who had fallen ill with yellow fever. His temperature soared, he vomited continually and could barely lift his head from the pillow. After several days, jaundice set in. Still the birds continued to bicker and sing.

My mother and I took turns reading aloud The Meditations of Marcus Aurelius, to which Papá had frequently turned when troubled: "Think of the universal substance, of which thou hast a very small portion; and of universal time, of which a short and indivisible interval has been assigned to thee; and of that which is fixed by destiny, and how small a part of it thou art."

Mamá soothed Papá's fever with cold cloths and held his hands for hours, as if trying to transmit through her fingertips her own vitality. She made Papá caldo gallego and gave him black Spanish olives to suck. Slowly, his health improved, although he was never the same again.

On his first day back to the cigar factory, Papá's step was plodding and faltering, and I was certain he could not walk the entire mile to the outskirts of town. I accompanied him, bracing his elbow. Friends greeted him along the way, ignoring the sweat that rolled from beneath his hat, and this seemed to encourage him.

When at last we arrived at the factory and Papá, with great difficulty, climbed the three steps to his platform, the room erupted with hoarse cheers. "¡A-güe-ro! ¡A-güe-ro!" the workers chanted, clapping and stamping their feet to the rhythm of our name.

"Please, hijo." My father finally turned to me, his voice barely audible. He raised his palm to the crowd, and the room became silent, suffused with smoke and the sweet smell of cedar. "Read for me today."

He handed me a heavy book, its red leather faded, its spine broken from so many readings, and I took his place at the lectern. I turned to the first page. The smoky air made my eyes water. Words scattered before me like a frightened school of fish.

The workers strained toward me. My voice was small, hesitant. Down below, a paper fan fluttered. I reached the second paragraph and stopped.

"Go on, Ignacio," my father whispered.

"There was a king with a large jaw, and a queen with a plain face, on the throne of England; there was a king with a large jaw, and a queen with a fair face, on the throne of France. In both countries it was clearer than crystal to the lords of the State preserves of loaves and fishes that things in general were settled forever."

SPRING MIGRATION

✵

HAVANA

MARCH 1991

It is the time of the spring migration. Reina Agüero opens the French doors of her father's study and steps onto the small square of balcony three stories above the pavement. She searches the sky for the slightest hint of morning but finds none. The moon is still firmly in charge. At this hour, the trade winds clear the air of the day's rude accretions, and it is good to breathe.

Reina cranes her neck to the left, toward the dark moving silhouettes of treetops sheltering the dead in Colón Cemetery, toward the ancient poinciana guarding her mother's grave. Then she looks to the right, past the floating procession of wrought-iron balconies, past the slow-changing colors of traffic lights directing the rhythm of cars on the Paseo Aranguren. If she listens closely, Reina can hear a car sputtering down the Avenida de los Presidentes. Isn't someone, she thinks, always trying to escape?

The street is deserted except for a light in the old mansion on the corner. It is a building of associations now, for poets and painters, sculptors and ceramists. Its walls are optimistically lacquered with murals. Is it forgetfulness or necessity, Reina speculates, that keeps the light burning?

Pepín Beltrán is asleep on her bed, snoring loudly as he always does after they make love. Although he insists that he is aroused as ever by the discordant new landscape of her skin, Reina has noticed that Pepín lingers longest by his own dermal donation, stitched in the glossy hollow of her back. Most of Reina's nutmeg color is gone, replaced by a confusion of shades and textures. A few patches of her skin are so pink and elastic, so perfectly hairless, they look like a newborn pig's.

At the hospital in Santiago de Cuba, doctors from around the country came to admire her exceptional recovery, the thickly puckered rind of her behind. But after a while, their prurience disgusted Reina, and she barred them all from her room.

Reina doesn't particularly mind her skin, mismatched and itchy as it is, but she cannot tolerate its stench. No one else seems to notice, but to her it reeks of dry blood and sour milk. She recalls hearing of animals in the wild spurning their own kind when touched by an unknown odor. Now Reina understands why.

She tries to mask the odor by rinsing smoked grapefruit through her hair. But the relief is only temporary. The stink ruins all her familiar pleasures. Gone is her rapture. Gone her hot, black scent. When Reina makes love, nothing, not even Pepín, whose hands erase all borders, whose mouth clashes against hers in love, can make the bliss return. Perhaps it was her own scent, Reina thinks, that had stirred her all along.

It is the first day of her period. Reina is proud that

despite her age and incongruous skin, her monthly blood, at least, is still intact.

Remnants of a bird's nest dangle from the chandelier in her father's study. Reina remembers how Papá used to leave the French doors to his room wide open so that families of birds could flit back and forth with their twigs and bits of thread or twine. They fed on the crumbs of his sandwiches and the mashed-potato croquettes he messily ate at his desk.

"Tell me what you want, and I will tell you who you are." Her father had read those words to her once from a book in his lap. She was too young to understand the question, but she remembered it nonetheless. Well, what is it she wants now? Reina wonders whether it's nostalgia to yearn for her mother, nostalgia to gather her shadows all these years. Why else would she choose to live like this, amidst the debris of her childhood and Papá's dead specimens? What truths can they possibly reveal to her after so long? Can they tell her why her mother died, why her sister was sent away?

Reina remembers how, after her mother's death, everyone's vision splintered. There was a bird that hovered over Mami's burial plot at the Colón Cemetery. Her father pronounced it a common crow. Constancia, fresh from the farm in Camagüey, insisted it was electric blue. Reina wanted to believe her sister, but *she* saw a bird on fire, tiny and bathed in a violent light. It broke the air around them, invited an early dusk. Reina recalls how the emptiness seemed to surround them then, a sad bewilderment that has never lifted.

The day before, Reina had accompanied her father to the Flores y Jorganes Funeral Home on Obispo Street. She carried a prized snakeskin in a little felt sack to place in her mother's coffin. But Papá wouldn't let her anywhere near Mami.

The odor inside the funeral home made Reina catch her breath. In one room, she saw a man with a preposterous mustache, naked and covered with leaves. In another, a plump woman with no fingertips, resting on a sea of satin. Next to her, a pale sliver of a girl lay in a frosted-pink coffin. It was early morning, but Reina remembers thinking she could already hear the moon, its long, threading wail of solitude.

Quietly, Reina slipped away from her father while he was talking to the funeral director. In the last embalming chamber, her mother lay on a rusting pedestal, her throat an estuary of color and disorder, as if a bloody war had taken place beneath her chin. Reina stared at her mother, forced herself to see her whole again, to breathe the lost incense of autumn in her hair.

There were footsteps in the hallway. Reina quickly kissed her mother's cheek, then snuck out to the patio, into shrill daylight, and released the papery fragments of her dried snakeskin to the wind.

When Reina returned from the hospital in Santiago de Cuba, the local Committee for the Defense of the Revolution insisted she volunteer for night duty since she was awake anyway, but Reina refused. Like her cursing, blinded, half-mad *compañeros* at Céspedes Hospital, Reina decided to do nothing more for the revolution.

Reina cannot say when her discontent took root. Pepín, for one, blames El Comandante. After all, it was he who invited the trouble by allowing the exiles to return to Cuba for visits. What those *gusanos* brought in their crammed suitcases—photographs of ranch homes and Cadillacs, leather shoes in every color, watches that told the time in China, even extra-strength aspirin—began rapidly to unravel the revolution. In no time at all, good citizens started skipping the May Day rallies, refused to cut their quota of sugarcane.

Over the years, Reina had hoped her sister would return to Cuba, but Constancia always found an excuse not to come. Instead she sent packages every Christmas, with instant vanilla pudding, cubes of beef bouillon, and the strawberry sourballs she knew Reina loved. Constancia referred to her husband and her children only in passing, updating what Reina hadn't known to begin with. Heberto finally passed his kidney stone; Isabel had dyed her hair indigo, like Indonesian cloth; Silvestre had changed his name to Jack. Curious details.

Reina realized then that she understood as little of her sister's life in America as she had in Cuba. When they were children, Reina had wondered why Constancia had been sent to live so far away. But her mother told her only that she and her sister were meant to live apart.

Six years ago, Reina had a chance to leave the country. She was on a trip to Venezuela with a Cuban delegation of master electricians, to install generators along the Orinoco River, where the mosquitoes feasted on every inch of exposed flesh. By the end of the second week, all her colleagues had defected, and Reina returned to Cuba alone.

Now it's nearly impossible to leave the island without the express permission of El Comandante himself. Escapes have become more daring, the repudiations more scorchingly severe. Last year, Osoris de León, a former lover of Reina's from Tunas de Zaza, a decorated hero from the war in Somalia, fled the island in a stolen government helicopter and landed on the roof of the Miami airport's Holiday Inn. A group of backslapping exiles were waiting for him, and soon Osoris was giving interviews deploring the revolution on Radio Martí. Now Reina's daughter, too, has left Cuba. Her Dulcita, a desperate *jinetera cualquiera*.

Reina wonders what José Luís would think of his revolution now, of Dulcita's defection on the arm of a detestable tourist. José Luís had been one of El Comandante's most trusted aides, his link to sympathetic youth throughout the country. He was only fourteen when he left high school to join the rebels in the Sierra Maestra. Reina discovered José Luís several years later, gaunt and foul-mouthed, subsisting on oranges from her boarding school's grove. She hid him in a local dovecote, far from Batista's men, and later in her bed. When Reina found out she was pregnant, she begged him to marry her.

"Do you think we can keep anything we love, Reina?" José Luís demanded.

When Dulcita was four years old, Reina heard that her beloved had drowned off the Isle of Pines, learning to swim. It was then that she gave their daughter his last name: Fuerte.

Reina knows that Dulcita resents her father, the veneration he still receives as a Hero of the Revolution. As her daughter grew older, his picture stared back at her from her history books, his slogans were extolled while she endlessly harvested lemons or yams. All Dulcita's life, it was José Luís Fuerte this, José Luís Fuerte that, until it made her ill.

If he was so great, why didn't he ever see me? Dulcita was six years old when she asked Reina this. They were on a train headed for Matanzas, to the first of Dulcita's many boarding schools (she was kicked out of eleven altogether). Reina tried to explain to her daughter the nature of longing, the nervous pressure in the heart that never wanes. How could she tell her that José Luís simply hadn't wanted children, that it was nothing personal against Dulcita herself? Finally, Reina told her daughter that she was born of a grand passion, that at one time, nothing had mattered to Reina but her lover's face.

When he died, Reina knew somehow that José Luís had chosen it. Death, she is certain, begins from within. It doesn't wait onstage like a retired general, eager for the podium, but overcomes a body cell by cell. For a few people, this happens long before the accidents and wrinkles, long before the conjugations of regret.

Reina settles down next to Pepín and closes her eyes. Voices gather in her head, scattering senseless codes. Since the burning atop the mahogany tree, voices come to Reina late at night, unfettered by logic, utterly imprecise. *The stars have died, murdered in their nests. Yours are the creased lies of solitude.* Oye, mi hijita, *patience condemns*. Sometimes, like tonight, they creak out a chorus or two of the national anthem:

> *Al combate corred, bayameses*
> *que la patria os contempla orgullosa:*
> *no temaís una muerta gloriosa,*
> *que morir por la patria es vivir . . .*

Sleepless and adrift in the dark, Reina circles and soars over the decades of her life, much like the bats and owls her father once so assiduously studied. She hisses and creaks and scolds herself for what she sees, for what she might have changed, for what she cannot. She avoids the image of her dead mother in the funeral home, which appears as something dangerous and blindingly hot far below, and averts her eyes as if from the direct rays of the sun. Is it for this that she's remained so long conscious?

When she opens her eyes, the voices and images recede. She is thirsty again. Reina drinks water straight from a Mexican pitcher Pepín brought back from a trip to Tampico, then sucks on the last lumps of ice. She paces the chilled marble floor in her bare feet. La Virgen de la Caridad del Cobre has definitely failed her. The rooster flew off with some curse. Pepín insists that the powder he bought from that *bruja*, La Sequita, saved Reina's life. Perhaps he is right, but for what?

Reina reaches in the bottom drawer of her father's desk and pulls out his passport, carefully stored in a wax-paper envelope. It was issued to him in 1948, the spring before her mother died. Reina examines the photograph, the flash-frozen expression. Papá was forty-three when the picture was taken, a sturdy man with brilliantined hair unfashion-ably parted in the center.

A faint blue permit from the United States is stamped on the first page. Reina vaguely recalls a trip he and Mami were planning to the deserts of America. But she can't recall why it was they never went. The succeeding pages of Papá's passport are blank. It seems to Reina that this passport, filed away for years with her father's other important documents, tells the truth of their lives as nothing else does.

Reina wonders, too, whatever happened to the little bone her mother used to carry in a red flannel pouch at her waist. Mami would let her touch the bone sometimes, let her rub a finger against the mushroomy knot at one end. Reina never learned where the bone came from or why her mother kept it.

In the closet, Reina unearths Papá's twelve-gauge shot-gun, in its velvet-lined case. She removes it from its cradle and holds it tight against her shoulder. Then she aims the gun at various targets in the room: the *periquito* her father had shot in a virgin forest near Guantánamo; the opaque globe of streetlight burning just outside her window; Pepín's oblong face, heavy with sleep.

There is a portrait of her mother on the desk. She is much younger than Reina is now, with round cheeks that end in a jutting little chin. Mami's hair is loose and wavy and falls past her shoulders, past her smooth white throat. It seems to Reina that her mother is always calling to her from this photograph, whispering her name.

Constancia grew to look remarkably like their mother after her death. She seemed to absorb Mami's erratic vigor, the spidery movements of her wrists. Even her inflection changed, from a nasal steadiness to the halting, feathery music of Mami's voice. Reina remembers how at the funeral, Constancia frightened all the mourners with this spectral impression. Reina wasn't scared, though. After never knowing her sister, she longed only to love her. Of course, Constancia wouldn't allow it. A week later, her sister went back to looking like herself.

Reina replaces the gun in its case and carries it downstairs. Outside, the wind is sharp, but she doesn't feel its sting. It seems as if she, like the gun, is trapped in black velvet. She walks rapidly to the Avenida de los Presidentes, then turns onto La Rampa. Not a soul anywhere. She passes the white-domed Coppèlia ice cream parlor and the harsh lights of the Habana Libre Hotel. A thumping music drifts down from its rooftop bar, the bar where Dulcita met the Spaniard, but Reina doesn't hear it. She passes ministries and travel agencies, restaurants, cabarets, and movie houses, all closed.

When she reaches the seawall of the Malecón, she stops. The air is rich with salt, and she swallows it hungrily. Reina feels as if the air is filling her heart, expanding it, giving it courage. A block away, a fisherman patiently casts his line, but Reina pays him no mind. Slowly, she steps back from the seawall and, with all the force she can muster, hurls the twelve-gauge shotgun far into the starless night.

MIAMI

The evening gowns flaunt their hothouse colors, as if forced to bloom in artificial light. Jades and saffrons, vermilions, glamorous blacks. The women inside them turn and hesitate, rustling their skirts with a deafening allure. The men wear white guayaberas with stoles of discreet embroidery. Their skin has absorbed the sun their wives take pains to avoid. It is Tropical Night at the club on the bay, and the orchestra plays a cha-cha-chá so hot it nearly scorches the pork.

Constancia pulls her husband to the dance floor. He is diminutive, like her, and she is dressed in white, like him. Together they look like a first communion date. Heberto is a good dancer, but often reluctant. Constancia is not, but excessively enthusiastic. She lurches too far to the right on a turn, but Heberto reels her in with a practiced air. Then he steadies her with a palm to the small of her back and leads her across the room.

Heberto's chest glows through the front of his linen guayabera like a wet forest. He moves gingerly, still bruised from the pounding Constancia gave him in the back of the Cadillac.

"*Carajo*, you almost destroyed me," he accuses his wife without warning, rubbing his solar plexus. Heberto maintains that he doesn't remember what happened to him before Constancia found him tied up and unconscious in the yacht club warehouse.

"*Por favor*, Heberto," Constancia counters dismissively. "You were already half dead. You're lucky I got there in time."

According to Gonzalo Cruz, the midnight assault on Heberto was executed by a fanatical exile group that got wind of his selling contraband Cuban cigars in New York. Of course, Constancia thinks, they must have sent some Latin Mata Hari to do the job. How else would Heberto end up stark naked in her car?

Constancia assumes that Heberto and Gonzalo know more than they claim, but how can she prove it? She mistrusts the brothers' growing chumminess, their endless, rum-fueled tête-à-têtes. Look where it's gotten Heberto in only two months!

The trumpets and congas call and respond. Soon Constancia and Heberto are back on the dance floor. His hips take in the extra measure of rhythm. Hers remain a quarter beat behind. Constancia leans forward and presses her mouth over her husband's, tastes the blackness inside. She wonders at that moment if all creatures face their doom opposite men.

Constancia wants to tell Heberto how the methods of ornithologists have changed since her father's day. That instead of guns they string up nets in the jungles now, stare at the birds face-to-face. Then they press their thumbs hard on the exotic birds' breasts to stop the dainty motors of their hearts.

"You don't need to die yet," Constancia says instead, more softly than she intended. Her own chest aches with too much exhaled air. *No te vayas, mi cielo.*

The swell of a new mambo takes hold of the room. A woman dancing alone in an atomic-red dress bumps up against Heberto. She's at least twenty years younger than anyone there. Everywhere she moves, the dancers lose their step. Heberto stops in mid-turn, stares helplessly in her direction. Then he faces Constancia, the anger spreading unexpectedly from his mouth. "I won't loiter around here like a bum!" he shouts. Then he swivels into step again, an orchestral extension, and dips Constancia clear to the floor.

Heberto is leaving on Tuesday. Constancia blames Gonzalo for this. She knows firsthand how persuasive a salesman her ex-husband can be. Thirty-five years ago, Gonzalo came courting her, ferocious with dreams. He cut open a vein in his leg to impress her, brought her a wreath of dead bees. He said: *Mi vida, te lo juro,* I will know what you need.

Constancia considered him a hazard, like languor or sunstroke, and resisted his contagion. But it only drove him toward her all the more. The day Gonzalo took her hand, he left a live stain. It colonized her arm, overpowered her heart. Constancia and he shattered all language their first months together. Then Gonzalo had nothing left to say.

Heberto had joined Gonzalo's underground exile group, La Brigada Caimán, shortly before the attack in the pink Cadillac. The organization takes credit for every plot and bomb against suspected Communists, whether it's responsible for the violence or not. Gonzalo boasts that La Brigada Caimán stages military rehearsals in the Everglades in preparation for a final takeover of Cuba. The big invasion, he hints, could occur this very summer.

Constancia can tell that her husband is overcome with a sickness of possibility, with the promising grandeur of a quasi-historical calling. Already he's bought brand-new guerrilla fatigues and a hunter's knife for his utility belt. How could she have predicted that Gonzalo's crude appeals would so stir Heberto? She considered her husband a strict *comerciante*, with little use for leisure or politics. In fact, he never seemed to enjoy anything unless there was a likely, definable yield.

"Don't be ridiculous, Heberto," Constancia sniffs as they wait their turn at the banquet table. "There's nothing left to inherit in Cuba, nothing left to divide."

Her husband loads his plate with hunks of *lechón asado*, *arroz con frijoles*, avocado salad, and *yuca* in garlic sauce. Then he serves himself a huge portion of flan for dessert.

Constancia thinks of how self-delusion is integral to even the most senseless endeavors by men. "We moved to Miami so you could relax!" she insists. Instantly, she realizes it's the wrong thing to say.

Heberto refuses to tell Constancia where he's going, but he expects her to pack for him just the same. Constancia shrank his underwear too tight for wearing, hid the laces for his army boots. When he goes to apply his deodorant, Heberto will find grade A honey in its place.

"Men always confuse patriotism with self-love!" Constancia hisses between bites of fried plantains. It's a perverse form of idealism. Why else all the primping and medals, all the oiled and spit-shined leathers? In her opinion, war should be strictly personal, like philosophy or sexual preference.

· · ·

Later that night, Constancia approaches her husband, who is feigning sleep in their bed. She slips off her evening gown, slides naked across the sheets. Then she pushes herself to standing, plants one foot on either side of Heberto's head. Constancia stares down at her husband, at the pleated humidity of his face. Slowly, she lowers herself until he must breathe her entirety. She rocks on her heels until the whole bed trembles, unsettled with her desire.

Constancia knows her husband is perplexed by her sexual urgency of late. It's as if a vital pleasure has reasserted itself since she found him inert in her Cadillac. Now she feels as if there were no history, no memory, no future between them except death.

The next morning, Constancia follows Heberto across the Rickenbacker Causeway in a rented sedan from the hotel down the beach. Her convertible, she decided, is much too conspicuous for pursuit. The bay is flawlessly blue, an immaculate abstraction. Sailboats graze the water with starched rectitude. Constancia notices how distances are distorted by this blue, like an unreliable mirror.

Her husband is headed north. Constancia hates to drive on the I-95, but she's committed to this chase. The traffic is erratic, clots of cars followed by mile after mile of clear highway. The jumble of downtown skyline increases her restlessness. Miami is too young a city for peace. Nine cruise ships are docked on Dodge Island, hung with banners and triangular flags. Every Saturday night, Constancia spies the ships advancing along the horizon, imperceptibly, like time itself.

Constancia is driving seventy miles per hour behind her husband. She knows he won't see her. Heberto goes too fast, never checks his rearview mirror, carelessly changes lanes.

Besides, Constancia is in disguise, much too garish to be recognized. Her hair is swept up inside a flowered turban, her sunglasses are oversized. She wears fuchsia lipstick well past her mouth's outline.

Her husband continues north, past signs for the airport, past exits Constancia might have guessed he would take. Then, to her surprise, Heberto heads west toward Bird Jungle. Constancia visited it one afternoon when Heberto went fishing. She found a *guajiro* there who told her everything he knew: that the bones of the loons are most like those of the first birds who flew; that on the Chincha Islands of Peru, five million cormorants roost; that of all the birds in Cuba, the quail dove wore the most riveting blue.

Heberto continues past Bird Jungle, past Le Jeune Road, to the entrance of Hialeah Park. Although the racetrack is closed for off-season, men with hoes and mowers meticulously work the grounds. The gatekeeper waves Heberto in as if he were a regular customer. Constancia stops a half mile behind. Moments later, she follows her husband inside.

Constancia wanders through the deserted clubhouse, brackish with last season's smells, and raps on each betting window. She inspects the men's rooms, the ribbed cage of the grandstand. Everything is empty of Heberto.

Outside, in a garden of bromeliads, a spotted iguana suns itself on a rock. Constancia remembers the black iguana she saw once, hung to dry from a *yagruma* tree in Pinar del Río. Her father explained that the black iguanas were nearly extinct because the *campesinos* killed them to ward off bad luck.

The paddocks are green with tending and recent rains. A duet of frogs sits in a puddle, courting or complaining, she isn't sure which. Flamingos are everywhere, awkwardly preening. Constancia suddenly longs for a horse to brush. For years, her father used the same two mares on their collecting expeditions. Gordita was plump and parti-colored and fond of peeled grapes. Epictetus was the color of chestnuts and loved a good chase. Both horses died on the same day in the Zapata Swamp, driven mad, her father said, by relentless mosquitoes.

Her mother died with the horses that day. Her father said that Mamá had drowned after they'd separated to better catch the evasive ruddy ducks. He said Mamá slipped and hit her temple on a log, that she breathed in the swamp water, unconscious, until she died. Constancia remembers watching Papi's face as he told her this, his flat, decided eyes. She remembers thinking that Mamá may have died, but she'd be impossible to bury, that she'd remain in their lives forever, sulfurous as her absence.

When Reina insisted that she'd seen Mamá in the funeral home with a shattered throat, Papi denied this was possible. Reina screamed like an animal blinded and tore all the blossoms from her favorite tulip tree. Then she went from house to house, pulling up the neighbors' gardens, scattering petals and bees.

When their father sent them to the boarding school in Trinidad, her sister took to sitting in the rain, numb as a wildflower, sucking on fallen leaves. Constancia wanted nothing to do with Reina, rebuffed her overtures, refused to hear another word about Mamá. Constancia felt jealous of her sister's grief, for she felt nothing at all.

A year later, Papi finally confided to Constancia that what Reina had seen was no lie. Their mother had shot herself in the Zapata Swamp, he said, aimed the gun at her own throat. He made Constancia promise never to tell Reina, that the secret would only reopen wounds. This frightened Constancia more than his original version, because now she knew she couldn't rescue Papi, knew for certain that he would die next.

Constancia crosses the Hialeah racetrack in the noon heat. High above her, in the announcer's box, she spots a waving pair of spangled high-heeled shoes. She is uneasy with the implications. This is one discovery about her husband she refuses to suffer. Constancia rests by the edge of the pond inside the track's ring. Then she tears a frond from a stubby palm and carefully wipes the lipstick from her mouth.

It is late afternoon. Heberto has not yet returned home. Constancia climbs a stepladder and, corner by corner, removes the Cuban flag her husband tacked up on their bedroom wall. She shakes it out until it billows like a freshly laundered sheet. Then she folds it into a diminishing square against her chest. Constancia mistrusts flags, understands all too well their steadfast passion for the dead.

Constancia goes to the living room and selects a record from her collection of twentieth-century Cuban symphonies. The music peels back raw regions of misery, wires lesions from nerve to nerve. When she listens to the rumbling drums, her every season is disturbed.

Her son was seven years old when Constancia gave him a set of bongos to play. Silvestre banged them and banged them until he could feel the beat. Then he claimed he could still hear things.

"Like what?" Constancia asked him.

Silvestre imitated the roar of the ocean, called out like the vendors plying fruit near the Malecón: *¡Mangos preciosos, mangos deliciosos!* Constancia realized then he was just remembering the sounds, the way amputees still felt their missing arms and legs. Finally, Silvestre imitated Constancia's voice, loud and in Spanish: *Be a little man and don't cry, Silvestre. This is much better than becoming a Communist.*

In 1961, it was rumored in Cuba that children would be rounded up and shipped to boarding schools in the Ukraine. Panicked, parents sent their sons and daughters to orphanages in America, where they hoped to retrieve them after the crisis passed. Constancia sent Silvestre to Colorado. That winter, it was so cold in Denver that her son wore layer upon layer of the clothes Constancia had packed for him. A few other children spoke Spanish. They were at the Catholic orphanage for the same reason as Silvestre: so the Russians wouldn't get them.

In less than a week, Silvestre was in the hospital with a 107-degree temperature and a bad swelling up and down the right side of his body. By the time his fever subsided, he was irreversibly deaf.

A year later, Constancia left Cuba and went with Heberto and baby Isabel to pick up her son. They found Silvestre sequestered in the orphanage infirmary. Constancia refused to believe that Silvestre could no longer hear anything. She clapped her hands behind his back, expecting him to jump. When he didn't, Constancia tore up the room, guilty and grief-stricken, and ended up temporarily hospitalized herself.

There's a picture of Silvestre on the coffee table, framed in polished silver. He is sixteen and dressed in a light-blue tuxedo and an extravagantly ruffled shirt for his junior prom. Constancia remembers dropping him off a block from his high school, then sneaking into the gymnasium later to watch him dance. All the students at his school were deaf, but they rocked to the blasting music anyway, responding to the vibrations from the waxed wooden floor. Constancia spotted Silvestre slow dancing with a tall, buxom girl in a floor-length dress. *She looks nothing like me, nothing at all,* Constancia thought. He nuzzled the girl's neck, and they soon began kissing, Silvestre straining slightly to reach her lips.

The spectacle revived Constancia's sorrow, stunned her with the fidelity of certain unshakable pain.

Constancia turns off the stereo and twists the dial from the twenty-four-hour tides report to *La Hora de los Milagros'* nightly update. There is a follow-up on the Virgin sightings in Cozumel, which local boosters are comparing to the miracles at Lourdes and Guadelupe.

The Virgin, apparently, is still partial to the laundry room at El Presidente Hotel, where she's appeared nine times to the laundress Bernarda Estrada, cloistered now with the Sisters of Mercy. The Virgin also manifested herself twice to kitchen assistant Consuelo Barragán, each time as she was peeling potatoes for the hotel's acclaimed lobster stew. And on the south tennis courts of the Hotel El Cozumeleño, groundskeeper Gustavo Rubio has sworn on the grave of his mother that he saw the Virgin hover six feet above the net, swinging her right arm as if in a powerful serve.

Constancia remembers her own religious devotion, encouraged at first by her nanny, Beatriz Ureña, and then by her ragtag assortment of uncles in Camagüey. There were rituals on the *finca*, men dressed in white, chanting, always chanting late into the night. When Constancia was eight, she jumped from a municipal trolley to show her Tío Dámaso that Jesus would make her fly. Instead Constancia landed on a mango vendor's cart, smashing his careful display. For weeks, she attracted stray cats with her sweet, fleshy scent.

Another time, Constancia carved her thighs with her grandfather's pocket knife, engraving shallow crosses that healed into tiny crucifix scars. But nobody, not even the suggestible nuns at the Santa Ana Convent, would believe they were stigmata.

After her father killed himself, Constancia stopped praying altogether. She knew then that with luck, she might control only the minute precisions of her life. Everything else would be out of reach.

There is a pound of ground beef in the freezer. Constancia defrosts it in the microwave and heats a swirl of olive oil in her largest skillet. She sets a pot of water to boil for the rice. The garlic is dry, but she minces it anyway, chops an onion, the remains of a glossy green pepper, sautés it all in the pan. She browns the meat next, adds a can of tomato sauce, pimientos, stuffed olives, a half box of raisins.

As the *picadillo* simmers, Constancia returns to the balcony with a paring knife to watch the approaching storm. The heat presses against her face like a warm hand. She thinks of something Isabel told her a week ago (where does her daughter learn these odd facts?): that if every person on earth wanted to take a vacation in the galaxy, there'd be thirty solar systems to choose from apiece. Constancia repeated this statistic to Heberto, but he didn't seem the least bit impressed.

Last month, Isabel sent them a gift for their thirty-second anniversary: a collection of dead wrens in jars of formaldehyde, dressed in woolen booties and shawls. Her daughter knitted the pastel outfits herself. Isabel said that since she'd stopped her pottery, she's been experimenting with more conceptual pieces, involving traditional handicrafts. *Anniversary Birds*, she said, was evidence of her new artistic direction.

Constancia cuts through the balcony screen in five places. The metallic gashes curl inward like injured leaves. Constancia wonders whether she could ever kill herself. She would do it differently from her parents, choose a high open place, a suitable cliff, a sunny stretch of Mediterranean coast. Certainly no place where they could find her broken body for her husband and her children to lament.

Constancia takes a step forward and flattens both hands against the torn screen. Heberto is leaving the day after tomorrow. It's against nature to choose death, yet the alternative, this slow lifetime of dying, hardly seems dignified at times. Her limbs feel heavy with blood. Constancia tries to recall her dreams of last night, but she can't remember a single one, remembers only the weight and disturbance of having dreamed them.

The sun's absence spreads down the beach, then approaches itself wave by wave. It is a colossal disregard, indifference afire. It leaves behind a landscape no ordinary darkness can hide.

THE LEATHERBACK

❋

My parents celebrated my thirteenth birthday the way they did every important event in our lives, with ceremony and fanfare. Papá baked me an almond torte with marzipan parrots he'd ordered from a sweet shop in Havana, then the two of them serenaded me for an hour like a pair of mariachis. Mamá sang in her squeaky, scratchy way, so unlike her mellifluous speaking voice, and Papá slowly forced out his baritone until "Happy Birthday to You" sounded more like a speech than a song.

I'd expected a gift, but none so spectacular as the full-color, single-volume British encyclopedia Birds of the World. One thousand forty-three pages in all. Years later, this exquisite volume was stolen from my office at the University of Havana. The illustrations turned up in the markets throughout Cuba, framed in cheap wood and sold for pennies to guajiros as *decorations for their homes. I know this because I bought several of the illustrations myself in Guardalavaca and Morón.*

After dinner, my father and I walked through the balmy streets of Pinar del Río, stopping here and there to greet a friend or admire the latest binoculars in the window of the camera shop. This aimless strolling went on for an hour or more, unusual for my purposeful father. It seemed that Mamá had instructed Papá to discuss with me the ways of nature— me, a keen observer of the animal kingdom since I could walk! Papá coughed and strained uncomfortably with his words until I found myself waving my hands the way he did when he was impatient or anxious.

"De acuerdo," he said. "But in case your mother asks you, tell her we've spoken."

Since his bout with yellow fever, Papá often asked me to substitute for him at the cigar factory. I was no longer so nervous before a crowd, and the cigar workers complimented me on my voice—not nearly as sonorous as my father's, they said, but high and distinct as chimes. It was not what I wanted to hear, but I accepted their praise just the same.

On one such day, I organized the morning's reading: two local newspapers, a movie magazine, the latest newsletter from the International Cigar Workers Union, and Papá's favorite recipe for Galician-style scallop pie, which called for a special type of scallion grown only in Spain. My father had taken to sharing his culinary expertise with the cigar rollers, who greatly appreciated his cooking tips. Once, when Papá had tried to demonstrate how to prepare the perfect torta a la española *on a portable burner, the director stopped him mid-lesson for creating a fire hazard. A banner reading* NO COOKING ON THE PREMISES *still hung, frayed and yellowed with smoke, in the back of the hall. In the afternoon, I would continue with the*

Spanish translation of La Bête Humaine, *which Papá had begun the week before.*

After lunch, a new employee walked through the factory doors. She was the very image of a voluptuous carnival reveler I'd once admired in a nineteenth-century engraving. The young woman, who wore a gingham dress and a starched white kerchief, took a seat in the front row and removed a circular blade from her purse. The foreman brought her a large pile of tobacco leaves. She was a despalilladora, *whose specialty it was to strip the stems from the leaves.*

Up on the platform, all my old nervousness returned. I felt as if the despalilladora *alone sat below me, judging me with her lustrous eyes. I cleared my throat and began to read:*

> *"At eleven-fifteen, dead on time, the man on duty at the Europe bridge gave the regulation two blasts on the horn to signal the approach of the express train from Le Havre as it emerged from the Batignolles tunnel. . . ."*

I felt exceedingly hot, stifled, but there was no window I could open, no place I could turn for air. I noticed that the despalilladora *did not smoke cigars but that she inhaled the smoke deeply, with satisfaction, as if the wisps encircling her were fresh breezes from the sea.*

> *". . . Soon the turntables clanked as the train entered the station with a short note on the whistle, squealing on the brakes, steaming and running with water from the driving rain that had been pouring down all the way from Rouen. . . ."*

A distressing prickliness spread through my body, starting in my chest, where my heart knocked loudly, then to all my extremities at once. In an instant, my skin was coated with sweat and every vein in my body jumped with blood. Down below, the despalilladora *stared at me, her eyebrows raised in concern, her circular blade poised in midair.*

I awoke flat on my back in the offices of El Cid's general manager. My mother stood above me, passing a hand over my forehead. It smelled good, of vanilla, of the creamy soaps she used. She helped me sit up, straightened my collar and tie, then looked me full in the face.

"You're in love, Ignacito," Mamá whispered so no one else could hear, and held me tight against her.

Nothing came of my obsession, which lasted the better part of a year, except that I missed many days of school, spying on Teresita Castillo. My sentiments, opulent with insecurities, bred in me humorlessness so severe as to border on pathos. How could I laugh when I feared more than anything being laughed at myself?

I learned that Teresita had recently married and moved to Pinar del Río from another part of the Viñales Valley. Her husband, Rodolfo, a slight man with an unexpected, sinewy strength, drove a truck for a box factory and was gone for days at a time on cross-country deliveries. I imagined saving Teresita from this unworthy mite, offering her a life by my side, but I had just then started high school.

Each time Teresita and I met—never by chance, since I knew her schedule down to the minute and occasioned to see her several times daily—she asked about my health, as if I were somehow sickly or prone to fainting spells. This ate at me more viciously than any acid, which, in my despair, I thought of swallowing. If I could not win Teresita's love, I would settle for her pity. Pity, I'd learned from reading so many of Papá's novels, often proved a fertile, if shallow, soil for romance.

Such foolish thoughts, such a foolish heart! It would be

almost comical if, looking back, I did not feel a twinge of the anguish I once felt.

My mother was kindest to me during this time, which is to say she left me alone, asked me no questions, and made certain I ate despite my distraction. Papá was less comforting. He lost patience when I pestered him for details about my beloved. I wanted to hear only superlatives about Teresita Castillo. That she was the best despalilladora in the factory, the quickest and most efficient with her knife. That she was the kindest of all the cigar workers, the most generous of heart. But my father would not condescend to tell me what I wished to hear.

During the time I was in love with Teresita, Papá did not ask me to read for him at the factory. My mother must have ensured this with gently pointed threats.

Shortly before Easter, Teresita confided to me that she had an infestation of bats in her roof. What marvelous luck! Of course, I knew all about her bats from my constant spying, but I did not let on. Most Cubans in those days were quite tolerant of bats—a simple fact of life, after all. This was unlike the attitude prevalent among Americans and even a few Europeans, who erroneously credited bats with all manner of antisocial behavior. Still, the number of bats in Teresita's house had grown immoderate and the stench too pronounced to ignore.

I arrived at Teresita's house just before nightfall, dressed in my father's borrowed waistcoat and jacket, looking more appropriate for a state dinner than a mass extermination. She invited me in, kindly ignoring my appearance, and offered me something to drink.

"A whiskey, if you have it. Or a cognac. Por favor." I immediately regretted this.

"Would a little rum do?" she asked me, straight-faced. I wanted to kiss her in gratitude.

"Yes, yes. Thank you."

I took small, burning gulps of the liquor.

"This is about the time they begin stirring," Teresita said. I stared at her, uncomprehending, my face and chest on fire. "The bats," she emphasized. "Can't you hear them?"

In fact, the bats were squeaking and scuttling above us with a rapidly intensifying clamor. A moment later, the sounds melded into what sounded like the buzz of a gigantic beehive.

"There they go!" Teresita announced above the din. "¡Mira!"

Outside the window, a stream of bats poured into the air, forming a huge gray-black whirlpool. Around and around they went, as hundreds more took flight, circling at high speeds before flying off in every direction.

"Tedarida murina," I said. "They're the best fliers on the island." I wanted to tell Teresita that the bats were the second most plentiful in Cuba after Molossus tropidorhynchus, *that they occupy much the same position among their kind as swifts do among birds, that their long, narrow wings row through the air so rapidly that the bats oscillate from side to side, that their habitat extends to Jamaica, Santo Domingo, and Puerto Rico.*

Reluctantly, I told her how to plug the roost openings with straw and cement, where to place the rat poison for maximum fatalities, what to do about the persistent stink. It made me sad to tell her all this. On my way home an hour later, still slightly drunk from the rum, my love for Teresita Castillo began to fade.

That summer, partly to console me for love's failure, my parents took me to the south coast of Cuba for my first solitary expedition. From there, I connected with a steamer that ferried me across the Batabanó Gulf to Nueva Gerona, the capital of the Isle of Pines. Before I boarded the ship, Papá handed me a wicker hamper laden with foods he'd prepared himself: shrimp tartlets, fresh bread with anchovy paste, lamb sausages, and a still-warm seafood stew. It occupied twice the space of the satchel I carried for my entire trip.

As I crossed the turquoise waters of the gulf, past archipelagos of tiny islands with fanciful names, I thought of what the first explorers must have felt at the sight of a new horizon, at the roar of possibilities in their heads. How they imagined the vast riches that awaited them, all there for the taking with a musket and a strong pair of hands.

On the steamer, an American woman with two young children befriended me. She'd been living on the Isle of Pines since 1913, when her husband had bought a grapefruit plantation. On warm summer nights, she sighed, the aroma of citrus coated every particle of air. Señora Crane recommended that I visit the Punta del Este caves. They had recently been discovered by survivors of a shipwreck, she explained, and contained paintings from pre-Columbian times. In the biggest cave, pictographs of red and black concentric circles were connected by arrows pointing east.

In my exalted state and the Isle of Pines' unforgiving heat, I found it impossible to sleep. I calmed myself with nightly swims along the northern beaches, brilliant with black sands. It was on my fifth night, as I floated lazily in the ocean, that something mammoth swam by me, grazing my leg. I panicked, quickly calculating the odds of a shark coming so close to shore. That afternoon, I had cut my foot on a shard of marble at Bibijagua Beach, and the wound was still raw.

Cautiously, I paddled my way toward shore, keeping my injured foot above the water as best I could. I reached the beach, breathing so hard I thought my lungs would collapse.

It was then I saw her. Her ridged back and the enormity of her flippers made identification easy, especially in the moon-

light. She was over eight feet long, a half ton of slow magnifi-
cence. The leatherback turned her wrinkled, spotted neck and
gazed at me, as if gauging my trustworthiness. I could see her
eyes clearly, the inverse widow's peak of her beak. She proceeded
up the beach, dragging herself with her front flippers, stopping
every few feet to rest. In her wake, she left a long, wide ridge
of sand.

It was exceptionally rare to see a great leatherback on our
shores. The turtles breed primarily off the Gulf of Guinea in
West Africa and lay their eggs in the shallow waters around
Ceylon. Even then I knew that a leatherback turned up in
Cuba no more than once every several years, and almost never
to spawn.

When the leatherback found a nesting site, she sank her-
self deep into the sand, rotating several times until she had
shaped her hollow. Again she faced me, as if warning me to
come no closer. Then she continued to dig her egg pit, using one
flipper and then the other, curling the edges inward to force up
more sand.

After what seemed interminable digging, the giantess
brought her hind flippers together, craned her neck forward,
and began to sway slightly to a private rhythm, finally laying
her eggs in the sand. When she was done, the exhausted mother
filled in her pit. She patted the sand until she erased all traces of
her nest, then wearily made her way back to the sea.

All night I searched the waves for a sign of her, but only
the steady surf answered my scrutiny.

At dawn, a fat scavenging gull dropped onto the leatherback's
buried nest. I cursed the bird and threw a fistful of sand at it. A
moment later, more gulls appeared, suspended in formation
overhead, and a stray dog nosed its way down the beach.

What choice did I have? I sat on the leatherback's nest all

*that day and all the next night, guarding the eggs from preda-
tors, guarding the eggs for her. I imagined her babies racing for
the surf later that summer, and I still wonder sometimes how
many of that hatch survived. Perhaps only one or two. Those
turtles would be fully grown by now, parents themselves, idly
traversing the seven seas.*

TRAVEL IN THE FAMILY

❁

*R*eina *works through* the warm April night, rummaging among her father's books, papers, and animal skins. The French doors to the study are wide open. It seems to her that tonight this room is an intimate part of the city, not sealed off by plaster and stone but one of its small vital organs, an essential cavity. For once, Reina is glad of her insomnia, of the gentle solace of the dark. The past she combs through is long dead, sloughed off from Papá's life like the desiccated skin of a snake.

Still, dozens of his specimens are left to inspect, all creatures native to Cuba. Most of these Reina will donate to the Natural History Museum of Gíbara. The best-preserved of the lot she will bequeath to the Carlos de la Torre Collection in Holguín. Her father had been friends with de la Torre, the greatest Cuban naturalist of all, an expert in mollusks who once gave a remarkable demonstration at the University of

Havana. Blindfolded and with astounding alacrity, de la Torre distinguished ninety-two shells with only his fingertips. And he was old, too, nearly blind enough not to need the blindfold.

Reina wonders who would remember de la Torre today. All of her father's friends are dead, their bones long enrolled in the earth's myriad cycles. Dr. Sergio Manubens y Quintana. Dr. Mario Sánchez Roig. Dr. Victor Rodríguez y Fuente. Dr. Eliseo Pérez Tovar. Dr. Isidoro Castellanos Solís. All superb scientists in their day, now an anonymous bit of fish muscle here, a breath in the lung of a migrant bird there. To be forgotten, Reina decides, is the final death.

Papá, no doubt, would have been surprised at her devotion, surprised that it was she and not Constancia who had taken care of his treasures all these years. Her father used to speak of Constancia as perfection in absentia, intrepid and talented, although Papá never explained why she couldn't return home. With Reina, he always maintained a more formal demeanor. He read to her frequently and worked to sharpen her reasoning abilities. What he could not do was deter Reina from loving him.

Reina puts on her work jumpsuit, consoling even without the customary weight of her tool belt. She laces her rubber-soled boots, then slips on her official government windbreaker, which she hasn't worn since the burning at El Cobre. Reina hops in place, first on one foot, then on the other, enjoying the exorbitant lightness at her hips. Then she unhooks the metal ring of keys from a nail on the door and eases herself into the night.

Bus after bus goes by as Reina strolls east on La Rampa. During the day, she frequently waits two hours for a ride and still can't elbow her way on, for all the people. Who can explain such planning? Empty benches line the Avenida de los Presidentes. A woman of indeterminable age rattles toward her, pushing a wooden cart piled high with rancid bundles. She is dressed in tattered layers of many colors. Reina thinks the woman might have looked festive from afar, like an apparition from medieval times, but up close there is no mistaking her misery. Around the corner, a slick black Plymouth slides by, inflating the air with the faint notes of a *danzón*.

At La Rampa and L Street, Reina heads south toward the University of Havana. She remembers one Saturday she accompanied her father to his office while Mami was away visiting friends. Reina played for hours with Papá's stuffed birds and bats, careful not to disturb him. She conducted unlikely marriages among the furred and feathered creatures, threw a treetop party, mourned the *cordoníz* at its imaginary funeral.

That afternoon, Papá turned to her, his eyes a complicated gray like the winter sky outside. Reina remembers the height and curve of his forehead, the twist of his polka-dotted bow tie. She had a little earless owl in one hand and, in the other, a bat so tiny it looked like a butterfly.

"Please be so kind as to tell me," Papá began, as if solemnly addressing a graduate student, "what makes us different from those creatures you hold in your hands?"

Reina was thoroughly puzzled. Her father had often held long discourses on the nature of instinct and intelligence, but she was much too young to follow his arguments. She merely picked up a word or a phrase here and there. Normally, he did not ask her questions, much less expect a response. Reina wondered if Constancia would have known what to say.

Papá's breathing came in steady, labored puffs. His breath filled the room, dictated its warmth and moisture, its chemical composition. Then suddenly he dropped his gaze and looked out the window, which neatly framed a leaning royal palm.

"Receptacles," he whispered, as if remembering something from long ago. "Thousands of receptacles." His voice rose, impossibly slowed. His back was still turned. "We . . . are . . . not . . . bees."

Then he returned to his work with a renewed ardor, leaving his senseless words to dance in Reina's head.

Reina makes her way to the biology building, in the middle of campus. Posters with revolutionary slogans wash over the walls like a static sea. The main entrance and the side doors are locked. Reina rolls her pants to her knees and, fueled by the aberrant strength of her insomnia, hoists herself up the side of the building. She begins to climb, wedging her feet between the immense limestone panels, scaling ledge after ledge until she reaches an open window near the top.

It takes her a moment, but Reina finds a light switch and flips it on. She is disoriented. There's no office or classroom here, just a crude exhibit of invertebrates against the far wall—sponges, polyps, flatworms, rotifers. In one corner, in an encrusted glass case, a Gila monster and a giant salamander stand face-to-face; in another, a large family of pin-pricked coral shrimp is on display.

Reina remembers a story her mother told her once, about how the nebulous lights Christopher Columbus saw from the poop deck of the *Santa María* were probably Bermuda fireworms. "Twice a year the fireworms mate," Mami explained, "and turn miles of the Caribbean a phosphorescent green." Then she held Reina's face in her hands and spoke to her sharply: "You don't know how much of what you see, *mi hija*, you never see at all."

Her mother used to tell her many stories like this, but from her head, not mostly read from books, like Papá.

From the time Reina was an infant, her mother took her all over Havana. She used to carry Reina in a sling as they wandered along the Río Almendares, which meanders to the sea between Vedado and Miramar, then on to the Bosque de la Habana, with its lush subtropical trees and chalk-white cliffs. Her mother would point out the lizards and snakes hiding in the logs and piles of leaves, turn over stones to examine every manner of insect.

As Reina grew older, she and her mother would visit Chinatown on the weekends, especially the Teatro Gran China, in the heart of the red-light district. They would sit through the histrionic plays, not understanding a word but drawn to the extravagant tragedies and the wonderful, dissonant music.

When Dulcita was a few days old, Reina fashioned a sling from two hospital pillowcases and carried her daughter along the same path she and her mother used to take by the Río Almendares. But the river was filthy, shimmering with mosquitoes and algae, the trail clotted with garbage and rotting fruit. This was not what Reina had remembered.

Reina moves down the hallway, desperately flicking on lights everywhere. If only she could brighten the place fast enough, she might get a glimpse of her mother bent over a specimen or quietly writing at a desk. In the buzz of unexpected illumination, the burden of the biology building trumpets itself: a sink full of petri dishes, velvety with mold; the mildewing skins of dozens of discolored birds; a haphazard skeleton missing key bones.

The glare of lights only increases Reina's confusion. Nothing is familiar to her, nothing seems in its rightful place. She races from room to room like a howl in the night, desperately searching for her father's office. Would her mother be there, stuffed and inert like everything Papá killed? Her throat patched over with grafts of skin? Her riding boots shined to catch light? Would the greens of the world lie dead in her eyes? And around her slender neck, a hand-printed sign reveal her species, the date and place of her capture, her normal habitat?

By the time Reina reaches the ground floor and pushes open the enormous bronze doors of the entrance, she is shaky and feverish. The science building is ablaze in a thunderous light. Reina feels as though she, too, were lit from within, burning with a forged history. She waits to see whatever her disturbance will bring. But nothing happens, nothing at all.

At precisely five-thirteen in the morning, Reina approaches the grandfather clock in Papá's study. With a flourish, she removes the black cape with which she'd draped it earlier that night, as if it were a voluble parrot. Then she records the hour in a small spiral notebook. Her mission is clear, although her motives are still ambiguous. Reina knows only one thing for certain: she can no longer stay in Cuba. She trusts that the rest of what she must learn will announce itself in time. She envies her daughter's clarity in leaving the country, her willingness to go to any lengths to get what she thinks she wants.

Reina gathers her soap, her toothbrush, Papá's ancient gold razor, and steps down the hallway to the bathroom. Reina prides herself on completing her day's grooming in just under five minutes. The key, she's discovered, is to accomplish a multitude of bothersome tasks—brushing her teeth, blowing her nose, wiping clean her ears, and urinating—all while in the shower. Despite the disruption of months in the hospital, Reina maintains her exacting schedule.

Today she dresses in her soft flannel skirt, a short-sleeved white blouse, and a silk vest with bone buttons borrowed from Papá's wardrobe. She fastens on the hoop earrings that somehow survived the lightning. Her black patent shoes, which she wears only on special occasions, are thick-heeled, with oversized buckles, a coachman's footgear from another era.

Outside, it begins to rain hard, linear and relentless, like self-important men. Reina reaches for her father's ancient umbrella. The visa and emigration office won't open until eight o'clock, but Reina is prepared to wait. She marches down the dormant streets, twirling Papá's umbrella with a surety of purpose. The rain subdues the stink of her skin to a bearable mixture of vinegar and suede, and this pleases her.

Soon Reina takes her place among the dissenters at the visa headquarters on Avenida Bélgica. Her passport picture, taken six years earlier for her trip to Venezuela, no longer resembles her. She wants to clarify this discrepancy, explain the condition of her malodorous skin, but no one bothers to ask for an explanation.

Why do you wish to leave Cuba? It occurs to Reina that this question, third down on the emigration application form, requires from her an answer lengthier than the inch of blank space provided. Her father used to say that bureaucracies preferred the tyranny of clear-cut solutions, of irrefutable knowledge, a defined time and place. "True questions," Papá told her repeatedly, "always insist on better questions."

"Come back in three months, and we'll inform you of the status of your application," the clerk says automatically when Reina hands her the application form.

"But you haven't even looked at my papers."

"I don't make the decisions. I only accept the petitions."

The young woman's hair is arranged in an old-fashioned bun, but her uniform, revolutionary crisp, is all modern angles.

"Then I'll just stay here until I get word."

"*Compañera*, I told you to come back in three months. We won't have anything for you before then."

"I'll wait over there," Reina indicates the plank bench in the foyer.

Reina is uncharacteristically polite during the four days and nights she camps out in the visa and emigration office, refrains from raising her voice or resorting to threats. She simply states, as one official after another pleads with her to be reasonable, that she will not quit the premises without first receiving permission to leave the country.

The secretary of the interior initially vetoes her trip on the grounds that Reina's record is badly marred by her daughter's defection to Spain and that her own skills as an electrician are still considered essential for the revolution. But Reina remains intractable.

During the day, she passes the time playing cards with the dissenters, sharing their coffee and cold *yuca* fritters. At night, Reina rests on the same plank bench, her thoughts whirling above her like a lumbering galaxy through space. She thinks about Dulcita, the loneliness that must descend upon her every evening in Madrid. Reina received a postcard from her daughter a week ago. Dulcita wrote that she'd seen a billboard on the Calle de Alcalá that said, *Jesus rents grace.*

On the fifth morning of Reina's vigil, word comes down from El Comandante himself: "Let the old mare go to America if it pleases her. What use is she to us now?" And with that unimpeachable directive, Reina is finally given her departure papers.

• • •

In all the years they've known one another, Reina has never set foot in Pepín's house. The night before she leaves Cuba, she appears on her lover's doorstep in her wrinkled flannel skirt. His wife answers the bell. Gloria Beltrán stares up at Reina. She needs no introduction. After nearly a quarter century, she knows who it is. Even before her husband's indifference, even before their children left home for places they'd shown her on maps, cold places in Eastern Europe or Russia or places hotter than Cuba in summer, she had imagined this woman's face.

"He's in the bedroom," Gloria says stoically. She's a psychologist at the 26th of July Elementary School and accustomed to speaking in comforting tones. She leads Reina to her husband.

The room is neat, rectangular, the paint a faded pink. A chandelier hangs askew over a sagging double bed. Beyond the shut window, a trellis of bougainvillea can be seen dominating the courtyard below. Reina thinks of something Pepín told her years ago, that there's an unlicensed spot in the brain that if manipulated just right could keep a person happy for decades.

She closes the door, waits until she can hear Gloria's footsteps retreating down the hallway. Then she reaches with both hands and guides Pepín's mouth toward hers.

Their lips are dry, hot, flammable. The air in the room is close, suffused with a stale, floral, female scent, as if roses had withered on the dresser or under the bed where they lie. Then Reina and Pepín make love for the last time, tenderly as only old lovers can, briefly sheltered from the long and rumoring night.

MIAMI

There is a faint whirring that Constancia cannot identify in the slow, surrounding white. It sounds just below the surface, enameled, perhaps, and slightly metallic. Her eyes are closed, but she can hear the surgeon's breathing, muffled and near. His crimson scissors sing neatly through her skin. He pulls and relayers the delicate flaps, so flimsily rooted, dips and loops his special dissolving thread, a bloody pointillist.

Constancia listens to the pressure of the surgeon's supporting fingers. They creak and groan like miniature glaciers, alive against her face. Constancia is inside the whirring now, immediate as fury. The surgeon severs roots and useless nerves, reinvents the architecture of her face. Oh, the noise the tight crown makes, newly slotted to her skull! It drowns all entering sounds.

Constancia resists the deafening white, but then, as if

by a divine capsizing, she surrenders to its peculiar peace. There's a secret art to the senses, she decides; nothing is directly perceived. She understands then that time arcs differently for those intimate with blood.

It is six in the morning. Constancia awakes from her dream and goes to the bathroom. She switches on her vanity mirror, finds her face in disarray, moving all at once like a primitive creature. Her neck and temples itch furiously, erupting with bumps each time she attempts to scratch.

Constancia takes a deep breath, sprays herself with a plant mister of salt water she keeps nearby for extra hydration. Then she checks the mirror again. Her face has settled down, but it appears different to her, younger, as if it truly had been rearranged in the night. She rubs her eyes, pinches her cheeks. Her eyes seem rounder, a more deliberate green. Then it hits her with the force of a slap. This is her mother's face.

Constancia turns off the lights and nervously climbs back into bed. She senses a sudden coldness at her center, as if she were freezing from the inside out. Her blood is congealing, her nerves are a fine net of ice. For a moment, Constancia fears she may no longer exist. "A! E! I! O! U!" she shouts, as loud as she can. If she can still recite her vowels, Constancia reasons, she couldn't possibly be dead.

Since Heberto left last month on his clandestine mission, Constancia hasn't been herself. She's lost without his sturdy presence, volatile though he was in the last weeks before his departure. If only her husband were here to reassure her, tell her she looked as lovely as ever. Then Constancia would reward him, slip her hands down the front of his pants, breathe warmly in his ear: *You are a traveling jewel merchant in Cienfuegos. I am a rich, lonely housewife with an unfaithful husband. Sell me a ruby ring,* mi cielo. Lately, her fantasies have been getting more and more outlandish. Casts of thousands. Exotic locales. Raw close-ups of flagrant masculinity.

Constancia gets out of bed and changes into her swimsuit. A walk on the beach will help, she thinks, clear her head of delirium. Perhaps she has too much time on her hands. Perhaps she should call and apply for that Avon job, after all. As she passes her reflection in the hallway mirror, she barely stifles a scream. Her mother's face hovers in the glass, appearing as frightened as Constancia herself.

She hurries to the closet and pulls out a stack of bedsheets, then drapes every mirror in the house with expanses of pastel linens. Still, it's impossible to avoid her reflection entirely, the reluctant dialogue with light on every surface in the house.

Outside, the sun feels like a hunter aimed at her skin. Constancia strolls along the beach, moving her head carefully, as if in a levitated present, willing herself not to touch her cheeks. She wonders if her mother's face could have built up incrementally overnight, layer by cumulative layer, like limestone or unbridled coral.

Above her, the seagulls appear strangely magnified, streaking the sky with their arrogance. Constancia's condominium building, circular and nineteen stories high, is set back on the sand. Incongruent details loom up from it in sharp focus, as if linked by a commonality not yet apparent to her. On the roof, an American flag flutters from its sleek pole.

Constancia greets a passing neighbor, but he doesn't seem to recognize her. Her voice is off—higher, girlish, with a queer, feathery lilt. Every breath feels as though it's forcing itself through a lump in her chest.

The sea shimmers an aquarium blue. Constancia knows that Miami is replete with marine biologists and other so-called ocean experts. She recalls that showy Frenchman on television with his cameras and oxygen tanks, his melodrama business of underwater science. But like her father, Constancia is wary of the sea. Papi joked once that they shared an irrational fear of devolution, that somehow in the ocean they might return to an earlier life form, lobsters, perhaps, or irritable squids.

The night her father died, Constancia stopped dreaming altogether. Not until she was pregnant with Isabel many years later did Constancia begin to dream again. Her first dream was simple to interpret: a barren landscape, mud dried to cracks, the persistent drone of midday. A slender shoot appeared, tenderly green, and then another and another, until the earth was ablaze with the density of life.

She wonders now why her first pregnancy didn't disrupt her dreamlessness. All the while she carried Silvestre in her womb, Constancia felt him as a nerve inside her. She'd had to fight an impulse toward edges, tried in vain to steady her erratic heart. It didn't help that her son grew up to look exactly like Gonzalo. By the time he was twelve, Constancia found herself spying on Silvestre in the shower, lifting the blanket on his naked, sleeping body, running a finger along his quiet hipbone.

Constancia's love for her daughter was entirely different, an easy, radiant devotion. Her balancing necessity.

Back home, Constancia digs in her rattan armoire for Heberto's Instamatic camera and takes thirty-one photographs of herself. Then she sends the undeveloped film to her daughter in Hawaii. Constancia can always count on Isabel to tell her the truth. Her daughter has no sense of the usual proprieties, is invulnerable to ordinary temptation. Constancia could no sooner get her to wear lipstick than she could build a hydrogen bomb. Each time she attempts to persuade Isabel to do or say or wear something at odds with her nature, the reply is unfailingly negative.

Constancia checks her horoscope in the newspaper. As usual, it gives her no clues. "Everything lives at night in secret doubt. Something tells you that to die is to wake up." Constancia considers the Miami *Bugle*'s astrologer unusually poetic but not the least bit illuminating. She decides to dress in her navy-blue Adolfo suit, accenting it with a checkered silk scarf and a choker of pearls. The outfit reassures her, makes her feel substantial, armed for the worst. It is difficult to indulge self-doubt looking this good.

Constancia drives to the yacht club in her pink Cadillac convertible, the top down, the radio bursting with a raucous merengue. She swivels slightly to the beat, knees together, in her bucket seat. The guard waves her in to the parking lot, and she is somewhat heartened. If she looked like a total stranger, he certainly wouldn't have let her pass.

In the clubhouse dining room, there's a *palomilla* steak special for lunch. Constancia orders this with French fries and the house salad, blue cheese dressing on the side. Perhaps her diet is interfering with her perceptions. All the Cuban food she's been ingesting lately, so heavy on the grease and meat. That must be it. Her fat intake has dramatically increased. She calls over the waiter and promptly cancels her steak.

There's one other diner besides her, devouring a key lime pie. It is her husband's favorite dessert. Constancia silently promises a battery of saints that she'll bake a pie for Heberto every day of his life if they return him to her in one piece. Now whom should she petition, Constancia wonders, to get rid of her mother's face?

Constancia picks at her salad, allocates a drop of dressing for each leaf of romaine. At eleven-thirty, the regular clique of Cuban ladies comes in for their heavily sugared espressos. Constancia waves to them, but she receives only chilly smiles in return.

"¿No me reconocen?" Constancia asks, walking over to their table, desperate for acknowledgment.

But the five ladies simply stare at her, blank with surprise.

Constancia rushes out the door and starts up her car. There is nowhere for her to drive, but she wants to drive anyway, far from the ocean and its grammar of ruin. She longs for a small body of water, self-contained, secure.

She remembers a trip she and Papi took to the caves outside Matanzas early in 1948. Armed with torches and fishing nets, Constancia trailed her father deep into an underground cavern until they came upon a pool of water so still it appeared frozen. Carefully, Papi cracked through a surface coat of lime to discover crystalline waters where thousands of pale fish swam, looking, Constancia thought, as if they'd devoured stars.

"They're blind," Papi said. In fact, the fish were so sensitive to the slightest movement or sound that it took nearly three hours to secure a dozen specimens.

Outside the cave, another surprise awaited them: a group of rural guards had surrounded the entrance. Their leader, a thickset sergeant missing a thumb, demanded an explanation. Word had spread quickly of their trek to the caves. There could be only one reason, the locals decided, and they wanted part of the treasure. Only after Papi produced his sodden identification papers and held up the booty of fish did the sergeant, with a profound sigh of disgust, agree to let them go.

It begins to rain as Constancia drives toward the mainland, but she doesn't put up the top. Instead she pulls a map of Miami from the glove compartment and searches for the tiniest lake she can find. There's one in Hialeah, right off northwest Sixty-second Street. The roads begin to swell with the downpour. Constancia gets soaking wet, but she continues to drive anyway. The roar of the rain is a kind of silence, she thinks, a dark, temporary precinct. To the north, the horizon looks as if it's below the level of the sea.

Constancia turns left on Dr. Martin Luther King Boulevard and passes a bright-yellow house. She impulsively stops. She knocks on the door, drips a puddle of water where she stands. No one answers, so she enters the house, and waits. Inside, everything is yellow; floors, walls, ceiling, all yellow. There's a yellow cotton sofa and five yellow-painted chairs. By the window, a lone sunflower grows in a yellow ceramic pot. Above her, a ceiling fan hesitantly stirs the air.

A plump man, no taller than five feet, appears in the hallway, dressed in white, a prim white cap on his skull. His name is Oscar Piñango.

"How does my face look?" Constancia demands, as if he could tell her everything.

"I can see destruction is dear to you."

"Is it that obvious?"

"All afflictions are obvious."

Constancia follows Piñango down the bare hallway, trailing rainwater, to a room entirely devoted to La Virgen de la Caridad del Cobre. There's an electric fountain in the center, lit by amber spotlights, and, on the altar, a white sheet cake with a crenulated yellow border. Pumpkins of all sizes are draped in beads and arranged at the goddess's feet. The santero calls La Virgen by her African name, Oshún.

In Cuba, Constancia had heard of Oshún, of the goddess's fondness for rivers and gold and honey. She unclasps the pearls from around her neck and offers the necklace to the santero. Piñango motions for her to place it with Oshún's other propitiations, between the *ochinchín*—the shrimp-and-watercress omelet—and a six-pack of orange soda. Then Constancia kneels before the altar, giddy with the mingled scents of urgent devotion.

"It will please her," Piñango says, unsmiling. His round bulk shivers as he beckons Constancia toward a straw mat. He lights a good-quality *claro*, oddly feminine between his stout fingers, and puffs on it five times. He sucks in his lips until they disappear entirely, then offers the lit cigar to Oshún for extra *ashé* in reading the shells.

"You carry your enemies here," he tells Constancia, tapping his upper chest. "You have power but no strength. You are tired from too much useless vigilance."

The santero dips his middle finger in a bowl of water and sprinkles the floor to refresh the divining shells. His voice deepens as he prays in Yoruban, first to Oshún, then to the other *orishas*, until they are properly honored one by one. Then he gathers the cowries and touches Constancia's blessing points so that the gods may perceive her burdens.

"The shells never lie. Through their mouths the *orishas* disclose their purpose."

Piñango gently shakes the cowries before throwing them on the mat. The pattern falls in *ofún*, where the curse was born. This is the principal ruling. Then he throws the shells twice more. The message doesn't waver: *oddi*, where the grave was first dug, where the grave was first dug.

The room grows warmer. Constancia removes her checkered silk scarf. It's damp and it reeks of salt. The santero continues to pray. Her luck is not good, he says. There must be a *lariache*, a solution, a circumvention, perhaps, but none is forthcoming. Black smoke from Oshún's cigar ripples through the room. The odor is brackish, rotting, nothing at all like tobacco. Constancia finds it difficult to breathe.

Suddenly, the cigar catches fire, fueling the air with its hot fossil stench. Constancia is held still by the sight of the flames, by the spike of pain in her throat. Piñango shakes a maraca, beseeching Oshún, until the air slowly clears and a fine yellow ash coats every surface in the room.

THE NATURE OF PARASITES

❀

The Great War had been over for two years when I left Pinar del Río for the University of Havana. It was the days of the "Dance of the Millions," when the price for sugar had soared so high that many Cubans became millionaires overnight. The rich erected marble palaces along the Paseo del Prado and other fashionable boulevards of the capital, and in the late afternoons, they could be seen cruising their fancy foreign cars up and down the Malecón.

It was a time of unseemly extravagance, and it had little to do with me, a sixteen-year-old scholarship student from el campo. Few in Pinar del Río had benefited from the sugar boom. At El Cid, where my father continued to read at his lectern, half the cigar workers had lost their jobs to falling tobacco prices. Those who remained were fearful of losing them to the modern cigar-rolling machines from America.

Papá, as usual, was involved in union policy and wrote

editorials for the Boletín de Torcedor, *the cigar worker union's newspaper, extolling the glories of revolutionary Russia. What relation this had to the workers' daily concerns was unclear to me, and Papá and I argued frequently over what we considered each other's misguided politics.*

By then, Mamá had developed arthritis, which curtailed the hours she could teach flute, and I saw in her reddened joints the nascent disfigurements that would plague her last years. She grew more remote too, as if her inactivity enabled the sadness of her past, of her lost daughter, to finally overwhelm her.

It was understood that I would work while I was at college, and within a few days I found a job that suited me perfectly: night usher in a movie house on Avenida Galiano. It was a garish theater, in keeping with the times, and I was required to wear a uniform festooned with enough braids and tassels to command an entire battalion. The work itself was easy, and the perpetual darkness accustomed me to working at night, an invaluable advantage when I began to research bats in earnest.

Most nights, after guiding patrons to their seats, I joined the projectionist in his fetid cubicle, where I studied as best I could. The movies, mercifully, were silent in those days, although I still had to contend with the melodrama of the organ. Occasionally, I would peek through the projectionist's window when the music rose to a crescendo, but I never understood those who would choose to sit through this dark make-believe when the whole world was waiting outside.

In the spring of my freshman year, the renowned biologist Dr. Samuel Forrest, of Harvard University, came to Havana to teach a course on tropical zoology. Word spread quickly of his need for a field assistant, and the best graduate students signed up for an interview. Although I hardly expected to capture such a coveted position, I, too, signed up to meet the great man.

The next week, a dozen hopeful young men milled outside his office. For three hours we waited, as one shaken student after another emerged from his interrogation. "What does he want?" those of us who had remained outside asked. But the only clue came from one exceedingly frustrated student: "He wants your opinion on the universe!"

"Please sit down," Dr. Forrest said wearily when it was finally my turn. He was quite obese, and his eyes, blue as a quail dove's feathers, were accentuated by a high, lineless forehead and woolly muttonchops.

"Could you tell me, please, Señor Agüero, which of our brethren in the animal kingdom you most admire?"

I thought at first that I'd misheard Dr. Forrest, or that he was in a mood to test my humor. Why else would he ask me so facile a question? He looked up from his notes and blinked impassively.

There were many creatures I was particularly fond of: the tree ducks that had saved my father's life; the regal hawks of Cuba, circling their inspiration beyond the mountaintops; and of course, my lovely leatherback, who one humid night on the Isle of Pines entrusted her eggs to my care. Instinctively, I knew not to mention her to Dr. Forrest, to hide my sentimentality at all costs.

"Parasites," I offered.

"Parasites?" Dr. Forrest seemed surprised. He smiled tightly, whether out of amusement or disdain I was not yet certain.

"Yes, sir. I believe they are the most original of all animals."

"Go on," he said, serious now, as if he were trying to gauge my audacity.

"Consider intestinal worms, or beetles, or even fleas, for that matter." I grew bolder. "A good parasite must exploit a *host that is larger, stronger, and faster than itself, with minimal disturbance. Every fiber, every function of its being, is inscribed with this necessity—"*

"—of quiet boorishness." Dr. Forrest smiled more broadly.

"Precisely." I laughed.

He leaned forward in his chair, tugging his left mutton-chop. I continued, encouraged by Dr. Forrest's unwavering attention.

"The difference between us and lower life forms, I believe, comes down to the fact that humans have developed a variety of receptacles and containers for their needs, and animals have not. It seems to me that building vases or suitcases or skillets indicates a unique human ability to plan for the future, to predict the behavior of matter in ways wholly distinct from animals. A bee, after all, has been constructing its same tiny cell for one hundred million years."

"Very interesting," Dr. Forrest said. "And now a personal question, if you don't mind, Señor Agüero. Are you a Catholic?"

"No," I answered quickly. In fact, I'd been trained by Papá to be suspicious of all organized religion. Only later did my father acknowledge that politics, too, could be a form of religion in extremis.

Dr. Forrest stood up and thrust a plump hand toward mine. "This concludes our interview, Señor Agüero. It will be a pleasure working with you."

That night, I quit my job at the movie theater.

For the next six months, I accompanied Dr. Forrest as he criss-crossed the island by boat and train and horseback. Everywhere we went, Dr. Forrest bemoaned the loss of Cuba's lowland forests. Although the island could not support the luxuriant foresta real of Central or South America, he said, its vast areas of calcareous soil once sustained a heavy and varied sylvan growth. The only true forest remaining in Cuba was in the higher mountain ranges of Oriente province, to this day so steep and inaccessible as to offer refuge to many precious species.

Sadly, it was mostly in the cities and their environs that we could appreciate the charms of the island's tropical flora— the broad groves of royal palms, the great red-green mango trees, offering the densest of shades, and every variety of exotic flower. There continued to exist large areas of granitic and serpentine savanna lands in Cuba, but only because they were unfit for agriculture. With their groves of jata and cana palms, these regions were home to a relatively meager bird and animal population.

I remember well our first trip into the heart of the Zapata Swamp, the relentless rustle and hum of its invisible creatures, the air thick as pudding in our lungs. I followed Dr. Forrest as he eased one foot in front of the other across the surface of saw grass and bulrushes, the formidable muss threatening to engulf us at any moment.

On another trip, Dr. Forrest asked me to collect ordinary house bats at an abandoned cavalry barracks outside Matanzas. Dr. Forrest intended to preserve a series of their embryos so that he might study the early development of their teeth. Protected with heavy gloves, I managed to fill two sacks with live bats and returned to the Hotel El Mundo, where I left my restless cargo in the bathtub.

"After we have had our luncheon," Dr. Forrest said in his proper, drawling Spanish, "we shall kill the bats and search for their embryos."

During our meal, Dr. Forrest was expounding on the finer implications of Freud's theories, when a terrible clattering and commotion came from the hotel kitchen. In an instant, the chef, two assistants, and a waiter came storming through the swinging doors, pursued by a swarm of Molossus tropi-

dorhynchus. *Dazed by the light, the bats buzzed and dropped over the banquet tables, splattering soup and sending the cutlery flying.*

"Naturam expellas furca, tamen usque recurret," Dr. Forrest said, shrugging off the incident. He was fond of philosophizing in Latin.

On another expedition, camping in the backcountry of Sancti Spíritus, Dr. Forrest was pleased to catch an iguana for our dinner. Now, I knew that in Central America, where Dr. Forrest had spent a considerable portion of his career, iguana meat was considered a delicacy. But I found my repugnance difficult to overcome. You see, when iguanas are hung to dry, a brown gurry like coffee grounds runs from their mouths, reminding me of my father's yellow-fever vomit.

That night, Dr. Forrest roasted the iguana over a campfire and offered me a slab from its back, liberally sprinkled with salt. I could hardly refuse. I swallowed the meat whole, barely allowing it to slide down my throat. Then I excused myself, hid behind a white ixora, and disgorged my meal on its splendid snowball blossoms.

Despite this and numerous other mishaps, Dr. Forrest always treated me as a friend and a competent colleague. In time, and with his patient encouragement, I became both. My debt to him is immeasurable. The modest successes I enjoyed under his guidance nurtured my confidence as a scientist.

Dr. Forrest had begun his vocation in the latter half of the nineteenth century, when great scientific advances had kindled the enthusiasm of thousands: Darwin's theory of evolution; Mendel's law of heredity; the identification of light as an electromagnetic phenomenon; the law of the conservation of energy; and not least, the development of the spectroscope. When Dr. Forrest came of age, it was science, not politics or economics, that held the key to conquering the universe. Science was his mission, and soon enough, it became mine as well.

Perhaps my most extraordinary discovery under Dr. For-rest's tutelage came toward the end of his stay in Cuba. It started one May evening at the University of Havana biology library, where I came across a page of field notes tucked inside a 1907 edition of National Geographic magazine. The notes, which had no date or name attached, were written in a clear, minus-cule hand and stated that in the scrub between Morro Castle and the little fishing town of Cojímar, a deep pool could be found containing shrimp that "looked as if they had been boiled." This struck me as curious, because all the cave shrimp I had studied with Dr. Forrest were pallid. Only deep-sea shrimp sported the dark-red color the notes described.

The next day, I set off in search of the mysterious shrimp. The morning air was warm, and I walked briskly to hasten the adventure. I felt rather ridiculous relying on the anonymous notes, but Dr. Forrest had taught me that no expedition was ever futile. Over the years, he had happily followed many a campesino—he counted them among the finest observers of nature—with only a vague promise of observing something new. Dr. Forrest dismissed no clue or wild tale without first investigating the matter personally.

I hurried to the harbor and hired a rowboat to take me across the bay to Morro Castle. I landed at the steps on the shore, near the Battery of the Twelve Apostles, then trudged through the coastal forest of beach-grape trees until I came to a broad area of bare rock. In the middle was an open basin of the purest water, where, it appeared, the roof of a cave had fallen in. The depth and crookedness of the channel made it difficult to see beyond a foot or two.

I stirred the water with the long-handled net I had brought, and before long, tiny crimson shrimp came out of their hiding places and swam closer to the surface. The shrimp were striking, their wispy legs tipped in white, as if they had acci-dentally stepped in paint. Over and over, I dipped my net, but *the creatures were nearly impossible to catch. After several arduous hours, I finally secured twenty specimens.*

That evening, Dr. Forrest seemed impressed with my shrimp. He sent them off to a Miss Barbara J. Winthrop, an authority on crustacea at the United States National Museum in Maryland. Before long she wrote back, identifying the shrimp as a new genus. She had also taken the liberty of suggesting a name for them: Forrestia agueri.

PART TWO

A Common Affliction

ORIGINAL GEOGRAPHY

✵

THE EVERGLADES
MAY 1991

Heberto Cruz is unaccustomed to the crushing sun, to the drip and suck of the swamp, to the stinging heat behind his bloodshot eyes. Clots of incessant mosquitoes, whining, tormenting, settle and resettle on his blood-lit face. Heberto trudges on in his water cracked boots, the submachine gun slung diagonally from hip to shoulder blade, a pink fungus blooming on his thumb. Heberto trudges on, taken with a sense of his own new significance.

Constancia, he knows, is skeptical of his mission. Of course, she would be. She hid his razor, shrank his underwear, embroidered epithets on his socks. Glorious vainglorious—what does it matter what his wife thinks? He is here now, isn't he? Here with men of action, helmets afire. Here with hundreds of militant, *ordained* men. The stench for miles a privilege of endurance. He is here, no? Not any previous elsewhere. Not rocking in his boat, pathetic and pleading with the moon. Not constrained behind his counter, dispensing expensive cigars. Not surrendering himself to the erratic republic of Constancia's bed.

After all, Heberto thinks sourly, what has safety brought him but more fruitless safety?

It's late afternoon. Clouds rush in from the south, booming with thunder. In a moment, all is water and refraction, every variation of vertical. Lightning steals down from the sky in brilliant filigrees. The men shout instructions, hold fast to cypress trees. Heberto stays put. He knows that the only protection from the storm is time. Except for this clandestine mission, it makes no sense to be in the swamp this time of year, when only a few misguided tourists from Europe visit. But this heat, this training, is meant to toughen him, to prepare him for the invasion ahead.

Invasion. The word makes Heberto hard as a young man. He can feel it. The tight ridge of expectation in his groin. His contracting *cojones*, the same ones his father accused him of not having. Heberto puts his hand over his heart and imagines it roaring with life. Tireless. Inexhaustible. Vibrant with a fugitive rhythm.

For him, there'll be no more waiting on the sidelines in this shabby empire of exile. Soon he'll confront himself in the ultimate exaltation—focused, vehement, without memory. Nothing less will satisfy him.

Years ago, Heberto had wanted to join his father and exiled brothers in the Bay of Pigs invasion, longed to commandeer one of the Cruzes' secretly donated ships. But Constancia threatened to leave him and move to Spain. "I won't sacrifice myself for your *politica dichosa*!" she screamed, packing her hard-shell suitcase. And so Heberto stayed home.

Heberto's older brother died a hero in the Bay of Pigs. Leopoldo Cruz drowned in the stampede toward shore, while the skies remained empty of American planes. At the last minute, President Kennedy lost his nerve and pulled the promised air support. Gonzalo, the youngest, was shot in the leg. His knee was so badly mangled that he still walks with a pronounced limp. Gonzalo could have fixed his leg years ago, but he prefers it damaged, the pretext it gives him to boast of his valor. Their father, Arturo, who watched the invasion through binoculars on the deck of his cargo ship, left Cuba good only for dominoes and a dulling nostalgia.

For years afterward, Heberto's father treated him coolly. Heberto's shame came bullying during idle hours, and so he kept busy until his every minute was accounted for, until there was nothing of any importance left to do. The winters in New York City helped, the ice and blindness one long third of the year. With each passing season, Constancia, like any woman with her own money, grew more confident at his side, and Heberto was besieged by all that had escaped his life.

At one time, Heberto had loved Constancia, desired her with a ferocity that frightened him to near passivity. Above all, he wanted to protect her. She'd been Gonzalo's first wife, and she had suffered with his brother. Heberto didn't want to make Constancia suffer anymore. But over the years, as his passion waned and his wife bloomed with self-assurance, Heberto couldn't shake off the disconcerting feeling that somehow he'd inherited his brother's spoils. Heberto had even raised Silvestre, Gonzalo and Constancia's son, put him through that expensive deaf college in Washington, D.C.

For once in his life, Heberto wanted something that was entirely his own. Was this so much to ask?

When he first moved to Miami, Heberto had avoided Gonzalo, the putrid skin of his brother's final illness. But their father's death brought them together again. The night of the funeral, Heberto drove Gonzalo back to the hospital. His brother invited him up to the terminal ward for a drink and, with a snap of his fingers, had an orderly bring them two bottles of seven-year-old Cuban rum. They drank slowly, deliberately, emptying the night, smoking *coronas* (Montecristo No. 3's) and reminiscing until dawn.

They remembered their mother, María Josefa Escoto de Cruz, so brittle and decorous and constantly weeping. *Una neurasténica*, such women were called in her day. María Josefa died in her sleep the same day her trim, coiffed hair turned all white (this was no biological impetuosity, a neighbor said; María Josefa had been planning it for weeks). Her three sons were still in their teens. Heberto and Gonzalo reluctantly agreed, drinking and smoking and nearly weeping themselves, that their mother had loved only their older brother, Leopoldo.

They recalled, too, the night their father took them to a whorehouse near La Chorrera in Havana. Heberto and Gonzalo were only eleven and nine, but Papá made them watch him fuck an opulent mulatta with Oriental eyes, made them watch as his prodigious *cojones* bounced against her immense, quaking, plum-colored ass. The heat that rose from their coupling nearly stifled the boys' breath. Finally, Papá ordered the woman to suck his *pinga* for what seemed an eternity, until he groaned and slumped forward like a lanced bull. *Así jode un hombre,* Papá said with satisfaction, and taunted his sons to follow suit. When they backed away, terrified by the whore's acres of naked flesh, Papá laughed at them and called them *maricones*.

On the way home, Papá told them that any woman who sucked their *pingas* was a whore, that they should remember this and not be made fools of.

For years afterward, this image of his father haunted Heberto, disturbed him on the rare mornings when he could remember his dreams. On his wedding night, in a baroque room lit with leaning tapers, Constancia tenderly bent over his loins. Heberto brutally pushed her away. "Don't ever do that again!" he demanded, then turned his back on her. He suspected his brother of corrupting Constancia, of humiliating her the same way their father had the slant-eyed whore.

The nights in the swamp are worse than the days. Heberto sleeps fitfully or not at all as the lanterns burn, glaucous with insect repellent. The other men dream angrily from the mouths of their tents. Every night, Heberto secretly lights a Cuban cigar, a *panatela*, away from the encampment. When it comes to cigars, at least, Heberto sets politics aside.

He was glad to know that Gonzalo, who considered himself an unerring exile leader (he's known as El Gallo for his success with the ladies and his willingness to take on any foe), also succumbed to the transcendent pleasures of a hand-rolled Cuban cigar. That night in the hospital, they'd shared their country's finest rum and *coronas*, and their lives began to intertwine once more.

Who can defend Cuba today? Its daily, ordinary evils? Gonzalo had asked Heberto this behind a cloud of fragrant smoke. *Nobody,* Heberto answered, growing more and more despondent as he inventoried his own inaction over the years. *The revolution is an accident of history, entirely reversible,* Gonzalo continued with an eloquence that astonished Heberto. *Everyone on the island wants a fresh start, a radical change of destiny, a pair of brand-name blue jeans. Anything less is insupportable.*

By morning, Heberto wanted desperately to fight alongside his brother, to break free from his leashed life. He was tired of everything. Of the part in his hair, combed just so. Of his useless, uncalloused hands. Heberto wanted a role in Cuba's salvaging. He'd blow up bridges, if he had to, swallow the necessary bricks. For him, there'd be no hesitating, no more anxiously looking back.

Beneath him, the river of grass does its continental slide. The rhythms of the dark seem all wrong to Heberto, clashing and without syncopation. Back in his tent, each of his legs twitches to a separate tempo inside his nylon sleeping bag. He hears the cries of the spectral birds, the alligators' ungainly slinking into mud. And though panthers are exceedingly rare here, Heberto imagines again and again their soft, circular padding around his tent.

Nobody is too holy to die, Heberto tells himself. Perhaps a distinguished death might redeem the stolidity by which he's lived. To live with death, he believes—to live with it like a hot breath on the back of your neck—is to truly live. No matter; this time he would be deliberate. Yes, for once, Heberto Cruz would be deliberate, and he would be saved.

KEY BISCAYNE

A vat of *Constancia's* new face emollient simmers on the kitchen stove. She adds a cup of ground papaya stones, folds in the petals of a dozen yellow roses. Seventy-two royal-blue bottles crowd her Formica counters. Each is affixed with a label featuring a cameo of her mother's face (now her own) beneath the ornate logo *Cuerpo de Cuba*. Constancia inserts rosewood stoppers in the bottles and winds them with silk cords and tassels to give them the appearance of heirlooms.

It is seven in the morning. Constancia turns up the radio, half hoping to hear news of her husband. Heberto left nearly two months ago, and she still hasn't heard a word. A moment later, she switches to the early edition of *La Hora de los Milagros*. Constancia learns that in Xcalacdzonot, a village not far from the ruins of Chichén Itzá, a brindle cow named Chuchi has begun reciting the Lord's Prayer during its morning milking. At first, the miracle was dismissed because

Benito Zúñiga, the cow's owner, is known in those parts as an incorrigible prankster. But the village priest, a man indisposed toward excessive religiosity, confirms that the otherwise ordinary Chuchi is indeed reciting the Our Father, if somewhat indistinctly.

Constancia rubs a bit of the hot emollient on the slant of her cheeks and considers the case of the praying cow. She traces a faint line across her forehead, on the hint of a crease between her eyebrows. Last month, she awoke and discovered that her mother's face had replaced her own. Since then Constancia has slept only four hours a night, and her energy has increased to an exhilarating degree. She finds the soft stretch of Mamá's flesh over hers oddly sustaining, as if she were buoyed by a warm tidal power.

Still, Constancia's moods pendulate unpredictably, from this sense of contentment to an uncontrollable desire to scratch off her face. She wonders how long she must carry her mother's visage, shoulder the burden of Mamá's youth in full bloom (she was thirty-four when she died in the Zapata Swamp) alongside her own midlife perspective. What penance this is: to wear Mamá's mouth, her eyes, like a spiteful inheritance, to suffer the countenance that scorned her, that banished her to a lonely childhood of uncles and horses.

And the question persists: Where has her own face fled? *For every action there is an equal and opposite reaction.* Her father taught her this, an immutable law of physics. If it's true that nothing is lost in the greater balance sheet of energy, then her face must be somewhere—slipped through some cosmic sluice, tucked deep into a cold black hole, urged away by unknown codes of affinity. Perhaps, Constancia hopes, it's only a rare menopausal side effect.

Constancia waits an hour for the emollient to cool before pouring it through minute funnels into her royal-blue bottles.

The cream is sharply fragrant, like a season distilled. Constancia sweats in the heat and daze of its strange amplifications, in the long-ago summers in Cuba it conjures up. She remembers her Tío Dámaso standing before the wood-fire stove at the ranch, stirring his famous plantain soup. Although her grandfather and uncles raised horses and cattle, they were practically vegetarians. And there was an unspoken rule that pork would not be tolerated in their home. Not even *chicharrones*, the crispy pork cracklings that Constancia loved.

At times, when she recalls those isolated years on the ranch, Constancia senses the room, the air, indeed everything around her, rotating slowly, imperceptibly, as if she were a small white sun, the cynosure of a modest new galaxy.

Fortunately, it hasn't taken Constancia long to interest Miami's department stores and specialty shops in her home-made lotions and creams. Her initial strategy has been simple: to keep quantities of the products strictly limited in order to stimulate demand. Her first success, an eye repair cream called Ojos de Cuba, sold out in forty-two minutes at the Bal Harbour shopping mall. And her foot bath, Pies de Cuba, received a two-column rave in the beauty section of the Miami *Bugle*'s Sunday magazine.

Constancia intends to launch a full complement of face and body products for every glorious inch of Cuban woman-hood: Cuello de Cuba, Senos de Cuba, Codos de Cuba, Muslos de Cuba, and so on. Each item in her Cuerpo de Cuba line will embody the exalted image Cuban women have of themselves: as passionate, self-sacrificing, and deserving of every luxury. Last week, she found a defunct bowling ball factory she plans to convert into a cosmetics plant with money from her account at the Nicaraguan bank.

Constancia credits the emergence of her mother's face

over hers with her business acumen. Her ads (glossy, soft-focus affairs with antique mirrors and tropical foliage) appeal to her clients' memories, to the remembered splendors of their Cuban youth. Her motto—*Time may be indifferent but you needn't be*—appeals to their anxious vanity. Hardly a subtle approach, she admits, but highly effective.

Already, Constancia has received dozens of letters from women who confess that they feel more *cubana* after using her products, that they recall long-forgotten details of their childhoods in Sagua la Grande, Remedios, Media Luna, or Santa Cruz del Sur. Perhaps it is Mamá's questioning eyes that spur these reminiscences, or the sight of her long, unguarded throat. Politics may have betrayed Constancia's customers, geography overlooked them, but Cuerpo de Cuba products still manage to touch the pink roots of their sadness.

Constancia is not immune from these sudden reveries herself. The last time she applied her eye cream, she vividly recalled her mother's funeral, the electric-blue dove that hovered over the burial pit, helplessly thrashing the air, her sister's unrelenting grief. Papi held a clod of wet dirt to throw into the grave, but aimed it at the dove instead. The bird drifted interminably until it came to rest on Mamá's coffin. "It's still moving!" Reina shouted, but Papi paid no attention. He grabbed a shovel from a cemetery attendant and quickly filled in the grave.

Constancia rearranges the condiments in her refrigerator to make room for the fresh batch of emollient. She uses no preservatives, so it's essential that she keep the cream cool, especially in this weather, which spoils everything so quickly. As she lines the shelves with her royal-blue bottles, Mamá's face stares back at her in dizzying miniature. Constancia considers how far she's traveled away from her mother, only to find that she is waiting for her in each new place.

Lately, Constancia has begun wearing vintage clothing. Fitted suits from the forties, strapless summer dresses that flare out at the hips. She buys old brooches and drop pearl earrings, crocodile pumps made in Havana years ago. She doesn't remember her mother dressing like this, doesn't remember much of Mamá at all, except for the day she returned home, eight months pregnant and bruised. Constancia likes to imagine herself as her mother might have been, on Papi's arm, attending a scientific conference in the capital. The hall would rumor with her presence, unsettling Papi's colleagues with her disturbing beauty.

It is afternoon by the time Constancia loads up her Cadillac for her first delivery of the day. She thinks of Heberto as she fills the backseat with three Styrofoam chests, vaporous with dry ice. What would she ask him if she were allowed only one question?

Today she'll deliver Cara de Cuba to accounts in Kendall, Coconut Grove, and South Beach. Her other clients must wait several more days for a shipment. Constancia knows that people will endure almost anything for a product they consider precious or rare. Whenever she pulls up to a shop in her pink Cadillac convertible, steps out in her forties dress and open-toed pumps, all traffic instantly stops.

The sun weaves the air with thick, unbearable light. Constancia drives her convertible with the top up and the air-conditioning on full blast to protect her fragile cargo. How different this is from her childhood traveling days, when she and her father braved every inconvenience Cuba could offer—torrential rains, black clouds of mosquitoes, dirt roads or none at all, and the beastliest heat in the Western Hemisphere—in pursuit of their endangered creatures.

On one trip through Pinar del Río province, she and her father came upon an upland pasture pockmarked with hundreds of singular-looking burrows. Some of them were rough and unfinished, while others had a smooth, patted appearance. The rough ones, Constancia quickly discovered, were filled with tarantulas, quite common in Cuba. But the smooth ones, about eight inches deep, each contained the rare toad they were seeking: *Bufo empusus*. The toads, which looked much larger than their burrows, used the tops of their heads to seal off their homes, like precise lids.

That night, as they camped out under a sky collapsing with stars, her father expounded on the relative merits of the Greek philosophers. Abruptly, though, he changed the subject. *Analyzing people is infinitely more taxing than distinguishing among even the subtlest variations of subspecies.* It was true that with a quick glance, Papi could identify a creature's essential habits—its food preferences and mating rituals, its nurturant or aberrant behavior. *Human beings are distressingly unpredictable. They have a natural propensity for chaos. It is part of their biology, like a capacity for despair or profound joy.* Her father paused, looked up at the quickening wounds of a million stars. *There is a comfort,* mi hija, *in knowing what to expect.*

Constancia was perplexed. Her father's pronouncements were usually circumscribed—to the present, to natural history, or to abstract philosophies. Papi never alluded to her mother or her half-sister in Havana, not even in passing. Constancia struggled with the burden of this emptiness, of sharing no past but the land's and no future but the creatures soon to be in her and Papi's possession. But the pleasure of her father's presence, his reassuring voice, frequently overrode her discontent.

· · ·

Constancia takes U.S. 1 south toward Kendall. Her client's boutique is situated across the street from a serpentarium. Constancia is tempted to visit it—some of her most enjoyable memories are of catching snakes with her father—but she fears her emollient won't withstand even a moment's exposure in this heat. A banner outside the store announces the day's arrival of Cara de Cuba. A long line of elegantly dressed women are waiting to buy her product. Constancia pulls up in her pink Cadillac and removes a Styrofoam chest from the backseat. The women burst into applause. A scuffle breaks out at the front of the line, and a security guard rushes in to break up the fight. The owner tells Constancia that the first clients started lining up at dawn and are feeling somewhat testy.

At the Coconut Grove store an hour later, customers learn that only two dozen bottles of Cara de Cuba will be available for sale, and another fracas ensues. One woman tears through the back window of Constancia's convertible and grabs the last chest of lotion, meant for the South Beach shop.

On an impulse, Constancia drives to the Good Samaritan Hospital in Coral Gables. Her ex-husband, Gonzalo, is still dying on the eleventh floor. She tells herself she'll insist on learning Heberto's whereabouts, that she won't leave until she knows when he's coming home. She blames Gonzalo for Heberto's departure, for inciting her husband to become a bold, impassioned man.

Constancia is reluctant to visit Gonzalo. In fact, she hasn't seen him since his father's funeral, in January. He looked quite feeble then, but his presence stirred her nonetheless. Secretly, Constancia feared he might reignite a passion inside her, impossible to quench. Gonzalo may have left her long ago, may have lied to her so consistently it was a kind of truth, but Constancia never forgot him. Never forgot him or forgave him.

Over the years, their son yoked Constancia to Gonzalo as if to a living steer. She suspects that her decision to send Silvestre to an orphanage in America was more for her benefit than for his. By then, she was resigned to her marriage with Heberto—so predictable, kind, and quietly efficient in bed (he was sanitary too, unfailingly rinsing and powdering his penis after every coupling). Yet each time she and Heberto made love, Silvestre knocked on their bedroom door, wanting something. The sight of her son, his eyes the same capricious brown as Gonzalo's, continually revived Constancia's despair. Not until Silvestre was in Colorado, deaf and nearly dead of a fever, was she able to get pregnant again.

At the hospital, Constancia is surprised to see how robust Gonzalo looks for a terminal patient, although the nurse tells her it's mostly water-swelling. His head seems large and hard to balance, his fingers monstrously tumid. Worst of all are his eyes, dim and sticky with mucus.

Gonzalo doesn't recognize Constancia at first. But as soon as she speaks, he opens his arms in welcome. *"Ah, mi golondrina!"* he coos, using his old pet name for her. Gonzalo always maintained that he could remember a lover best by her voice.

Years ago, Reina confided that she'd slept with Gonzalo once, after he'd divorced Constancia. His penis was so small, her sister complained, a mere boy's, that she could hardly feel him inside her. Constancia was astonished. She'd always considered Gonzalo's penis impressive, certainly more so than Heberto's. But she'd had only two lovers all her life. How could she imagine what Reina's other conquests had accustomed her to?

"Are you aware of the deadly attraction certain infective agents have for the liver?" Gonzalo asks, staring intently at Constancia.

"Where's Heberto?" she demands, trying to quell the anger in her voice. "He left with your pirates in March, and I still haven't heard a word!"

"The trees are disappearing," Gonzalo whispers, turning toward the window. The clouds are pink and fleshy in the sky. Constancia follows his wandering gaze and notices a patch of cabbage palms in the hospital gardens, two jacarandas, a single bottlebrush tree.

Gonzalo picks up the telephone as if prompted by an invisible signal and calls a fellow patient down the hall, a mystic named María del Carmen, who, despite a pneumectomy, continues to smoke through a hole in her throat.

María del Carmen shuffles in on paper slippers. Her head is shorn, her nails are geometrically lacquered in gold. She insists that the Holy Ghost oversees the body's purification systems and tells Gonzalo that he, too, must shave his head so that the Spirit can descend upon him with a minimum of friction.

"So you think I should cut this off?" Gonzalo flirts with Constancia, flicking the ends of his scraggly hair. There's a drop of spittle on his chin. "Do you think it would make a difference?"

Constancia says nothing. She tries to reconcile the sight of Gonzalo with the slim brown body that once defeated hers, that left her prepared for more than she would ever receive again. She studies his fever charts, the registry of his manifold disease. It occurs to her that in all these years and through six disastrous marriages, Gonzalo has sought no solace but adventure. Her own life, in contrast, has been a pursuit for ever more exalted security. Which appetite, she wonders sadly, is the more meaningless?

María del Carmen pulls a razor and shaving cream

from a fold of her hospital gown and gets to work on Gonzalo. She begins with his widow's peak, methodically shears him from the hairline back.

Gonzalo is in a sentimental mood. He recalls the first time he saw Constancia, sitting at her receptionist's desk against the picture window of Havana harbor. It was 1956. She wore low-heeled sandals, and her tiny feet were visible beneath her desk.

"I looked at those China-girl feet and knew right then I would marry her," he says to no one in particular.

No sooner does María del Carmen exit, her razor held high in triumph, than Gonzalo begins rubbing himself freely, prompting his little sex to swell beneath his hospital gown.

"This summer, your husband will be a hero," Gonzalo says in his most seductive voice. He looks down at his inconsiderable bulge, then stares at Constancia expectantly, as if offering her an unparalleled opportunity for patriotic duty. "Really, *mi vida*, you should be thanking me."

Constancia takes a step toward Gonzalo, absorbs a wave of his humid decay, of the scent of mint shaving cream still damp on his skull. She wants to reprimand him, demand Heberto's return, but something makes her stop.

She bends over him, slips her right hand beneath his hospital gown, grips the solid familiar warmth. Constancia stares into her ex-husband's face, dissolving now with pleasure, then quickly pulls her hand away. She covers her nose and mouth with it, inhaling deeply, and hurriedly leaves the room.

Constancia guides her battered Cadillac back toward Key Biscayne. From the interstate, she spots the riotous blur of a poinciana in bloom. Most of Miami's poincianas are still dormant, heavy with dark seed pods. In another month, the city will be ablaze with their brilliant displays. Constancia prefers the deep scarlet of the royal poincianas best. Papi showed her once how each one of its red flowers has a token white petal, which unfolds when its pollen is ripe. The white petal serves as a nectar guide for bees and birds and other pollinators.

Constancia crosses the Rickenbacker Causeway in her pink convertible. The top is down, and her hair whips loosely in the wind. What a relief it is to escape the oppression of possibility in Gonzalo's hospital room.

Around her, the bay slackly merges with dusk. The tide is low, and an army of iridescent crabs scrambles along the shore. Shirtless men in cut-off shorts gather the crabs in tin buckets as spirals of smoke rise up from barbecues on the beach. The fading light lingers on the water before dying altogether. The hour spreads quickly, emptily, in all directions at once. As the heat of the day grows quiet, the darkness absorbs the horizon and all other illusions.

Constancia counts the traveler's palms along Crandon Boulevard. She wants to stop and tug at the base of each leaf stem, tap the quart of water trapped inside. She and her father drank frequently from the trees during their travels, quenching their thirst, refilling their empty canteens. They ate their seed pods, nutty and slightly bitter, often sheltered themselves with their enormous, wind-torn leaves. Papi told Constancia that *guajiros* thought that in the wild, the palms were a natural compass, always aligning themselves in an east-west direction. Later, Constancia was disappointed to learn that this was not actually true.

She signals left, heads toward her condominium on the beach. The guard waves her in, and she parks in her usual spot. Heberto's plain Chevrolet sits idly in its space. There's nothing of interest in the mailbox. No postcard from her husband. No letter from her daughter or from her son in New York. Only coupons from the pizza place down the block. Slowly, Constancia climbs the nine flights of stairs to her apartment. She does this once a day to keep her legs in shape.

A telegram is taped to her front door. It seems to bleed into the blond wood around it. The message is from her sister, Reina, in Havana. It says that she will be arriving in Miami via the Bahamas the following night.

Dulce Fuerte

MADRID

Here in *Madrid*, the sky is a constant placid blue. No violence to match my own. It hasn't been pretty, this rush of purpose deflated. To leave Cuba I had to burn everything I know. Memory, I'm convinced, is the worst of traitors.

Two weeks with Abelardo, that sickening ridge of spine and tailbone, and I left him for good. A wilderness of patience, and then I left him for good. Sometimes I wonder what I've gained besides this new bargain with solitude.

I stole everything I could from Abelardo's widowed sister, pocketed her greasy cash, pawned the jewelry. This was after our fistfight. She pulled my hair, called me a Communist whore. I knocked her down a flight of stairs. She survived by landing on an elderly neighbor just back from retrieving her mail. Abelardo had nothing worth stealing.

It didn't take me long to find a job. I'm the woman hired to clean the mansion and love the lonely two-year-old girl.

My uniform is a disaster: baby pink with a scalloped apron and white, spongy-soled shoes. Let's just say my presence is a tolerated intrusion.

The weather inside the house is restless. It's obvious there's a divorce in the making. I prefer it when the Señor and Señora leave me alone with the girl. Her name is Mercedes, and she is spindly and inscrutable for being so tiny. She barely speaks, so I tell her what I read in the newspapers. How the polar ice caps are melting and the half-degree rise in the temperature of the earth's surface is killing off countless forms of life.

We go for walks in the afternoon. Mercedes always stops in front of the cutlery store and stares at the gleaming display. Little cleaver, I joke, you'll grow up and kill your parents. I think of how all evil begins with the first absence.

Nobody knows where I am. It's as if night has descended on me with a velvet anonymity. Of course I don't use my real name. Not that I think Abelardo and his Franco-worshiping sister are looking for me. Not that I think anyone is looking for me. But more to try on a fresh identity, plant a tentative new root. Sometimes I wish everything I wanted could be arranged this easily.

There are no paintings or books on the walls of the house where I work. Only mirrors, dozens and dozens of them ricocheting with light. I've reached the point where I can finally ignore my reflection, even when cleaning a mirror head-on. Believe me, it's a relief to be this invisible.

The Señora preens in her mirrors every evening, adjusting her sparse blond bob. Mercedes sits beside her, pulling her own baby, batlike ears.

Somehow this is more than I intended, and less. I'm on another clock, suspended in time, expecting privileges I thought automatically came with risk. But it's a place with rules I don't understand. I look for clues in the shredded bullfight posters, in the separatist graffiti, in the conversation I overhear in the meat department of El Corte Inglés. Each word is a map I track toward the same blank wall, thickly covered with moss.

Sunday is my day off, and I go to El Retiro and walk around the man-made lake. Every ripple from a diving swan sparks little internal ceremonies of doubt. There's a Gypsy woman on the promenade, whom I usually sit with for an hour or more. She's young, no older than I am, with coarse skin and two-different-color eyes. I smoke cigarettes and listen to her garbled Spanish, watch her nimble leather fingers snap my future into place.

"You are thin, but there is too much fat in your blood," she begins each session, her gray and brown eyes serious.

"Tell me something new," I asked her the last time.

"I look in your heart and read only questions." She stopped shuffling her cards and pointed to a knave with a red collar of bells. "Who is this man still whispering in your ear?"

"Che Guevara." I laughed. Then I lost patience. "Look, how should I know? You're the Gypsy!" I was down to my last cigarette. I needed something to eat. I thought of how antibiotics were losing their effectiveness against disease.

The Gypsy slid her cards together in a haphazard pile. "No charge for you today," she said, and sullenly turned away.

Last week, I took Mercedes to El Prado. Except for the archives in Santiago de Cuba, where my father's picture hangs with other artifacts from the revolution, I'd never been to a real museum before. I've never even been to a church. Who the hell can keep up with all those martyrs and saints? In Cuba, we were taught that religion is a refuge for the weak and the ignorant. But then I saw Raphael's *Cardinal*, and I knew that wasn't right at all.

"Look at that man's face, Mercedes."

"Man," she repeated in a loud voice.

"Everything you need to know about ambition is right between his eyes."

I come from a long line of atheists. My mother puts her faith in electricity and sex. And my father's anticlerical slogan for the revolution—"Make them grow palm nuts!"— is still exhorted in Cuba today. My maternal grandparents were scientists and dismissed organized religion out of hand. "Religion is a form of willing delusion," Mamá used to say, quoting her father. Both her parents died within two years of each other back in the 1940s, but Mamá could never tell me why.

Sometimes I wish I could've known my grandparents. My mother makes them sound larger than life, like those billboards of Che intoning that we do more for the revolution. They traveled all over Cuba, studying birds and bats and other animals. Mamá says her parents were famous in their field, that scientists from all over the world came to visit them in Havana. I wonder if anyone still remembers them.

Some days I feel the hot mist of the past on my back, all the generations preceding me, whispering *this way and this way and not that*. There should be rituals like in primitive societies, where the elders confer their knowledge on their descendants bit by bit. Then we could dismiss all the false histories pressed upon us, accumulate our true history like a river in rainy season.

My mother has passed along only fragments of her family's past, a few quotes from ancient philosophers, a questioning nature that, more often than not, has gotten me into trouble. Of my father's family I know nothing. (His parents were "laborers," the revolutionary books say. Like who the hell isn't?) Mamá didn't have much time to fill in the gaps. She was always working, illuminating the remoter parts of the island. She has an unusual gift for light. As for me, I spent practically my whole childhood in boarding schools, wearing navy-blue uniforms, picking lettuce or lemons or yams and reciting useless facts.

Everything at the museum cafeteria is so expensive that I buy only a bowl of gazpacho to share with Mercedes, and all the saltines I can stuff into my pockets.

"Hot!" she shouts, meaning spicy, so I pour a little water into the soup to dilute the taste. This suits Mercedes just fine. I've been teaching her how to eat with a spoon, and she slurps the gazpacho with relish.

I notice a man watching us, but then he gets up to leave and I think nothing more of him until he slides into our booth with two trays of steaks and stewed vegetables and portions of wobbly flan. He is exceedingly tall. Even sitting down, he is taller than most people. A planetary height. His features are so bland I can't get a fix on him. It's like staring at a peeled potato.

"I'm here in Madrid for two days only," he says finally. I place his accent as Swedish or Norwegian, and in fact he's from a suburb of Stockholm.

Nothing is free, I think, but I'm so hungry I cut off a piece of steak. Mercedes grabs the flan nearest to her and squeezes it in her fists.

"She's not my daughter," I announce, and then wonder why I feel the need to explain. "I just take care of her."

The man says nothing but continues to stare at me. A blood blister sprouts on one thumb.

"What's your business?" I ask in English, and it puts him immediately at ease.

"Pharmaceuticals." He straightens up and looks ready

to sell me something. "We have antidotes for many diseases. Baldness. Lung infections. Moroccan skin fungus."

"I'm glad to say I won't be needing any of your products," I say, back to Spanish. Mercedes starts laughing, squawking like a little parrot, as if she understood my joke. Her face and smock are smeared with flan.

"You have beautiful hair," the man sputters, as if seized by a sudden revelation, then he looks down at his immense hands.

His eyes are a delicate pink. Like a rabbit's, I think. Or a secret sorrow.

Mercedes and I accompany Bengt to a bullfight that afternoon. His company gives him tickets for entertaining clients, and so we have excellent seats. The matadors' costumes shimmer in the sun like grandiose insects. Four bulls are lanced with minimal fanfare, unleashing a torrent of hoots, cheers, and seat cushions. It's hopeless to read what pleases the crowd. Only disgust is unmistakable.

The fifth bull is small, overheated, glossy with anger. Again and again, it charges the young matador. He loses his footing, and the crowd jeers. The second time he slips, the matador is furious. He holds his sword high in the air, poised to kill, but the bull knocks him down and smashes his leg with its hooves. The matador slashes back frantically, severing the bull's ear and gouging out an eye.

For a moment, the bull stops, stunned. Then it charges wildly around the ring as blood pours from its skull. The fans go crazy, cursing the matador and every one of his ancestors. It takes a dozen men to finally kill the beast. When the ambulance pulls into the stadium to pick up the wounded matador, the crowd hurls rocks and bottles, and the medics barely escape with their lives.

• • •

It's nearly midnight when I sneak out of the mirrored house to meet Bengt at his hotel. He orders room service, then spends an hour watching me eat. Roast duck in olive oil, sweetbreads with pepper sauce, a half loaf of bread spread with pounded salt cod.

"May I feed you dessert?" Bengt asks shyly. There are a dozen *yemas* arranged like ovaries on a silver tray. He takes my hand and leads me to the king-sized bed in the other room.

The night is sold, I think, and begin to undo my clothes. He stops me.

"Please lie down," he whispers.

I notice the dark expanse of his tongue, thick and swollen and overrunning his mouth. He gives off a sharp, trespassing smell. It makes me afraid.

Bengt removes my shoes but nothing else. For a moment, he fingers the scar on my thigh, where I donated skin to heal Mamá's burnt flesh. Then he sits on a chair beside me with the tray of sugared egg yolks and a silver serving spoon. Bengt cradles the back of my head in his hand, gently, as if I were sick and needing assistance. With the other, he spoons the first *yema* into my mouth. It dissolves on my tongue with a moist, precise sweetness. Then he spoons another, and another after that.

Tranquillity is nothing less than the good ordering of the mind. I repeat this twice to calm myself down. I think of my mother reading her philosophers aloud, her face lax with nostalgia as if she herself had lived in ancient Greece or Rome. What was the last thing she told me before I left Cuba? Suddenly, it seems crucial to remember.

Seven *yemas*, eight. The egg yolks swell inside me like fat, sticky suns. Like the time I was fourteen and expecting a baby. Nine, ten, eleven *yemas*. *All things are changing; and thou thyself art in continuous mutation and in a manner in continuous destruction, and the whole universe too.*

Twelve *yemas*. Twelve. Bengt lets the spoon drop. He loosens his tie and covers his face with his hands. They seem radiant, trembling and sunken in light. Then he climbs into bed beside me and falls deeply asleep.

RARAE AVES

❖

During my last year at the University of Havana, my father was diagnosed with throat cancer. The doctors said he would live only a few months, but his will defied the prognosis. He survived nearly three years more. I decided to return to Pinar del Río to read to him. This was a luxury for Papá, who had spent so many years dutifully reading to others. Day after day, tome by tome, I read his entire library back to him.

My father, as always, took greatest comfort in the Greek and Roman philosophers—Plato and Epictetus—and, above all, in Marcus Aurelius. He delighted, too, in the poetry of Miguel de Unamuno and Rubén Darío, especially the poems in Cantos de Vida y Esperanza. Papá was not a religious man, but I suspect he discovered in those poems a path to a private solace.

Papá received countless visitors during his illness. His friends ignored his deteriorating health and shared with him news and gossip from the cigar factory. The talk of the day was of the vile cigar-rolling machines, those clanking monstrosities from America that were ruining the cigar workers' way of life. No amount of marching or rioting would rid the factories of them. It appeared that the jobs that had been lost would stay forever lost.

One night, during the carnival festivities, a band of costumed men broke into El Cid and smashed the cigar-rolling machines to unrecognizable hulks of metal. Later, explosives demolished the replacements from the United States. Papá, who had the soul of an anarchist but an accountant's practicality, had disapproved of his friends' plan. In the end, six of them went to jail.

The tradition of the lector also had eroded. After my father resigned, no other reader proved as learned as he. No one, despite the enhancing advantages of a microphone, commanded the respect he'd once enjoyed. I was flattered to be offered the position myself, but I could not accept it. The world I'd known as a boy, Papá's world, no longer existed.

Instead I took a job as a part-time hunting guide, to help my parents pay their medical bills. My clients were primarily North American tourists, indiscriminate and grossly underskilled to a man. To me, shooting animals is neither recreation nor sport but a necessity subsumed to either hunger or higher scientific purpose. Today younger naturalists use cameras and recording devices that make collecting more humane. But in my day, such equipment as existed was much too unwieldy to take along on field trips. One simply had to kill a creature to fully understand it.

Mamá implored me to return to Havana to finish my studies, but I refused to leave my father's side. Mercifully, Papá's degeneration was so gradual that we grew accustomed to it. His appetite diminished to nothing as he withered to eighty pounds. The cancer spread to his mouth and jaw until the bottom half of his face collapsed. He became disoriented and *spoke to me as if I were* his *father. When he reminisced, his bony fingers moved involuntarily, twitching with the memory of a hundred fine muscles. Papá spoke of the fiddles he'd helped his father carve on their kitchen table in the hills of Galicia, of the foul-smelling varnishes they'd distilled from the resins of trees. "It's the varnish, above all," he insisted, "that ensures a violin's resonance and longevity."*

Papá's final hour came unexpectedly. It was a late afternoon in September, and Mamá had just finished cooking a caldo gallego, *my father's favorite soup. When she brought him the steaming bowl, Papá pushed himself onto his elbows, inhaled deeply of the aroma, and hummed the opening bars to the "Witches' Dance Variations." My mother smiled sadly as she lifted the spoon to feed him. He grabbed it from her hand and began eating with unaccustomed gusto. Mamá and I looked at each other. Perhaps Papá's health would improve, after all.*

An instant later, my father threw the spoon to the floor and poured the remaining soup down the front of his dressing gown, his skin numb to its heat. His eyes and what remained of his mouth were open, but he could no longer see or speak. His face was a mask, stiffened with fear.

I offered to run for the doctor, but Mamá took my hand and asked me to sit beside her on the bed.

"Go, if you must, mi amor," she told Papá gently. "Your memory is safe with us."

Then she held his hands in hers as they quivered with the last of his life.

No sooner had I finished my doctoral studies and begun lecturing in the biology department of the University of Havana than General Gerardo Machado ordered the college closed. The professors had protested vociferously that they could not teach with soldiers in the classrooms, and so that despot tried to do away with higher education altogether. It was 1931, a dreadful year. Thousands of students were rounded up and many murdered in cold blood. One of my colleagues, the famous Bolivian zoologist José Garriga, was rumored to be a member of the secret terrorist group ABC. Early one morning, he was abducted from the university cafeteria and never heard from again.

Many professors fled to New York or Miami or the Yucatán, waiting for the violence to end. Others remained in Havana and found menial jobs to stay alive or support their families. The chairman of the chemistry department became a short-order chef. A physicist friend, Jorge de Lama, delivered ice for his uncle. Other colleagues worked as waiters, cane cutters, ranch hands, or shop clerks. I decided, once more, to return to Pinar del Río.

During the course of my father's illness, Mamá's arthritis had bent her back and disfigured her graceful hands. She lived on Papá's pension, the few pesos I saved from my meager salary, and the generosity of our neighbor Graciela Montalvo, a retired dressmaker. I took to hunting for food in what remained of the forests around Pinar del Río, shooting hutías and pigeons for our dinner. I planted a garden and harvested garlic, onions, bell peppers, and tomatoes. Our orange tree, too, was prolific. We survived better than most.

In those days, many people risked their lives to fight General Machado, a thug who financed his brutal regime with loans from American banks. His opponents organized rallies, planted bombs, sabotaged government buildings. I remember one local boy, Agapito Fernández, had his middle finger sliced off by the militia for refusing to divulge his union leader father's whereabouts. I heard these stories, and yet I found myself incapable of any useful action.

I justified my stance then by convincing myself that politics was a sordid arena, separate from science. My mother did not share my views. When word spread of the massacre of students at El Principe prison, Mamá joined the protestors in the main plaza of Pinar del Río. The following month, she marched to the police station to demand the release of Federico Zequeira, a former flute student falsely accused of treason. Later, Mamá wrote countless letters of complaint to U.S. Ambassador Harry Guggenheim and even to General Machado himself at the National Palace. It was a wonder she wasn't arrested.

Since I found it impossible to earn a living, I decided to return to my research. My new project was unprecedented: the cataloguing of every one of Cuba's nearly extinct birds. It was indicative of both my grand ambition and my equally grand ignorance to have undertaken this project during a time of virtual civil war.

Over the next eight months, with practically no funding except for what I could borrow, with an afflicted conscience, from my mother, I scoured the remotest corners of Cuba for rarae aves. I hitchhiked, jumped freight trains, cajoled guajiros into lending me their mules, slept in caves or beneath the canopies of immense ceiba trees. Cuba's landscape had changed so dramatically in only a decade that even the once populous birds that Dr. Forrest and I had collected were nowhere to be found, or found, at most, as singletons or in minuscule bands. There were no bird sanctuaries in Cuba, no sense that anything of value had been destroyed by the tractors and the plows.

I recall vividly ten days I spent observing a band of glossy ibises in the Zapata Swamp—certainly the last band in Cuba, at most three or four hundred birds in all. The long-necked ibises flew in from the east in undulating lines and landed on the rippling marsh. Then they worked their way toward shore, hunting for insects and snails. When they were frightened, the birds took to the air en masse, wheeling about in a magnificent display.

Mamá died of a heart attack while I was away in the Zapata. Señora Montalvo discovered her early one evening lying unkempt in her bed, the bed I was born in, the bed in which, long before, Mamá had surrendered her placenta to the black owl of night. By the time I returned to Pinar del Río, my mother had been buried four days. She lay beside my father on a patch of windy hillock, strewn with the brilliant lavender blossoms of twin poinciana trees.

I recalled then the story my mother revealed to me when I was nine years old. She said she hadn't wanted me to hear it from anyone else. Mamá told me that her father had banished her from the family when she was seventeen after a married man in Consolación del Norte had raped her. The culprit, the owner of a dry goods store, later became mayor of their town. That is how it was in those days.

My mother, who refused to join the convent or surrender her child for adoption, fled across the Cordillera de los Organos and started her life anew in Pinar del Río. It seemed to her a full-fledged metropolis then, especially to one who had grown up in tiny Consolación del Norte. With money she borrowed from a sympathetic aunt (who nonetheless warned her never to return home), my mother bought a used flute and supported herself by giving music lessons to the children of wealthy merchants. Her daughter, Olivia, was born in 1890. Four years later, the little girl drowned when the Guamá River overflowed its banks.

After Mamá died, I continued to live in my parents' home. Day and night I worked on my book, documenting the habits and habitats of ninety-six dwindling species, among them the Cuban paroquet, the wood ibis, the splendid camao (*Oreopeleia caniceps caniceps*), and Gundlach's hawk, one of the world's most seldom seen birds.

Around my small oval of clarity and order, the house fell into disarray. I didn't clean it or make repairs, and if it hadn't been for the kindness of Señora Montalvo, I probably would have eaten little. I looked as thoroughly disheveled as my surroundings. Occasionally, I left my study to walk in the woods, or to sell a piece of furniture to secure provisions. It took me many months to complete my book. By then, nothing remained in my parents' house except their hand-carved bed, Papá's philosophy texts, and a score of spiderwebs.

The afternoon I reemerged into the world, I found all of Pinar del Río nailed shut. The market was deserted, the streets were empty of vendors, the bakers had let their ovens cool. Garbage was piled high everywhere. Somehow I found the hush and stench even more disconcerting than gunfire.

Señora Montalvo told me that the chauffeurs of the Omnibus de la Habana had begun a general strike four days earlier. The streetcar motormen and taxi drivers had joined them. Then the stevedores, ferrymen, and longshoremen followed suit. She said that even the bellhops in the first-class hotels of Havana were going to work on roller skates. The island was at a complete standstill.

The pressure on General Machado intensified, until he was forced to flee the country. Hundreds of people stormed the National Palace, carrying off potted palms and long-stemmed cannas from the private gardens. Others raided the General's food supplies, as much from vengeance as from hunger, and hauled off a squealing razorback hog, which they unceremoniously butchered in Zayas Park. Many more looted the homes of Machado's cronies, the porristas, burning their possessions in impromptu bonfires.

The mood of revenge grew. Machado's henchmen were tracked down, beaten, and dismembered by mobs. Avengers found one notorious assassin, the man responsible for the massacre at El Príncipe prison, hiding under a kitchen sink disguised as an old crippled woman. They dragged his corpse, still wearing its black mantilla, through the jeering crowds of the capital. Many more days would pass before order was restored.

I sold my parents' house and, with the profit, published

five hundred copies of my first book, Cuba's Dying Birds. *It was a pleasure to finally hold the volume in my hands, to smell the fresh paper, touch the rough maroon binding. My name was on the spine, embossed in gold. It made all my work seem immediately less abstract.*

I sent my book abroad to the ornithologists I most admired. With all modesty, I must report it caused a stir in certain academic circles. Dr. Horatio Fowler III of Yale University wrote in Ornithology Today *that he considered my book ". . . one of the few instant classics of its time."*

That fall, when the University of Havana reopened its doors, I was promptly appointed a full professor of general science and biology. It was 1933. And I was twenty-nine years old.

A MATTER OF GIFTS

❄

KEY BISCAYNE

JUNE 1991

Reina unsnaps the top of her bikini and lies by the pool with her back to the morning sun. It's been over a month since she arrived in Miami, and already she's grown accustomed to the uneasy indolence of exile life. The Cuba she knows is fading in the luxury of her sister's existence. Only a suitcase stuffed with her father's mementos—taxidermic bats and birds, a few books and clothes, the framed photograph of her mother—remains of that disquieting time before her departure.

It seems to Reina that she'd been on the verge of some certainty in Havana. Now she wonders whether all certainty will be kept from her, wonders, in fact, whether certainty isn't truly disaster in disguise.

At the Miami airport, Reina was stunned to see a vision of her mother rushing toward her at the gate. Constancia looks so much like Mami now, down to the minutest details, that Reina couldn't help it—she studied her sister's face like a blind woman, tried to read with her hands the grace and terror that lay hidden there.

"What a strange way of being dead!" she finally exclaimed. It was her first direct utterance to Constancia in thirty years. Later, she stared at her sister for many more hours, considered her from every angle, until it made her frantic with grief.

Her first few nights in Miami, Reina slept in the same bed with Constancia, back to stomach, Reina on the outside protecting her slight, older sister, listening for messages from the dead. She and Constancia showered together, combed one another's hair, fed each other tidbits from their dinner plates. All the while, Reina kept watch over her sister's face as if it were a compelling tragedy.

Reina wonders whether Mami's face is only a superficial membrane, like her own patches of borrowed skin, or whether it penetrates further to the bone, to some basic molecular level. She can't help thinking how everything is fundamentally electric, how natural currents flow near the surface of the earth, telluric and magnetic, how she is pulled again and again into the charged fields of her sister's face.

If only Constancia would stop talking, stay mute sufficiently long enough for Mami to emerge. Reina finds intolerable the false expectations their mother's visage sets up. There is a part of Reina that wants to address Mami directly, to risk everything—even if it means eradicating her sister—in the hope of retrieving her past.

After their mother died, Papá sent Reina and Constancia to a boarding school in Trinidad. That first rainy winter, a forest of politeness took root between them, starching the air they shared. Each time Reina tried to talk about Mami, Constancia covered her ears and hummed the national anthem. Although they spent years together at boarding school, by habit or cowardice—Reina isn't sure which—she and Constancia never discussed their mother again.

Reina dives into the deep end of the condominium's pool with her eyes wide open. There's a dime and a gold hoop earring where the bottom slopes down. She plucks them from the concrete and leaves them on the rim of the pool. Then she swims with powerful strokes to the shallow end. One stroke, then two, and she's in the deep water. Two strokes more, and she's at the shallow end again.

This is a pool for pygmies, Reina thinks. Who else could be satisfied with these few drops of blue?

The sun is high in the sky. No interference from clouds. The ocean wrinkles with the slightest breeze. The city is in the distance, strangely flat and uninviting. Reina emerges from the water and shakes herself dry, a glorious titanic beast. Near her, sunglasses are lowered, shutters flung open. Her own pungent scent steams up from her mismatched skin.

At noon, Constancia calls down to Reina from the balcony, announcing lunch. It's delicious, as usual: *arroz con pollo*, fried plantains, a coconut flan for dessert, all served on fancy flowered plates.

"This is the century that Christianity has died out," Constancia declares, picking the petit pois out of her rice. "The metaphysical is taking over. People believe in miracles now instead of God."

Reina reaches over and mashes her sister's peas with a fork, sucks them off the tines. She looks up at the past trapped in Constancia's face and doesn't know what to say.

The phone rings incessantly during their meal. One call after another from Constancia's clients, impatient for orders of lotions and creams. Her sister is nearly finished retrofitting a bowling ball factory into Cuerpo de Cuba's new manufacturing plant to meet the clamorous demand. Reina has volunteered to help Constancia with the remaining electrical work.

There's a stack of photographs on the kitchen table, taken before Constancia's affliction. Reina thumbs through the pictures, carefully examines them one by one. Her sister looks good, well groomed, younger than her fifty-two years, her body pliant and pampered, Reina notes, but lacking the tone of true succulence.

"Do you think this will pass?" Constancia is moody, restless. "I'm not extinct yet, am I?"

Reina isn't certain she can stay with her sister if Mami's face disappears, isn't certain she can stay if it remains. She takes her sister's hand and pats it. It's a child's hand, lineless and smooth. What could there possibly be here still tempting the dead?

"I wish you'd stop that!" Constancia hisses all of a sudden. "You've been doing it for days!"

Reina realizes with a start that she's been unconsciously whistling. She recognizes the melody, a traditional *changüi* from Oriente she once heard a *negrito* sing in Céspedes Park. *He nacido para ti, Nengón. Para ti, Nengón.* His singing had made Reina cry.

"I've been ingesting small amounts of sterling silver," Constancia says, calmer now. She takes a denim pouch from her apron pocket, shows Reina the silver dust inside. "I heard on the radio that it soothes hallucinations."

Reina reaches for an apple from a bowl on the kitchen table. She doesn't want to say that the entire world should be eating silver dust, then, because everyone is hallucinating.

"Someone told me this might be an equatorial disease. I must have caught it here in Miami. There are lots of people from South America." Constancia pinches a bit of silver dust and sprinkles it on the tip of her tongue. Then she washes it down with a glass of ice water. "What I want to know is where *my* face went. Where has it disappeared to?"

Reina remembers a stray snatch of a poem, she doesn't know from where, maybe something her father read to her once. *Life is in the mirror, and you are the original death.*

Of course, she doesn't tell Constancia this.

"Ayúdame, por favor." Her sister decides to prepare a batch of Muslos de Cuba, her new thigh smoothener.

Reina isn't particularly interested—the smell and the steam give her a headache—but Constancia is so overwhelmed with work that Reina reluctantly agrees to help stir up a few gallons for a department store demonstration the next day.

"What are these for?" Reina asks, poking through a bowl of boiled avocado pits.

Constancia cracks the pits open with the blade of a knife and scrapes out the vegetal flesh. "Softens the subcutaneous cells of the thigh. Reduces the appearance of cellulite. Peel those peaches for me, will you?"

Reina leans over the tray of rotting fruit, waves away the cloud of feasting flies. She picks up a serrated knife and begins peeling. Reina is perplexed by the obsession women in Miami have for the insignificant details of their bodies, by their self-defeating crusades. She was appalled when Constancia took her to the Dade County shopping mall last Sunday. All those hipless, breastless mannequins, up to their scrawny necks in silk.

Don't women understand that their peculiarities are what endear them to men? Rarely do the most conventionally beautiful women have the greatest hold over their mates. Pepín, who adored Reina but remained an inveterate woman watcher over the years, admitted that he favored no particular female features. *Cada mujer tiene algo*, he liked to say. Every woman has something. The best lovers, Reina knows from experience, approach women this way.

"You don't have to worry; you never had to," Constancia sniffs. She opens a king-sized tub of cherry yogurt, ladles it into the steaming cauldron.

"But why should anybody?" Reina turns around, pulls up her terry-cloth cover-up to reveal her puckered thighs. "*Oye, chica*, since when did cellulite ever deter passion?"

Constancia grabs Reina's cutting board and scrapes the peach peels into the blender. It screeches like a malfunctioning drill. The skins turn brown and pulpy, altogether unappealing. Reina watches as her sister adds them to the bubbling emollient.

"I think every woman remains fixed at a certain age in her own mind." Constancia lowers her voice to a conspiratorial degree. "A rare time when she saw herself in the mirror or through her lover's eyes and was pleased."

Reina guesses this is her sister's best cosmetics-counter voice.

"Haven't you ever noticed how often women destroy pictures of themselves, Reina? That's because nothing conforms with our private image of ourselves. My products bring back that feeling. The beauty of scent and sensation, the mingling of memory and imagination."

"Not me, *mi amor*. I live in the here and now."

"Well, you're probably the only woman on earth who actually likes the way she looks!" Constancia snaps, stirring the thigh lotion with a steady rhythm of her wooden spoon. "Definitely bad for business!"

Reina retreats to the guest room and changes into her work jumpsuit. She's putting up shelves and plywood hutches for their father's stuffed specimens. She retrieves a hammer from her toolbox and secures another bracket against the wall. Her thumbs still feel a little sore from having been broken in the mahogany tree. Then she lines the shelves with arm lengths of aluminum foil she bought at the supermarket.

Reina is bewildered each time she goes shopping in Miami. The displays of products she'd forgotten or didn't even know existed. Red pepper spaghetti. Giant artichokes, looking vaguely medieval. Bread in countless textures and shapes. And anything, it seems, can be frozen or freeze-dried here. Instant, instant everything!

In the far corner of the room, on the topmost shelf, Reina displays the *periquito* Papi shot in a virgin forest near Guantánamo. Their father's spectacular *camao*, its mantle still an enviable blue, she places in a hutch by the window, next to an earless owl called a *sijú*. Reina fondles the elfin owl, her favorite of their father's collection, recalls the faint traces of light it left in a lace of leaves. She wonders if memory is little more than this: a series of erasures and perfected selections.

Over the dresser, where a decorative crucifix has been, Reina nails up the photograph of their mother that looks exactly like Constancia today. In fact, it's identical to the antiqued photograph her sister uses for the labels on her jars of lotions and creams. Mami is pale in the picture, so pale her complexion seems more conjecture than color. Reina remembers how the summer before she died, Mami's eyelashes whitened until her green eyes looked twice their normal size.

Reina works a neat row of nails in her mouth, then pounds them into the wall one by one. She adjusts another shelf against the wall. Working up a sweat, Reina strips down to her panties and an old-fashioned bra with conical cups. She's always wanted to work in the nude, considers clothing a nuisance at best. Nothing ever fits her quite right anyway, especially in this *nalgas*-denying country. Reina knows she looks best without a stitch, even now with her patchwork skin.

It's nearly four o'clock when Reina finishes with the guest room. She finds Constancia in the kitchen, dripping vanilla extract into the cooling thigh lotion. Reina urges her sister into taking Heberto's little motorboat out for a spin. "How hard can it be?" Reina asks. "No disrespect to your husband, *mi amor*, but how many astrophysicists do *you* know who go fishing on the planet?"

In Cuba, no one is allowed to go boating without a special permit, so Reina rarely got the opportunity to venture out on the open seas. Constancia is nervous because Heberto has been gone since March, on a covert mission against El Comandante. Reina suppresses her laughter. Nobody can bring that old *cabrón* down, much less mild-mannered Heberto Cruz. It amuses her to think that Constancia feels her husband has a fighting chance.

At the yacht club, Reina sets to repairing the rusting outboard motor before a crowd of hooting admirers. She buries her face in the motor, sharp-nosed pliers in hand, oblivious to the encircling commotion. Nobody has started the boat since Heberto's departure. Reina asks her sister for a spool of copper wire from her massive toolbox. She is always happiest with the toolbox at her side, even when she's making love. It increases her every pleasure.

Last month, she smuggled the toolbox out of Cuba by impressing the immigration officers at the airport with the name of a famous general she'd once seduced. Reina knows she could have bought a beach house in Manzanitas by selling her tools on the black market. *Coño*, it's impossible to get even a bandage in Cuba, forget a decent wrench. No way would she have left without her precious implements.

Constancia holds a stretch of wire for Reina to cut.

Reina patiently winds it through the motor, then pulls on the starter. The motor shivers and dies. She tightens two more bolts with her best adjustable wrench. Reina could be dropped anywhere with her tools, in a faraway galaxy with no water and a fraction of the earth's gravity, and some-how—she grins to think of this—she knows she would survive.

On the next try, the motor roars to life. Reina is pleased. Nothing, absolutely nothing, neither man nor machine, is immune to the resuscitative powers of her magic hands.

Constancia slips on her life jacket, but Reina doesn't bother to put one on. Instead she settles in the rear of Heberto's boat and motions for her sister to come on board. Then Reina steers her way out of the yacht club harbor as if she were born for nothing else.

The air is much too weary for wind. It's the middle of the week, and only two other boats are on the bay, sailboats barely moving in the distance. Reina has been on a boat only twice in her life, but she likes the perspective it gives her, the ocean's open contempt for destinations. Why hadn't she ever realized before the futility of living on land?

At Constancia's insistence, Reina veers left and putters through the canals of Key Biscayne.

"What would you do with this much money?" Constancia shouts over the whining motor, as if trying to impress Reina with the possibility.

Reina shrugs. She's indifferent to the mansions and yachts crowded together on the waterways. To have money and share this swamp with mosquitoes and water rats? *Por favor.* If she wins the lottery—and she's been playing reli-giously since she arrived in Florida—Reina would spend the rest of her life floating around the world, ravishing her choice of men. Certainly she wouldn't choose to live like this, cheek by jowl with the pathological rich.

Of course, if she won the jackpot, she'd split the money with Dulcita, coax her away from that Spanish buzzard in Madrid. Perhaps, Reina muses hopefully, she might become a grandmother. No, Dulcita is much too sensible for that. When she was fourteen and pregnant, Dulcita never said a word about it. But Reina could tell. Her daughter slept for hours in the afternoon, kept a box of stale crackers by her bed. Reina hoped that Dulcita, by some miracle, would decide to keep the baby. But she aborted it that autumn, like something fragile and seasonal.

"I want to be a grandmother," Reina announces as she speeds around a curve. "I want to be a grandmother and mambo all night!"

duality

Constancia turns to look at her, bemused. Reina is disconcerted by her face, by their mother's resurrected expression.

Anchored off a stub of jetty, on the deck of a yacht, a bare-chested man in madras pants types away at a portable computer. He looks up and blows a kiss at Reina.

"You're a goddess!" he shouts in badly accented Spanish, removing his baseball cap. There's a shock of gray hair on his head.

"*Caballero*, tell me something I don't know!" Reina shouts back, laughing.

The man tosses his cap in the air.

Suddenly, Reina longs for deeper waters to explore, and so she navigates her way out of the maze of canals and around the eastern tip of the island.

"Don't go too far, Reina! It's not safe!" Constancia protests. "Heberto never took the boat out of the bay!"

But Reina merely looks past her sister to the bristling blue concourse, to the broken arch of seagulls in the sky. She's impatient with Constancia's fear of adventure. Even at boarding school, her sister always asked permission for everything—to leave the breakfast table or cross the dirt road to wander through the orange grove. Then she married that boor Gonzalo, who cured her forever of any recklessness. Reina remembers how Constancia wore the loss of him like a spectacle, a holy medallion for everyone to see. But for Reina, the loss of her first lover, José Luís Fuerte, only whetted her appetite for more passion, like the ocean before them with its hunger for vulnerable men.

A concord of clouds solemnly assembles on the horizon. The sun recedes, and an unexpected wind raises tufts of monotonous waves. The little motorboat climbs and drops as the rain begins. Then nothing is visible but this realm of blue water and light.

"Turn around, Reina. *Tengo miedo.*" Constancia is shivering on her vinyl banquette, her hands raw from gripping the side of the boat.

The boat pitches in the deepening waves, spraying them with water. Reina's blouse is saturated, her sister's hair mats to her skull. The boat dips again. Another fierce spray drenches them both.

What was it Constancia told her at the boarding school? *Mercy, Reina, is more important than knowledge. Coño,* who had taught her sister that? Worse still, how could she have believed it? Their teachers had told them to pray for their mother's soul, to ask God for forgiveness. But Reina couldn't understand what their mother had ever done wrong.

She wants to tell Constancia again what she saw at the funeral home. Describe the colors of Mami's devastated throat. Force her to listen. Shout it loud in her sister's face. Mami couldn't have drowned, like their father said. No, she couldn't have drowned, which means their father must have lied. And if Papá lied, what the hell was the truth?

The bow of the boat tips steeply into a wave. Ocean pours in astern, up to Reina's shins. She's surprised at its beckoning warmth. She tries to imagine her mother, breathing her last breath of swamp.

Another wave slams against the side of the little boat. The motor floods and stops. Reina throws her sister a child's plastic bucket. "Start bailing!" she shouts. Constancia moves stiffly, her shoulders tight and square. The boat rocks hard in the waves. Reina inspects the outboard, unsnaps its casing. When there's only an inch of water left at their feet, Reina blows hard on the engine, emptying her lungs. She pulls the starter, and the motor turns over without a stutter.

Reina maneuvers the boat until they're heading southwest, toward the spangle of palms on her sister's tiny island, toward the dying twilight already fraught with stars.

MIAMI

onstancia stands outside her new Cuerpo de
Cuba factory in South Miami, gazing up at
the sky. Everything is heavy around her,
as still as the thickening clouds. An occasional, scattered
wind scratches the leaves in the palms. Only the birds move.
Constancia follows their trajectories, pretends the birds are
trailing colors until the sky fills with the bright lines of their
unintended grace.

In the distance, a storm disrupts the sky, skittish with
lightning and the low roll of thunder. Constancia wonders if
it's raining where Heberto is, what he's using for shelter,
whether he's had to buy more underwear. The tides, Constancia heard on the radio, are at record highs. The viscous
air is scented with death. Since her sister arrived from
Havana, it's rained in Miami nearly every day.

Reina is napping in the factory office. She's been up
since dawn, doing the last of the electrical rewiring. It was

no easy job converting this bowling ball factory into Cuerpo de Cuba's first manufacturing plant. Constancia is astonished at her sister's competence, her yeomanly concentration, the respect she commands from the awed construction workers. Balanced on ladders, twisting wires into place, Reina gleams with the quiet power of a perfect equation.

Yet there is something about her sister that Constancia mistrusts. To her way of thinking, anyone who can say "Wealth is ultimately futile" cannot be depended upon. After all, what can you possibly understand about people until you know what tempts them?

Her sister seems alarmingly content with the forty-dollar allowance Constancia has been giving her each week: for her lottery tickets (Reina plays with devout enthusiasm, tries endless combinations of numbers from her daughter's life), her chocolate bars (jumbo-sized Baby Ruths), and her diesel fuel (for her twilight rides on Heberto's motorboat).

Constancia wants to hire Reina as her factory floor supervisor, but her sister won't even consider it. Not even at six hundred dollars a week to start. She wouldn't take a cent, either, for all her work getting the factory ready.

"It's not the money, Constancia. I just can't see working with Mami's face like this. Her image parading past me every day, as if she were no longer mine."

"And my face?" Constancia felt a shiver pass between them.

"You can't help that."

"So you think I'm exploiting Mamá?" Constancia tried to decipher her sister's expression. Indulgent and sad, devoted, desirous. It irritated her to no end. "This is strictly business, Reina!"

"That's just what I mean."

• • •

Constancia climbs the short flight of stairs to her office. Reina has stripped off her clothing and is sleeping naked on the secondhand recliner. Constancia notices the echoes of burns on her sister's hips, her painfully cracked fingertips. Reina's skin looks fluorescent, on fire, like those films of the volatile surface of the sun. But then Constancia blinks, and her sister is only plainly radiant again, with her curious patch-quilt skin.

Last winter, Reina was struck by lightning in a giant mahogany tree on the outskirts of El Cobre. The electricity, her sister swears, still courses through her veins. In Cuba, Reina claims, she suffered from a tenacious insomnia, but here in Miami she has no trouble sleeping at all, particularly just before a downpour.

Constancia remembers how her Tío Dámaso once got hit by lightning as he was galloping through a field of dry grasses. The bolt struck a royal palm first, discharging a circular wave of electricity that traveled up through his horse, into his body, and out the top of his head in a fiery ball. Her uncle claimed he got smarter after the hit, that he developed an uncanny, if useless, ability to read everything backward.

Despite her skin, Reina has changed little in thirty years. Constancia is impressed by her sister's strength and stature, by her mesmerizing slabs of soft, beveled flesh. Reina occupies space with the confidence of tall men, issues an instant challenge to women. Her voice is deep, as it's always been, the sound of a sensuous cello. Constancia doesn't know why she ever felt guilty about not protecting her younger sister, why she didn't allow Reina to protect her instead.

Everywhere Reina goes, people watch her, whisper, point behind her back. Each time she sets foot in the yacht club, pandemonium breaks out. Constancia's female acquaintances have pleaded with her to keep Reina under lock and key. *We have enough trouble keeping our husbands in line without your sister coming around like temptation incarnate.*

Estela Ferrín, one of the regulars at the yacht club, even threatened to call immigration and have Reina deported. She suspects that her husband, Walfredo, an importer of German cars, has already strayed with the shapely electrician from Havana. In the past two weeks, he's lost nineteen pounds, dyed his hair a shoe-polish black, and calls out Reina's name in his sleep every night. According to his disgruntled partners, Walfredo Ferrín hasn't bothered to close a single deal on a luxury sedan in days.

Meanwhile, roses arrive for Reina by the dozens, red and humming, as if invisible microphones were recording their decay. Constancia's apartment is dense with the scent of a hundred dying blossoms. Her sister seems indifferent to the daily onslaught of flowers, to the magnitude of her attraction. Reina wants to open the windows to release the aroma, afflictive to her as weddings, but Constancia refuses to let in the fresh air. Instead she floats about late at night in a state of vague feverishness.

Reina's daughter, Dulce, is supposed to be just as stunning. When Constancia left Cuba, her niece was still little. She remembers Dulce as a sullen child, with a cleft in her chin and a fondness for pickled corn. Now Reina tells her that Dulcita is living in Spain, married to a senescent airline clerk she picked up at the Habana Libre Hotel.

"Levántate." Constancia leans in toward her sister. "It's nearly six o'clock."

Reina sputters awake. "I was dreaming I was a turnip, a famous one, a regent of Sweden." She laughs and kisses Constancia on the cheek. "Life was pretty quiet."

Constancia watches as Reina gets dressed, the ease with which she moves her body, the concert of muscles like something well reasoned. Reina's breasts are beautiful too, soft and generous. Today she doesn't wear a bra.

"The air-conditioning isn't working yet."

"Don't worry, Constancia. I'll have it fixed for you by Monday." Reina swings her toolbox in a gesture of certain triumph.

Constancia follows Reina across the factory floor, past huge electric vats ("vice cookers," Reina calls them) and a shiny conveyor belt, past row after row of industrial shelving, past boxes of royal-blue bottles pasted with their mother's pale face.

"Maybe you should create a perfume with my profile," Reina jokes, showing off her comely right side. "You could make it from coconuts and honeybees and the sweat of Brazilian monkeys. You know what they used to call me in Cuba?"

"I'm afraid to ask."

"Amazona." Reina flexes a biceps, feigns an aggressive stance. "*Créelo, mi amor*. It would be a big seller."

Outside, the sky ruptures with rain. Reina grabs Constancia's hand and drags her to the safety of the pink Cadillac. Reina settles in behind the wheel. Constancia always lets her sister drive. Somehow it seems inappropriate not to, an affront to her competence, despite the fact that Reina doesn't have her Florida license yet.

Her sister cruises north on U.S. 1. She convinces Constancia that they should stop for a bite to eat at the Américas Cafeteria on Coral Way. Constancia isn't very hungry, but she orders a *medianoche* anyway, with a banana milk shake and sweet plantains on the side. Reina orders the day's special, fried liver with onions, black beans and rice, an avocado salad.

The horseshoe counter makes everyone visible to

everyone else. Constancia studies the other diners in the glare of Formica, slurping and masticating and licking their fingers, and it occurs to her that eating should be strictly a private affair.

"You know what I miss most about Cuba?" Reina asks in a voice loud enough to make Constancia uncomfortable. "The little plazas in every town. In Miami, there are no places to congregate."

Constancia spears a fried plantain and puts it on her sister's plate. "I don't like to romanticize the past."

"You don't remember the plazas?"

"I think we remember a lot of things differently."

During their first days together in Miami, Reina asked Constancia to grant her small intimacies. Intimacies that Reina and their mother had shared. But soon Constancia found this too upsetting to sustain. Her memories of Mamá are altogether different from her sister's, hardly benign.

Reina eats the remainder of her liver and onions, washes it down with a bottle of dark lager. She leans back against her chrome-and-leatherette swivel seat. "I guess it's less painful to forget than to remember," Reina says quietly.

"I didn't say 'forget.' I said 'romanticize'!" Constancia snaps back.

If only she *could* forget. But certain memories are fixed inside her, like facts many centuries old. No amount of reconsideration can change them. Like the day her mother smeared a sticky blue paste on her mouth, which made her hallucinate for hours. Constancia complained bitterly to her father, but he was helpless before Mamá. In retaliation, Constancia tried to hurt Reinita—plugged her rosebud mouth with mud, dropped spiders in her crib. When Mamá found out, she ordered that Constancia be sent away.

Reina hisses for the waitress. "Do me a favor, *mimi*, and

bring me a *cafesito* and a *pudín de pan*. You want anything else, Constancia?"

Constancia looks down at her plate. She hasn't touched her sandwich. The plantains are cold and greasy-looking, scorched on one side. *"No, nada más."*

Reina stares at her, as if trying to see through the intoxication of their mother's face. "Sometimes we become what we try to forget most."

"What are you telling me?" Constancia's mouth tightens. "That I *am* Mamá?"

"No, *mi amor*, you're just worn out by mirrors."

That night, Constancia wakes up after only a few hours' sleep and pads over to the kitchen in her lambskin slippers. She sets out her cut-crystal goblets, her silverware and serving spoons, her china with the lily-of-the-valley pattern. She uses her good china for every meal, predawn breakfasts included. Not that her sister notices or takes care. So far, Reina has chipped two dessert plates, cracked an oval serving platter, ruined a silver fork prying English muffins from the toaster.

There have been other mishaps. A favorite silk blouse streaked with dishwashing liquid, her sofa stained pink with dime-store nail polish. Not to mention the countless electrical irregularities: clocks moving backward or stopping altogether, lights dimming for no discernible reason, the refrigerator coughing like a four-pack-a-day smoker.

Constancia sits at the kitchen table with her *café con leche* and a dish of whole-wheat toast. She drops three sugar cubes into the steaming mug. Constancia prefers cubes to loose sugar, the ceremony of the little tongs. Reina isn't home. This is no surprise. She must have slipped off for another post-midnight tryst with one of her paramours.

After breakfast, Constancia picks up a mister and

sprays her sister's roses until they look newly picked. *The flower indicates the crime*, her father used to tell her. After Mamá died, Papi wore violets in his lapel, violets with velvety dark centers. For years, every time Constancia did something wrong, she'd search for the nearest flower. Stealing was white carnations. Lilies were blasphemy. And sex meant *ave del paraíso* orchids—yellows, crimsons, the deepest blue-blacks—six hundred four orchids in all, for each time she and Gonzalo made love.

Constancia fills numerous bowls with apples, red as rampant lust, and places them strategically around the apartment. Oscar Piñango told her that apples absorb evil and all ill intentions, that Constancia should display dozens of them in her home each week. The apples should not be eaten, the santero advised, but Reina disregards his edict. She munches at least nine or ten a day—seeds, core, and all. The gods, she says, will forgive her this one transgression. In Cuba, there'd been no apples since the early days of the revolution, so Reina feels justified in devouring at least thirty years' worth in as many days.

On an impulse, Constancia plucks an apple from the bowl in the living room and lifts it to her mouth. A music starts up in her brain, a September music, somber and dark. Constancia drops the apple, dusts off a thick black record, José Ardévol's Symphony in F-sharp, and settles on the sofa to listen. These are the ruins she dreamed of when young, after Papi shot himself, after his ashes were strewn in the Zapata Swamp.

She reaches up to touch her face. When will her mother slip through? A word, a gesture, intact from the past? And what of her own oblivion? The memory of her previous self fluttering like a small satin flag?

Constancia looks around her apartment. It's decorated in every shade of white. White is all colors, she remembers her daughter telling her, black its total absence. Only the apples and Reina's red humming roses mar the perfection.

Isabel calls just as the sun begins to rise. Last week, she called at the same hour, informed Constancia that she was using photographs of Constancia's face in a collage she was fashioning with found bits of bird bone from the Paiko Lagoon. Then Isabel confessed that her boyfriend had disappeared every night for a month, that he avoided her swelling body, disproportionate with new life.

"*Cuéntame todo.*" Constancia knows her daughter wouldn't telephone again at this hour without a good reason.

"Austin's left me, Mom. He's moved in with a Chinese-Filipina dancer from the Don Ho show. She wears flesh-toned Lycra when she wears anything at all. Her family's been here since the reign of Queen Liliuokalani."

"Who?" Constancia prides herself on her knowledge of international royalty, but this queen she's never heard of.

"She's modeling for him. She's nineteen years old. She has tiny breasts." Her daughter's voice diminishes until it is barely audible.

"Get on a plane, *mi hija. Aquí te espero.*"

On Isabel's tenth birthday, Constancia took her to the American Museum of Natural History. Her daughter hadn't wanted an ordinary party. They visited the World of Birds first. Constancia pointed out three specimens her father had shot and shipped to the museum from Cuba years before: a haughty-looking bird with fuchsia plumage; another with stalk legs and a sprocketed bill; the last one so tiny Isabel had to squint to see it—a bee hummingbird with an iridescent throat.

Now poor Isabel is suffering the way Constancia once suffered. Those endless pregnant days weaving Silvestre in her womb. Gonzalo's absence banging inside her like a cheap tambourine. Nothing before or after him but a faint memory of what her body used to love. After Silvestre was born, Constancia watched the weather for hours, the tail end of day seeping into night. She had no energy for anything else. She heard a woman on the radio read a poem that spoke to her misery: *Love is a matter of gifts thrown in the fire, for nothing*.

Gonzalo returned to visit her when their son was eight months old. Constancia opened the cutlery drawer, aimed a carving knife at his heart. Gonzalo didn't wait to see where it would land. All the while, Silvestre slept soundly in his crib. It was the last day of May. Constancia longed for a change of seasons, a brief snowstorm, a swirl of dying leaves. Anything to mark this moment from the last.

Constancia wonders what Gonzalo would think of their son today. How long it would take for them to get to know each other. A month? Six months? Another thirty-three years? There's no substitute for the quiet culture of a life together, the endless days commemorating nothing, amassing history bit by bit. Only a few events irrevocably divide the past from the future. Like the time Constancia returned home and found Silvestre in the den, with a stranger's penis in his mouth. That same night, Silvestre moved out, explaining nothing. He was twenty-four years old.

Constancia hasn't returned to the Good Samaritan Hospital. Gonzalo calls her frequently, leaves *boleros* on her answering machine. His voice is like dark running water. Her hand still burns where she touched him.

It's dark in the guest room, funereal-looking with Papi's gloomy taxidermy. Reina's bed is unmade, as usual, her pillows and pastel sheets strewn with the black curly hair she indiscriminately sheds. Constancia has noticed that the hair on her sister's head and pubis is identical, thick and springy and intimate.

Constancia picks up the female *camao*, strums its gull-gray crown with her thumb. When her father shot it, the bird was practically extinct. Papi used to point out dozens of rare species to her on their collecting expeditions, told her tales about the fallen ones, the hunted ones, their every manner of demise. How the planters of Ciego de Avila used to feast on the tender flesh of the quail dove. How the Cuban macaws disappeared from Pinar del Río after the great hurricane of 1844.

Long ago, Constancia liked to imagine that she was the last dodo on earth, because her father loved nothing more than imperiled birds. Constancia pictured herself living in a silver cage in his study, subsisting on insects and rotten fruit. Her father would coddle her, stroke the feathers on her aching breast. What was it he said once? *Only lost causes merit any effort.*

Now Constancia feels extinct, like the many lost birds her father had lamented over the years, the birds that Cuba could no longer sustain, the birds they'd vainly searched for in the remotest corners of their sacrificed island. *Things cannot be murdered twice,* Papi liked to say. But Constancia isn't sure this is true.

She recalls one Sunday several months after her father died. The air was thin and dry in her dormitory room. The bells in the boarding school chapel rang for her presence, colliding with the distant ringing from Trinidad's oldest church, Nuestra Señora de la Candelaria de la Popa. Instead of rising with the other girls and dressing for morning mass, Constancia nestled deeper into her bunk and pulled the covers over her head.

Her bed was a small cemetery then, congested with

death. Her body felt heavy, her heart sank in its own slug-
gish blood. Her jaws were so weak she could barely open her
mouth, much less eat the fish croquettes the boarding school
cook personally delivered to her room in a futile attempt to
cheer her up.

There is a muffled scratching at the front door. The hallway
lights begin nervously flickering. Constancia slips on her
robe and finds her sister trying to break into the apartment
with a crowbar from her trusty toolbox.

"*Gracias, mi amor.*" Reina's hair is wild, every strand
standing on end; her patchwork skin is flushed. "I forgot my
keys."

Constancia follows her sister back to the guest room,
watches as Reina tears off her clothes and flops into bed.
Papá's dead birds stare from the shelves with their empty
agate eyes.

Reina yawns and pulls the top sheet to her chin. "You
know, it took me years to realize that not everyone would
want dead animals displayed in their home."

Constancia remembers how proud her father was of his
prize specimens, how he fussed over them, cleaned them
periodically with a glandular oil found only in certain
cetaceans, how he protected the skins from insects by
scrupulously wrapping them in chinaberry leaves.

Suddenly, Constancia decides that she, too, must attend
to Papá's lost birds. She grabs a washcloth from the hall
closet and moistens it under the bathroom faucet. The sun
climbs in the sky, spilling a river of light into the guest room.
Reina is already asleep in the twin bed by the window. Her
body rises and falls with a low, rhythmic scraping.

Constancia begins wiping every faded wing and
feather, methodically, as her father would have done, pol-

ishes each beak and hinge and claw. But no matter how much she dusts, the birds still look dead.

Only her mother looks alive in the guest room, in the photograph that Reina hung over the dresser. There's an invitation in Mamá's eyes, in the poised set of her mouth, as if she knew someone would ask her a crucial question long after she'd died.

THE WORLD'S SMALLEST FROG

❀

The first time Blanca Mestre walked into my biology class at the University of Havana, she sent a shiver through the room. There was something about her presence—quiet, luminescent, distracted—that stirred people, although it did not induce them to get close to her.

Her gifts had nothing to do with intelligence, which she displayed in impressive abundance, but were born of qualities much less tangible. Instinct. Intuition. An uncanny sense for the aberrational. Blanca had no patience for hypotheses or dry pontifications. For her, an unsolved mystery was sufficient enough invitation to science.

Blanca was most inclined toward chemistry then. The subject came naturally to her, and she seemed to have an odd, mimetic gift for inanimate substances. When she worked with sulfur, for example, her normally green eyes took on a yellowish tinge. If an experiment called for phosphorus, she vibrated with *its unearthly glow. And ordinary lead made her appear heavy and malleable and gray. It was as if matter spoke to Blanca directly, revealed to her its secrets.*

As a practical man, a man of science, I could not make sense of any of this. Yet how could I be logical when the very sight of this woman uprooted my heart?

Blanca was slight, as delicately boned as certain birds, and she had a cascade of blue-black hair that fell past her shoulders. Small purple burns marred her forearms, vestiges of chemistry experiments gone awry. She spoke little, as if unwilling to surrender to the unreliable realm of words. When Blanca was lost in thought, she often drew a finger across her throat.

Other men shared my infatuation with Blanca Mestre, succumbed to the peculiar vertigos she inspired. Amado Saavedra, a law student from a wealthy banking family in Ciego de Avila, suffered over Blanca's indifference toward him and eventually hanged himself from a manchineel tree after swallowing its deadly sap. That same autumn, Professor Isidoro de Grijalve, a renowned entomologist, became so obsessed with Blanca that he abandoned his wife and five daughters to dedicate himself full-time to her pursuit. His quest proved futile, and his illustrious career went to ruin.

There were others. A visiting Belgian herpetologist fell madly in love with Blanca and hired her as his assistant over other, more qualified candidates. The Belgian, who sported a mustache of caterpillaran proportions, did not manage to win her love on the many field trips he planned for them. But she proved a worthy apprentice of herpetology, nonetheless. Blanca was entranced by the distinctive camouflages of her subjects, by their versatile physiognomies, by their flagrant melding of the biological with the chemical.

On Fridays, when Blanca visited the central market in Havana, I used to follow her at a distance, stopping at the same stalls she frequented. I touched the same tangerines and sour-

sops, basked in the pockets of warmth she left in her wake. It was the only way I dared come as close as I dreamed.

There was another question I hoped my occasional spying might answer. What, por Dios, did the poor girl eat? Neither I nor anybody else at the university had ever seen Blanca ingest anything but milk, quarts and quarts of it, with thick hats of cream.

It turned out that Blanca ate only one meal a day, at four in the morning, the hour in which she'd been accustomed to breakfasting on her father's ranch. The menu did not vary: skirt steak, two fried eggs over rice, and a ripe mango in season. Between this and her vast quantities of milk, she seemed to require no other nourishment.

When at last I invited Blanca to become my research assistant, my colleagues were suspicious at best. Although I was immensely attracted to Blanca, I never would have hired her if she hadn't already proved to be a talented collector. She forged into caverns and woods without a backward glance, and her hands were especially fine, quick and useful. She could pack mud on insect bites, heal cuts and bruises with trim squares of moss, concoct elixirs for any ailment.

One evening, Blanca prepared for me a potion of five-pointed leaves that she boiled for an hour with a peculiar blue stone. Remarkably, my symptoms—acute abdominal pain and a spiking fever—disappeared almost instantly. That night, I dreamed vividly in black and white, instead of my usual color, and woke up temporarily forgetting my name.

Blanca and I traveled a great deal through Cuba our first winter together, initially by train but more often on horseback. It was 1936, and much had changed since I'd traversed the country with Dr. Forrest. I know it is unfashionable to admit this, especially in these days of fervent nationalism, but I missed the old British-owned railways. Certainly the uniformed waiters and afternoon teas could not have been more out of tune with local customs, but they were no less quaint for the incongruity. After General Machado took power, the country's train service severely declined and, sadly, never recovered. But even today, trains are still preferable to traveling by automobile. Cuba's roads, now as then, remain deplorable.

Our mission that winter was to document and collect sixteen targeted reptiles on the island before their native habitats were destroyed by new farmlands. Cuba supports more than seventy species of reptiles—fifty-two particular to the island, greater than any other in the Antilles—and nearly a third were already in danger of extinction. Blanca's and my findings were published jointly in a paper entitled "The Lost Reptiles of Cuba." I daresay it secured our reputations in international herpetological circles.

Blanca was especially partial to the world's tiniest frog, a lovely creature native only to Cuba, mauve with a yellow streak running the quarter inch from its nose to the insertion of its hind limbs. One day, near Hanabanilla, a pair of elderly campesinas *came upon us capturing the minuscule frogs in the woods. "¡Extraño ver personas tan grandes cazando animalitos tan chiquitos!" one woman sniffed to the other before walking on. Strange indeed it must have seemed to them to spy two grown people hunting such tiny game.*

Blanca did not touch the doves or hutías I shot to roast over our evening campfires. While I ate with the exaggerated hunger spurred by the outdoors, Blanca was content to drink fresh milk from her canteen. Occasionally, I succeeded in coaxing her to eat a bowl of beans or a baked yam to keep me company. But the food I cooked did not sit well with her. As always, she brought her own provisions for her predawn repasts.

Our constant proximity enabled me to note a streak of morbidity in Blanca. "Billions of insects die every second," she might say quietly as we prepared our campsite. Or, surveying a vast fertile valley in Oriente: "Everywhere, this reckless procession toward death!"

On the road, Blanca kept a fragment of bone in a worn flannel pouch on her belt. It was a human scaphoid, evident from the prominent tuberosity on one end. At times, Blanca seemed to consult the little wristbone, ask it for guidance. She would not tell me where she got it or what it was for.

I remember an expedition we took to a cave ten miles inland from Cienfuegos Bay. Blanca was squatting on her heels, the flannel pouch dangling from her waist, when she caught a blind lizard that neither of us had seen before. Less than an inch long and translucent as coconut milk, the creature had an archaic aspect and the probing habits of an earthworm. It turned out that the lizard was utterly unique. To my knowledge, no other specimen has ever been found. Blanca was pleased, but she did not seem the least bit surprised by this remarkable discovery.

Despite our many hours together, I gleaned only a few details about Blanca's past. She rarely spoke of her family, and then told only curious, tattered stories that hardly amounted to a history. She said she grew up on a pig ranch in Camagüey, that she was the youngest of seven children, and the only girl, and that she'd kept a series of pet crows. They were her favorite birds, she said, because they mate for life, look after their fledglings longer than other birds, and come to the aid of their wounded. Like me, she read Latin fluently and rode a horse expertly.

Later, I learned from Dámaso Mestre, the youngest of her brothers, that their mother was a mulatta descended, in part, *from French colonists who'd fled Haiti after the slave revolt of 1791. They settled in Santiago de Cuba with twenty-seven thousand other displaced French planters, imprinting the city with their culture, customs, and surnames. Her mother, whose maiden name was Sejourné, had been fond of French aphorisms. Au pays des aveugles, les borgnes sont rois. In the country of the blind, the one-eyed men are kings. It was a saying Blanca repeated often.*

According to Dámaso, their mother died in a freak accident on the ranch when Blanca was five years old. Eugenia Mestre's pistol went off in its holster, injuring the horse beneath her and inciting a stampede of pigs that trampled her to death. The ranch hands brought back her remains, soft broken remnants wrapped in a saddle blanket, and laid them on the veranda, where Blanca was playing. Only her mother's hands—brown, thick-nailed, and strong as a man's—were intact.

Their father, overcome with anger and sorrow, single-handedly slit the throats of the six hundred nine pigs that had taken part in the stampede. All the workers and villagers who ate the slaughtered pork vomited savagely for three days and nights. Several people died, including a twelve-year-old boy with a withered arm, but the others woke on the fourth morning cured of all minor maladies.

There were those who claimed that Eugenia Mestre had died a martyr or a witch, and for years, on the anniversary of her death, a memorial mass and countless cruder ceremonies were offered in her name. No one knows who painted the mural on the back of the town hall, but not even Críspulo Navarrete, the fearless chief of police, dared whitewash it. The painting featured Doña Eugenia, regal in flowing golden robes, stepping on the head of an agonized sow.

Ramón Mestre built an old-fashioned sarcophagus for his

wife, carving the stone himself and sealing it tight against worms. Blanca grew up in the shadow of her mother's coffin, which was erected outside her bedroom window. Her father began raising cattle and horses instead of pigs, but for years afterward, everyone continued to refer to his place as the pig ranch.

In Blanca's only photograph of her mother, Eugenia Mestre wears tan riding pants and polished boots to her thighs. She is a tall woman, narrow-hipped, with a large, high bosom. In the picture, her expression is mock fierce, as if she might crack a whip on your back, but her eyes betray the humorous pretense.

Blanca said she did not have a picture of her father, that she would sooner forget his sorry, dissolute face.

Late one night, while Blanca was setting water to boil for her rice, I crawled out of my tent to watch her fix her daily meal. There was no moon and only a scattering of faint stars, but this did not hinder Blanca's movements. She seasoned my charred skillet with a few drops of olive oil before frying her steak and eggs. Then she pulled off the skin of a mango as if she were merely slipping off its cape.

When the rice was done, Blanca piled her plate high with food and settled down by a pair of flat rocks. She spread a napkin on her lap and ate daintily with a knife and fork, her canteen of milk at her side. The night was unnaturally silent. The dying fire patterned shadows on her face.

I am not certain why it was this of all nights I chose to make clear my intentions. Perhaps the obscuring sky and Blanca's fine manners gave me courage. I smoothed my hair as best I could and, like a holy-day penitent, lurched over to her on my knees. Her hands were soaked with blood. A queer apparition. I realize now I should have taken a closer look, that she had spelled out her grief for me to see.

But then without preambles or guitar serenades, without bouquets of roses or confessions of love, without, in fact, any of the nonsensical accoutrements of courtship, I asked Blanca Mestre to marry me. And to my complete astonishment, she handed me her bloody knife and said "Yes."

POLISHING BONES

❧

*I*t *is Friday*, the best day for dispelling negative influences. Reina and Constancia follow Oscar Piñango around the Cuerpo de Cuba factory as he recites an oration to La Virgen de la Caridad del Cobre. He sprinkles a pungent elixir on the vats of emollient, on the bottling machine and industrial trolleys, even on the Agüero sisters themselves. Reina thinks she smells several of the same ingredients her longtime lover, Pepín, used to disperse throughout her father's apartment in Vedado—*paraíso, tártago*, and his favorite curse buster, *rompezaragüey*.

In the middle of the cement floor, the santero begins kindling a fire with leftover lignum vitae from the bowling ball factory. It's a dense wood, smoky and hard to burn.

"Open that door," Oscar Piñango instructs, pointing to Constancia's mezzanine office, "and all the closets and storage areas. Quickly."

The sisters dash around and do as they're told. There have been too many mishaps lately to take any chances: a family of dead bats found in a tub of elbow abradant; ointments and creams inexplicably curdling overnight. And during the first employee meeting, bloody chicken feathers floated down from the ceiling, prompting half the staff to quit on the spot. Only by increasing his salary prodigiously did Constancia convince her new manager, a young Wharton graduate named Félix Borrega, to stay.

Reina has noticed that Constancia, who rarely even breaks a nail, is becoming prone to minor accidents as well. Knives slip in her hands. Bottles shatter on the factory floor. Why, just this morning her sister got a burn the size of a sand dollar where she leaned too long on an electric vat. Today Constancia sent her employees home at noon (with full pay!), so that the santero could execute his purifications in peace.

Ochún yeye mi ogá mi gbogbo ibu laiye nibo gbogbo omo oricha le owe nitosi gba ma abukon ni omi didon nitosi ono alafia . . .

Oscar Piñango chants in monotone as he mixes a *sahumerio* to smoke out the evil. Incense, storax, mastic, garlic skins, brown sugar, all scorched in a censer over the wood fire. The smell stings Reina's nostrils, makes her lungs ache. The smoke clings to her hair. She wonders if her skin will absorb this stink the way it did the burning at El Cobre, whether it will replace that old distracting stench.

The santero lights fifteen yellow votive candles, all encased in glass. He places one at the factory entrance, two at either end of the assembly line, three by the vat of underarm exfoliant, and five on the shelves where the royal-blue bottles labeled with Blanca Agüero's face are arranged.

"These must burn for nine days straight." Piñango's

face glitters in the light, silvery and squamous as a river trout. "Do not move them, touch them, or blow them out — or the spell will be broken."

Then he takes the last two flickering candles upstairs to Constancia's office and announces that the *limpieza*, the cleansing, is complete.

Reina bends over to thank the rotund santero, and he kisses her on the forehead. She thinks that Piñango, too, smells smoked, like a fish cured overly long.

"Return to me before Oshún's feast day," he implores the sisters as they escort him to his canary-yellow Buick. "Do not miss the instant of recognition, I warn you. Or you will suffer, together and separately, each according to her affliction."

The fire continues to smolder on the factory floor. Constancia wants to pour water over it, but Reina dissuades her. "Give it an hour. It will extinguish itself."

"All I need now is for the place to burn down!" Constancia is still shaky from the recent string of crises. The timing couldn't be worse. Her first out-of-state shipment is due in two days.

Reina walks over to the shelves of empty royal-blue bottles. Their mother's face is tremulous in the candlelight. For many years, Reina couldn't bring herself to visit Mami's grave, although she imagined it time and again: the scallop of chiseled black marble, the plot swollen with rain. Every day that passed, Reina felt her mother die again.

"Did you ever go the cemetery?" Reina asks, still staring at the repeating pale faces.

"Not since the funeral, you know that." Constancia is agitated, already defensive. "Papi used to go frequently, though. He told me so."

Reina walks to the foot of the mezzanine stairs. She

flips open the metal clasps of her toolbox and removes her favorite pliers. Then she searches for a carton of Cuello de Cuba, Constancia's neck-mending potion (Reina imagines short-throated, reptilian-skinned women as its primary beneficiaries). She pulls out a jar, twists off the top, and begins coating her pliers with the mint-green cream. It's an excellent lubricant, Reina's discovered, much better than ordinary grease.

"I've asked you not to do that!" Constancia loses her temper. "People might get the wrong idea!"

"*Cálmate, mi amor.* There's nobody here but us." Reina knows how much it irritates her sister, but she continues to rub the luscious unguent into the hinge. "Did Mami ever show you her bone?"

"What bone?" Constancia asks tersely. She wants to grab the jar of cream from her sister, throw her pliers out the factory window.

"The one she kept in a pouch. A little bone, all yellowed, with a bump on one end. Like a root." Reina wipes a hand on her pants. "You never saw it?"

"No, I did not," Constancia sniffs, refilling the carton of neck cream and taping it shut.

"Mami said she'd give it to me when I grew up. I looked for the bone after she died, but it had disappeared. Maybe it was buried with her."

Reina first visited her mother's grave in 1962, fourteen years after her death. The headstone was perfectly clean, and at its base, a round earthenware pot smoked with fresh herbs. The burial ground was clipped and cleaned of weeds. Not a leaf anywhere stirred.

The next day, Reina returned with a bunch of violets and a Christmas picture of her daughter in a velveteen dress. Reina placed the photograph facedown on the grave. *This is*

Dulcita, Mami. Tu primera nieta. She's almost four years old. Then Reina knelt down and did something she'd never attempted before. She prayed.

"I saw a man at the grave." Reina faces Constancia, uneasily tests her pliers.

She recounts how tall and corpulent the stranger was, his skin a flawless evening black. His pants, made of fine linen, were sharply creased, and his tie was divided down the middle by a thin pink line. He wore an old-fashioned boater on his head and a silver watch on an endless chain, which he took out to confirm the time.

"He crouched next to me and looked at Dulcita's picture. 'She is very beautiful. And very wild. Like you, *mi hija*.' Then he stood up, pulled a handkerchief from his vest pocket, and began to polish Mami's headstone."

Reina recalls her mother's epitaph, the smoothness of the grooves beneath her fingertips.

Blanca Mestre de Agüero
1914–1948
In life and death, pure light

Each time she returned to the grave, Reina looked for the elegant man. But she never saw him again. She brought other photographs of Dulcita, planted a bird-of-paradise bush for her mother in the shade. The cemetery attendant could tell Reina little, only that long ago the same man used to visit Mami's grave every day.

Constancia picks up a broom, begins sweeping the cinders on the factory floor. They stir with a last flash of heat before dying altogether. As she sweeps, Constancia's head jerks back and forth inexplicably, like an energetic pigeon's.

"Papá looked too good after Mami died," Reina accuses her sister.

Constancia stops sweeping. She looks away, tries hard not to swallow.

"Excuse me, Constancia, but grief usually makes people look like hell!"

Reina remembers how their father's appearance conspicuously improved after Mami died, as if he'd stolen something of her life to replenish his own. His thinning hair grew back lush and black, as if someone were seeding his scalp in the night. The curve of his back slowly straightened, until he recouped every last inch of his six-foot height. As he strode along the great boulevards and cobblestoned side streets of Havana, women of all ages eyed him with more than casual curiosity. Even Margarita Vidal, the petite spinster next door, baked him vitalizing sweets, insisting it was her six-layer guayaba tortes that were restoring his vigor.

More royal-blue bottles are lined against the south wall of the factory, thousands of them, like a flock of migratory birds at a watering hole.

"Today's my last day here," Reina says. Her eyes smart in the still-smoky air. "I'm sorry, *mi amor*. But I can't help you anymore."

Constancia pretends to ignore her. "I heard on the radio this morning that all the chandeliers in a remote mountain village in Peru are hovering six feet off the ground."

Reina can't imagine how many chandeliers there could be in such a cluster of mud huts. One, maybe two at most, and then only if there's a church nearby. No, it doesn't make any sense. Nothing does.

Reina strides the two miles from her sister's condominium to the yacht club by the bay. It takes her less than half an hour. It's already dusk, and the worst of the heat is over. A hint of a breeze refreshes her pace. Men in cars honk their horns and stop on the road to offer her rides. Reina isn't wearing anything special, just white shorts and a tank top, but she might as well be walking naked down the road. Every inch of her body, Pepín used to tell her, is an open invitation to pleasure.

When she was a girl, Reina used to wonder where she'd gotten her dark good looks. Her mother was petite and transparently pale, her face a midsummer moon. Her father was big, like Reina, but plated with womanly flesh. Reina's hands were enormous at birth, the size of a five-year-old child's. Slowly, she grew into them, but after her mother died, Reina's hands spread and thickened again to luxurious disproportion.

What is bred in the bone has a mission all its own. One of her father's colleagues, Professor Arturo Romney, used to repeat this rhyme to Reina when he bounced her on his knee. She was three, four, five years old when he did this, harder each time, until he bruised her bottom. After her parents died, Professor Romney wanted to adopt Reina. He showed up at her boarding school with a shopping bag of tiny plaid skirts. When she saw him, Reina said nothing, only spat on his black lace-up boots.

Reina carries a portable radio hooked to the elastic waistband of her shorts. She'd seen tourists with these miniature radios in Cuba, swaying to rhythms hidden inside their headphones. But Reina never dreamed she'd own one herself. The sound of a mambo in high gear puts an extra swing in her gait. Reina likes to listen to the reactionary exile stations in Miami best. They play the best music and the most outrageous lies on the air. She's amused by their parading nationalism, like a bunch of roosters on the make. Who was it that said patriotism is the least discerning of passions?

The minute anyone learns that Reina recently arrived from Cuba, they expect her to roundly denounce the revolution. It isn't enough for her simply to be in Miami, or even to remain silent. These pride-engorged *cubanos* want her to crucify El Comandante, repudiate even the good things he's done for the country. What's the use of learning to read, they say, if all you get is that *comemierda* propaganda? Of course you get free health care! How else can you afford even a measly cotton swab on your salaries *de porquería*? The other day, Reina's vernacular slipped, and she called the Winn-Dixie cashier *compañera* by mistake. Well, all hell broke loose on the checkout line, and a dozen people nearly came to blows!

El exilio, Reina is convinced, is the virulent flip side of Communist intolerance.

By now, Reina is a familiar figure at her sister's yacht club by the bay. She's seduced a number of its more inspirited members, other women's men, but Reina doesn't dwell on unpleasant particulars. It's a well-known fact that ninety-seven percent of mammals are polygamous. Birds are another story, with their near-universal monogamy. But human beings are mammalian through and through. Why fight against nature?

Every day, bouquets of red roses arrive for her at Constancia's apartment. Reina is immune to the folly of her lovers' gestures, disdains the lack of imagination that sublime lust engenders. Why not cacti or carnivorous plants? That would be more to her liking. The married men are the worst, demanding all manner of commitment while remaining ringed through the nose. One *pobre infeliz*, Walfredo Ferrín, even offered her a new BMW to sleep with him again.

More distressing yet, every one of her conquests in Miami spells badly. Reina knows it's petty and prejudicial, but she can't tolerate a single consonant out of place. Now the men leave saccharine messages for her on Constancia's answering machine (like well-trained dogs, after the beep), something no self-respecting *cubano* would do back home even if they *had* the damn machines. All these factors, combined with a general conservatism among the men, make them suitable for a night or two's dalliance at best.

The most gifted of her recent lovers, Ñico Goizueta, a painter she met while he was whitewashing the clubhouse, loved her like a beast. He fought for her surrender, intimately feasting on her flesh until she was in a daze of sensation. Passion, he told her, is a frail interlude between the prosperities of loss. Still, Reina's pleasure didn't come. Afterward, Ñico sent her a dozen watercolors of their night together, paintings so gorgeously erotic that Reina felt on the verge of her past rapture. But her body continued to betray her.

Her sister seems discomfited by all the attention men shower on Reina. Constancia digs out the love notes Reina throws in the garbage, clips the stems of her roses, mists them regularly to prolong their life. When Reina announced that she'd won seventy-five dollars playing the lottery, it annoyed her sister no end. "You've never had to fight for anything!" Constancia lashed out. "You don't even know what it is to have to ask!"

The only time Constancia seemed in the least bit agreeable toward her lately was when Reina told her that she'd had a small part of her cervix removed. The doctors in Cuba said she may have a predisposition for cervical cancer, most likely caused by a sexually transmitted disease. Constancia seemed strangely pleased, as if Reina had gotten her due.

Whenever Reina stops by the yacht club, workmen and waiters line up on the dock to watch her. One wiry busboy, besotted with love for her, usually tosses her a complimentary can of beer. Boats stop in mid-throttle, women in mid-sentence.

Reina waves briefly to the onlookers, but today she's in no mood to banter. She removes the canvas cover from Heberto's boat and starts up the motor, which she's repaired and rebuilt to whirring perfection.

The headwaiter points to the black horizon, to the intervals of sheet lightning illuminating the sky, but he knows better than to try to dissuade Reina from leaving. Already, she's skittering out of the harbor, stitching a path on the gray, choppy water. Reina enjoys the feel of the ocean's mindless engine beneath the boat's hull. She follows the slick backs of dolphins mounting the waves, the mannered drifting of pelicans.

Reina wishes her daughter could be with her, could breathe every ounce of this invigorating blue. She touches her right forearm, where Dulcita's flat strip of thigh is patched in from elbow to wrist. It seems to pulse in the early-evening light. Reina is curious about how her daughter is faring in Madrid, if she's worn out yet from her compromising. For a moment, Reina is stricken with fear, but then she senses that Dulcita is alive, unhappy but alive. Tonight she will write to her daughter, invite her to come and swim in this healing blue.

In Cuba, the ocean is off-limits to all but government-approved fishing and tourist boats. People can swim near the shore if they want, but anything farther is strictly forbidden. It is essential, El Comandante has said many times, for one and all to stay close to land in case of a *yanqui* invasion. Now that she's in America, Reina can see how ludicrous the idea of an invasion had been. It's the last thing on anyone's mind here. People are too busy making money, too busy sorting through the hysteria of what to purchase next.

Around her, the borders of land are not at all enticing. It seems to Reina that everything comes to an end on land, rooted in accumulation. The sea is much more forgiving. Reina works the little motorboat through the waves. It heaves and tugs with the determination of renewed youth. Last week, Reina painted the boat blood orange, like a first love, or an accident.

Her outings on the ocean help soothe her troubled feelings. It's a form of visual cruelty, Reina thinks, that Constancia looks so much like their mother. Looks like her but shares none of Mami's attributes. Reina keeps expecting to be comforted by Constancia's presence, yearns to submit to a forgotten solace. Instead she is repeatedly disillusioned, met with only a cool proficiency of sentiment.

The evening collects the last of the sea's stray light. Reina turns off the motor and rocks in the violet haze of the bay. The city is in the distance, casual and glimmering. Civilization, she thinks, kills every original thirst.

It starts to rain, softly at first. Warm, interrupted rain that washes the long slopes of her body. Reina senses something loosening within her, becoming one with the water and the wind, with the delicate filaments of night. Papá insisted that Reina be weaned on her fifth birthday. If he hadn't done this, she muses, would she still be suckling at her mother's breast? Would she ever fall asleep with the assurance of that tranquillity again?

> *Naranja dulce*
> *limón partido,*
> *dame un abrazo*
> *que yo te pido.*
>
> *Si fuera falso*
> *mi juramento*
> *en poco tiempo*
> *se olvidará.*

Toca la marcha
mi pecho llora;
adiós, señora,
yo ya me voy.

Reina is adrift in her mother's lost voice. She closes her eyes, and the light is aquatic beneath her eyelids. Everything loses its shape in this melody, lazily waves in faded suspension, in the spiraling disorder of total peace.

When she was a girl, Mami used to favor moonless nights like this. They used to go to the roof of their building, where she kept a cactus, a night-blooming cereus whose blossoms only rarely erupted. Last year, desperate with insomnia, Reina studied the night-blooming flora of numerous towns in Cuba. She liked the sausage trees best, because their hanging crimson flowers always fell to the ground by midnight.

Who will remember Mami in thirty years? Who will remember her father? Who, Reina wonders, will remember *her*? We hold only partial knowledge of each other, she thinks. We're lucky to get even a shred of the dark, exploding whole.

The wedge of light strikes Reina's face. Outside it, all is black. Reina fell asleep in Heberto's motorboat and has been rocking in the sea for hours. There were trees in her dreams, forests of trees, twisted with branches sucking long and deeply from salt. Their language was harsh and clicking, improbably paused.

Reina's body is rigid with damp cold. She tries to spread her fingers, but her hands are curled tight into fists. There are others in the ocean, far away but distinct to her. She knows this. A Cuban woman her age, aflame in engine fuel. A teenager who surrendered his arm to a shark. Two families from Camagüey are adrift in the sea after a storm overturned their rafts. They will die momentarily, wash ashore on Key West at dawn.

When the huge yacht sidles next to her boat, Reina does nothing. A voice calls to her from behind the foggy light. It is male and familiar, but she can't understand the words, rounded and slit with alarm.

"It's the goddess!" the voice shouts. It is the man with the portable computer from the canals of Key Biscayne. He throws her a horsehair blanket, which raises more bumps on her skin.

"*Sí, soy yo,*" Reina whispers, adjusting the blanket over her shoulders. She touches her throat. It is burning with thirst. "*Soy yo.*"

Dulce Fuerte

MADRID

*S*ometimes *I think* I must be the wildest rumor going in Madrid. It's been months since I've seen that damn Bengt, and I still get phone calls from every Swedish pervert on vacation in Spain. You wouldn't believe what they want from me. In Cuba, sex was never so complicated.

Last week, La Señora intercepted one of my calls and got quite an earful. Some guy from Malmö into geese and Ping-Pong balls and God knows what else. I couldn't make it out for all her screaming. La Señora threw me out, with only a few *pesetas* in my pocket. What could I do? It was hard to say good-bye to little Mercedes, though. We'd gotten used to each other. She gave me kisses unannounced.

For several days, I hid out in a revival movie theater in the Salamanca district, which shows American films from the fifties. After the last show, I'd go to the women's rest room and unlatch the window so I could climb back in. I've been living on stale popcorn and licorice and all the orange soda I can drink. It makes me jittery, like the time I tried cocaine with a deejay from Toronto at a back table of the Tropicana.

This morning, the theater manager found me asleep in a bathroom stall. I'd been snoring so loudly he thought there was a plumbing problem. I was having the strangest dream, too: I was back in Havana, walking along the Malecón, when out of nowhere, thousands of big, black-lipped dogs start jumping over the wall into the sea. The city was younger in my dream, crystalline, as if freshly washed by rain.

I have no home, no job, no friends or family here. Only a stubborn fear. I've been wondering lately whether fear is necessary for survival, whether it sharpens the senses during storms of uncertainty. Or is it, as I suspect, merely another variant of weakness? Back in Cuba, the certainty was dismal, but it was still a certainty. It was hard to fall between the cracks, to starve outright. I haven't decided yet where I'm the poorer.

Today I'm hanging out at the Archaeology Museum until siesta time. It's peaceful in here, and cool. Summer in Madrid is a nightmare, dusty and bone dry. There are a couple of jeweled crowns on display that belonged to Visigothic kings. It's scary how long the Spaniards have been brewing trouble for the rest of the world.

My mother told me once how the early explorers had come to Cuba with their pestilential pets and nearly killed off the island's native species. She said that her father, my Abuelo Ignacio, held King Ferdinand and Queen Isabela personally responsible for the decimation. My *great*-grandfather originally came from Galicia, from the mountains somewhere. My mother says that he was one of the greatest *lectores* in Pinar del Río, that he read the classics to the cigar workers, organized unions, made a first-rate scallop pie. Why is it that everything interesting in my family happened long before I was born?

Sometimes I wish I could go back through all the blood and muscle to the origin. I read in the newspaper how scientists have traced genetic trails back millions of years to the first human beings in Africa. It makes me realize how we walk in their footsteps and everyone else's since. Thieves and czarinas, village chiefs and galley slaves, opera singers and oxcart drivers. Which one of my mother's philosophers said, *For I have been, ere now, a boy and a girl, a bush, a bird, a dumb fish in the sea?*

There's a soreness at my center I can't rub away. It opens and withers like a night-blooming flower. *Carajo*, I'm starving. I haven't eaten since the night before last, when I polished off a half pound of Gummi Bears. There's a good Cuban restaurant on Avenida Infantas, filled with fat expatriates. I'm tempted to go there, but I know the smell of fried plantains might make me do something desperate.

It's a Thursday afternoon, and the restaurants are crowded. My sense of smell is heightened from hunger. I can tell what's cooking five blocks away. The aroma of breaded chicken floats down from a balcony fringed with soot. River crabs and stuffed green peppers decorate the plates at a fancy sidewalk café. If I begged, I could probably scrape enough money together for *churros* and a hot chocolate, but nobody is serving them this time of day.

I sneak into the subway and know immediately where I must go. My ex-husband, Abelardo, will be taking his lunch at that depressing cafeteria down the street. He'll stay the afternoon to play bridge with the albino waiter. Abelardo's sister does her marketing on Thursdays. It takes her forever, because she bargains like a fishwife for every onion and hunk of ham.

Their building is narrow and dank, acrid with the incense of age. A decaying elm stands guard at the entrance. Overhead, a flock of blackbirds dissolves into the sky. A rust-colored wind whirls down the street, rustling garbage and dead leaves. I wonder what I look like in my grimy nanny's uniform. What would I think if I saw me? If I bothered to see me at all?

The lock on the front door of Abelardo and his sister's apartment is easy to pick. My fingers are useful and intuitive, like my mother's. I'm grateful to her for them, and for one or two things besides. Like her sense of humor. And the fact that she preserved my grandfather's apartment in Havana, mildewy with books and hundreds of birds he himself had shot.

Mamá kept a picture of Abuelo Ignacio in the bottom drawer of his mahogany desk. The drawer of impossibilities, she used to call it. There was the beaded bracelet my father wore in the Sierra Maestra. A cream-colored brassiere Mamá claimed still held Abuela Blanca's scent. *What we pass on is often as much a burden as a gift,* my mother told me. I used to wonder how I'd be able to tell the difference, how I'd ever know what the hell might save me.

Everything in Abelardo's apartment is the same as I remember it. The filmy, yellowing curtains in the kitchen, the crusts of dry bread collecting in the majolica bowl. Abelardo's sister is a compulsive feeder of pigeons. She wouldn't share a cup of hot water with a neighbor, but she keeps the local pigeons plump. There are two tins of rancid custard in the refrigerator. A box of cheese crackers in the cupboard. Four linked *chorizos* and a braid of garlic draped on two crooked nails.

I eat the sausages without bothering to peel off the casings, open a jar of briny olives, gulp down what's left of a strawberry yogurt drink. Then I break up the braid of garlic and stuff four of the bulbs into my apron. These will protect me, I think. They must. I steal a paring knife just to make certain, sharpen it on the edge of a rotting cutting board.

Their money is hidden in a plastic zippered case that's taped behind the armoire in my sister-in-law's bedroom. I found it there the first time too. They must have been certain I'd never return. Over a thousand *pesetas* in small bills. There's nothing else worth stealing, but I need a change of clothes. I dig out Abelardo's Sunday shirt, starched white and voluminous, and a pair of his leather suspenders. With his black ribbed socks rolled to my thighs, I look almost fashionable.

I search for somewhere to leave my mark. I want them to know, unmistakably, that I was here. But then suddenly it doesn't seem to matter. Instead I grab Abelardo's frayed airline cap and fix it on my head. I stuff a nylon satchel with my dirty clothes and immediately spring for the door.

On my way out, I glance at the cluttered table in the vestibule. There's an opened letter addressed to me. It's from my mother, postmarked Miami. *Mi queridísima hija* . . . , it begins, and I feel something breaking inside me, something lost and irreparable. Now all I want is for night to come; I want to hide in its scent like an orphan in a palace garden. I tuck my mother's letter in the waistband of my underwear and search the streets for a safe place to read.

An onslaught of bells disturbs the late-afternoon peace. On top of a hill to the north, an ugly little church is to blame. I used to escape into the cathedral in Havana when the sun was too brutal or my boyfriends occasionally got violent. I grew up believing every permutation of evil had been cultivated by bishops and priests. Still, there's a veneer of civility to churches. Perhaps this is their greatest solace.

Inside, the stone walls are moldering, embedded with a ringing only I can hear. I dip my hands in the holy water and wash off my face and neck. It smells of chestnuts and dying violets. There's an ancient woman in the front pew, bent over in prayer. At the shrine to Saint Elizabeth, a grossly pregnant woman stands with a hand on her hip, as if ready to scold the heavens.

I take a seat in a worm-eaten pew. The wood is soft, and I scrape it with my fingernails, make a paste between my forefinger and thumb. Then I rub it on my thigh, on the purplish patch where the doctors stripped my skin to mend my mother's burns. Mamá's letter sticks to my palms as I read. She's in Miami with her sister, my Tía Constancia, and she's playing the lottery every week with auspicious numbers from my life. Mamá says I've always been a lucky child. I become impatient with her handwriting, impossibly round and leaning backward. What the hell could she know of my life?

There's more news. A yacht club on the bay run by Batista's right-hand man. Vintage cars she's begun fixing with the tools she smuggled out of Havana. A mature man, Mamá says, part Indian, part German, part French, who reveres every inch of her flesh. She's learning idiomatic English from him too, from the lyrics to his old American records.

> *Yes, sir, that's my baby,*
> *No, sir, don't mean maybe,*
> *Yes, sir, that's my baby now.*

My mother doesn't ask me about Abelardo, assumes my unhappiness. No worthwhile woman can stay married for long, she told me repeatedly when I was growing up. Well, for once I think she was right. In the last few lines, Mamá begs me to come home. Home meaning where she is. She says that Miami's seas and skies are just like Cuba's, only fresher, bluer. *Everything here is so blue, Dulcita,* she writes. As if blue could take care of everything.

MIAMI

Constancia drives to the airport in her pink Cadillac convertible with the top down. It's a record day of heat in Miami, with next to no wind and the threat of rain sufficient to keep the humidity intolerable. More and more, Constancia is averse to artificial changes in temperature. In fact, she's convinced that air-conditioning is weakening the muscles of her diaphragm, keeping her perpetually short of breath.

At the airport, buildings and buses waver in the hammering light. Constancia parks the car near a construction site. The gravel beneath her high-heeled shoes sounds like a monstrous chomping, like her own bones giving way to some invisible jaw. She ties the sash of her old-fashioned hat tight under her chin and tentatively, like a tender-footed child on a shaly beach, picks her way to the arrivals gate.

It's freezing inside the airport. Constancia blows into her cupped hands to see if her breath is visible, then briskly rubs her palms together. She checks her watch. Isabel's plane is due in from Hawaii at two o'clock. She goes to a nearby phone and calls the factory manager. There's a critical shipment of spearmint due this afternoon. "Pressure the suppliers!" Constancia insists. "Make sure it gets here today, or that batch of Rodillas de Cuba will go to ruin!"

Constancia hangs up the phone and wonders suddenly how close she and her daughter ever were. Those chilly winter mornings in bed when they read storybooks together. Those slow hours pretending to cook alphabet soup in the tub. Did it all count? Or did they merely love each other?

Summer lightning crackles outside, causing a minor panic in the airport. Isabel's plane is a half hour late. The first passengers stream out of the gate, wearing straw hats and wilted leis. When you give birth, Constancia thinks, you cede your place to another. You say, in effect, when I'm gone, you will live, you will remember. But what is it exactly they're supposed to remember?

Isabel is nearly nine months pregnant. When Constancia was nine months pregnant, she ripped up all the photographs she had of her ex-husband, Gonzalo. Then she went to the seashore and fed the thousand pieces to the tides. Summer ducks stormed over, anticipating food. Constancia liked to imagine bits of Gonzalo's face ground down in the ducks' gizzards, upsetting their centers of gravity. She envisioned these ducks flying far off their courses, missing entire continents, every celestial clue.

Her daughter emerges from the gate, a glory of swollen flesh. She is wearing the largest pair of overalls Constancia has ever seen. Isabel is blotchy pink and luminous, like those portraits of saints in the midst of heavenly visions. She might divine water, abruptly erupt with poppies, harvest fat stars from the sky.

"Hi, Mom." Isabel hands Constancia a mesh bag with heavy, irregular shapes wrapped in Honolulu newspapers—the last pieces of pottery she worked on before she found out she was pregnant. Her daughter didn't make ordinary teapots or mugs she could give away at Christmas. She's never made a vase. Isabel has always been drawn to more free-form work, odd shards of clay and other materials combined to suggest something recycled, something tampered with or incomplete.

Constancia takes the mesh bag. She saw her daughter working once. Isabel glazed a chunk of clay, then fired it in a red-hot kiln until the color took hold. Later, she removed it with barbecue tongs and nestled it in a garbage can with dried eucalyptus leaves. When the leaves caught fire, she banged on the lid and waited. What comes out, Isabel said, is as much inspiration as destiny.

"You look good, Mom." Isabel carefully inspects Constancia. "Like some earlier version of yourself."

Constancia supports her daughter as she walks. Isabel's ankles and feet are inflated beyond recognition, shod in oversized hippie sandals. She manages only a slow slide-shuffle through the airport corridors. Constancia flags down a roving motorized cart for the disabled and bundles her daughter on board. Isabel has brought no luggage except for the few pieces of pottery in the mesh bag.

"No clothing?" Constancia asks, incredulous.

"Nope."

"No deodorant? No baby blankets?"

"Nope, nope. I sold everything."

Constancia looks hard at her daughter, at the quiet defiance she knows so well. She's convinced that by two years old, children have expressed all they will ever feel for the rest of their lives.

Constancia tells Isabel to wait on the curb while she brings the pink Cadillac around. The heat is stifling, made worse by the car exhaust. Constancia notices that her hands are moist and shaking. Is it possible she's going to be a grandmother?

As she pulls up in front of Isabel, the sight of her hugely pregnant daughter moves her. How does anyone recover from such an ordeal? Constancia helps Isabel into the car, pulls a pink chiffon scarf from the glove compartment to keep her daughter's unruly hair in place.

"Not exactly my style, but thanks."

"Don't worry, *mi cielo*. I have a new product—Cabello de Cuba Plus—that will tame your hair, turn it to silk!"

Isabel flinches forward. The baby kicks her hard, then twice more. Constancia wants to stop traffic, put her ear against her daughter's stomach, feel the tiny, wayward foot. Isabel says she took natural childbirth classes. Her instructor explained that having a baby was like pushing out a large grapefruit.

"¿Una toronja?" After all these years, Constancia is still astounded at the understatement of certain Americans.

Why doesn't anyone talk about the pain? The ruthless red pressure wrapped tight to your center? What is this conspiracy of stoicism women have about childbirth? Why doesn't she tell Isabel right now that it's like forcing out the largest mammal on the planet? Why doesn't she tell her that you never, ever forget.

Constancia maneuvers the Cadillac onto the I-95. Reina has likened driving this car to driving a tank she once commandeered in a military exercise outside Cienfuegos. She likes to tinker with the Cadillac, fine-tune all its gizmos and gears. Recently, Reina took a job as a mechanic fixing antique cars. She's found a *novio* too, a wealthy American who lives on a boat anchored off Key Biscayne. And this after she bedded half the yacht club, incited who knows how many divorces!

Ahead of Constancia, a brown sedan has its right blinker on. She knows that the driver, an elderly man in a starched guayabera, has no intention of changing lanes. It's one of the idiosyncrasies of driving in Miami. Cubans leave their blinkers on for hours, oblivious to the anxiety they create in their wake.

"Your aunt is at home, finishing up the baby's room," Constancia says. "She wants to surprise you." Reina is creating a mobile for the baby made from seaweed and a trio of Papi's stuffed bats. Constancia only hopes the thing doesn't scare her grandchild half to death.

Constancia visited her daughter in Hawaii last spring. She and her boyfriend lived in a cottage on the windward side of Oahu. The place was so small you couldn't spread your arms in the bedroom. There was a hot plate and a microwave but no stove, and a toilet that worked only infrequently. A redwood patio hung right over a marsh. Beyond it lay the constant blue of the Pacific.

Constancia doesn't ask Isabel about Austin or the Chinese-Filipina dancer. Behind her daughter's glowing health, Constancia can see the cold sliding ruin. Isabel's existence changed to mere scenery. Constancia remembers something her father said. *Every force moves toward death. Only constant violence maintains it.* Another one of his physics laws.

Near the tollbooth for Key Biscayne, Isabel spots the display of a life-size shark advertising the Seaquarium.

"Let's go."

"Now?" Constancia wants to accommodate her daughter, but the aquarium? In her condition? To be logical, she thinks, is to be continually amazed.

"Why not?" Isabel cranes her neck to get a better look at the fake shark. "I've never been."

"Whatever you say, *mi cielo*."

Constancia drives across the Rickenbacker Causeway, past the narrow stretch of beach lined with coconut palms, past the enormous marine stadium where women in sequined bikinis frequently water-ski. She visited the Seaquarium once during Reina's second week in Miami. It was a nightmare. Her sister volunteered for every marine demonstration: cha-cha-chá-ing with seals, feeding sardines to the sea lions, playing basketball with a four-ton killer whale. Reina flirted shamelessly with the attendants (gangly men with snaggle teeth and sun-bleached hair) and their aquatic wards alike.

Isabel wants to see the manatees first, and so Constancia pushes her daughter to their tank in a rented wheelchair stenciled with dolphins. The air is thick with chlorine and seaweed and the droppings of a thousand tropical species.

"Do I look like her?" Isabel stares at the lumbering mother manatee as she sucks in a leaf of butter lettuce. Her calf swims close by with its slow paddle fins, rolls onto its back like a shapeless acrobat.

"Now that you mention it, *mi cielo*. But I think it's only temporary. Definitely *not* a family resemblance."

Isabel laughs. Her voice scatters in the air like a spray of startled birds. Constancia likes pushing her daughter around in the dolphin wheelchair. It's as if Isabel were a baby again, compliant in her stroller. If only everything could remain this well defined.

In the outdoor turtle tank, a pair of loggerheads

are clumsily mating. The male is precariously balanced on the rear of the female's carapace. He tumbles back into the water but steadfastly tries to mount her again. Constancia respects his efforts but holds little hope for a new generation.

When she lived on her grandfather's ranch in Camagüey, Constancia frequently heard the great raw noise of animals in heat. In the spring, especially, when everything came to promiscuous life after the hibernating winter. Stallions and bulls, roosters and billy goats, birds of every size and hue. Trembling the nights and the white-hot days. Constancia was terrified that somehow she would be forced to surrender to a similar violence.

Sex was rampant in Cuba, and not only amongst the animals themselves. One day, Constancia saw one of her uncles (Ernesto, the second oldest) penetrate a little spotted mare from behind. He had to stand on a stump of a palm tree to do it, spit on his penis twice. Later, she saw many others from her hiding places in the restless shade of bushes. Her other uncles, farmhands, *guajiros* mostly, with horses and each other. Afterward, the mares would walk around snorting for an hour or more, with their tails slightly askew. She noticed nothing different about the men.

For a while, her grandfather used to ask Constancia to keep him company when he took his weekly bath in an outdoor tin tub. Constancia watched carefully from under the fig tree as Abuelo Ramón washed his penis, pulled the purplish foreskin back, meticulously rinsed it clean. Afterward, it hung there, withered and gleaming, like an unused limb. Abuelo would close his eyes then, tilt his head heavenward, breathing deeply, it seemed, of an old desire.

After heavy rainstorms, the ground around the tub would often be littered with figs.

• • •

In a few minutes, it will be show time for Lolita, the Sea-quarium's killer whale. Isabel wants to sit in the front of the amphitheater, even though signs everywhere warn of splashing. Constancia thinks how little her daughter's basic nature has changed despite her sorrow. Good-humored. Stubborn. No fear whatsoever of consequence.

Constancia pushes the wheelchair down a ramp to the front row and settles on a bench beside her daughter. Children run up and down the aisles, shrieking with anticipation.

"Have you considered other names besides Raku?" Constancia asks tentatively. She's not certain she can call her grandchild this, a sound like the mating call of some Amazonian bird.

Isabel shakes her head, eyes fixed forward for the first sign of the cetacean starlet. A moment later, like suspense incarnate, Lolita enters the underwater arena, circling, circling, maniacally circling, until with a leap unimaginable for a creature that size, she hurls herself into the air.

Splashing is not the word to describe Lolita's landing. Tidal wave, maybe. Tsunami. Not splashing. Isabel screams with hilarity and terror. That whale could have belly-flopped in their laps! Constancia sighs grimly. Her vintage linen suit is soaked with water and whale detritus. Meanwhile, Lolita is rewarded for her antic with a bucket of baby mackerel.

Constancia notices more water than necessary leaking from Isabel's wheelchair. At first, she thinks it's the whale water, but she finds it warm to the touch.

"Stand up, *mi hija*! I think your water broke!"

Isabel tries to push herself to standing, as more liquid pours down her legs. It *is* warm, and slightly sour from her daughter's womb. Constancia helps Isabel sit down again, presses her ear to her daughter's stomach. The crowd roars, as another wave from the leaping Lolita drenches them both. Constancia is oblivious as she listens intently for a sign from her new grandchild.

When Raku is born the following morning, he gives such a mewl of indignation that it breaks Constancia's heart. Her grandson, so tiny and wrinkled, with confused, swollen eyes. He latches onto Isabel's breast and sucks, quickly calming himself. Then he falls asleep against her, so fragile and sticky and impossibly flawless, it makes Constancia cry.

Reina visits in the afternoon, bringing a plastic shopping bag filled with odd gifts: a headdress of peacock feathers, an ancient chronometer that keeps perfect time, a bagful of lemons to squeeze into juice ("Helps avoid jaundice," she says). For Raku, she brings a pint-sized "starter" hammer and a tiny gold-and-onyx bracelet.

"I got this in Cuba years ago," Reina explains, fastening the bracelet on the sleeping Raku's wrist. "Payment for wiring up a black market satellite dish. The woman who gave it to me says it keeps away the evil eye. I always swore I'd give it to my first grandchild."

Isabel seems delighted with the gifts and gives her aunt a big hug. Constancia thinks the two of them look immense and flushed side by side, like hot giant rubies. She resists the urge to drag her sister from the room.

Constancia calls the factory from the hospital phone. For once, she's reassured. A cargo of head-to-toe products was successfully express-shipped to an American film star in Malibu.

Raku wakes up looking disoriented, as if everything had changed in his sleep. Isabel reaches for the baby and nestles him against her breast. "I can feel his little heart," she says, her face softening.

The nurse sticks her head in, offering formula, and advises Isabel to get some rest. Reina dismisses the nurse with a wave of her hand.

"My mother nursed me until I was five," she tells Isabel wistfully. "I wish she'd never stopped."

"I'll take home some formula just in case Isabel changes her mind." Constancia knows this sounds illogical and rivalrous but decides to hold her ground nonetheless.

"She won't change her mind," Reina counters evenly.

That night, Constancia stays with her daughter and grandson at the Good Samaritan Hospital. The maternity ward is only one floor down from the terminal cases, where Gonzalo continues to languish in festering splendor.

Constancia remembers her first days with her own son, the way his fists shook when he screamed, his pinched little mouth demanding milk. She didn't nurse him for long. She couldn't. Each time he suckled her breasts, Constancia felt a stirring between her legs. She tried to force her mind to neutral images, pigeons and peanut vendors, the calm of the ocean on a windless day, but it didn't help. The moment she felt the pleasure spread through her body, she pulled a startled Silvestre off her nipple and gave him cow's milk instead.

After her son moved out of the house, Constancia bumped into him all over New York: buying a pumpkin with a blind man on Columbus Avenue, roller-skating in the dead of winter with a thick-thighed *chinito* in Central Park. Silvestre seemed more annoyed than embarrassed on these occasions. When Constancia invited him and the Chinese man over for dinner, Silvestre gave her a look that said *Don't even bother*. In those days, he went by the name Jack. Jack Cross. Today Constancia left a message for him on his TTY machine, announcing the birth of his nephew. *Isabel gave the baby your name. Raku Silvestre Cruz.*

It is long past midnight. Constancia kisses her sleeping daughter and grandson, then sneaks up the service stairwell to Gonzalo's room. He, too, is sleeping, his mouth lax and soundless, his chest quiet beneath the hospital sheet. Constancia approaches the bed. The fax machine on the nightstand begins grinding out a message that wakes him up.

"Vente, mi vida," Gonzalo says in his dark river voice, reaching for Constancia's hips. He pulls her closer. His hands drift across her flesh like heat on snow.

"I'm a grandmother, Gonzalo," Constancia whispers. For a moment, she is tempted to stand before him, part her legs slightly, welcome the moist fever of his tongue. Instead she twists away, worn out from resistance and erotic illusion. *"Soy una abuela,"* she repeats, her voice growing stronger.

Then she smooths her linen dress and coolly leaves the room.

Constancia returns to the maternity ward and nestles into bed with Isabel and Raku. What is love if she can't feel it against her body? They lie together, mother and son and grandmother, as if tethered by invisible vines. Raku is asleep, wrapped in a flannel blanket so that his baby hands meet in prayer. A little Buddhist monk, waxy and lustrous as a sliver of moon.

If only Heberto were here, Constancia thinks, he wouldn't worry so much about another future. His vision would fill to the edges with their grandson's face.

After an hour of restlessness, Raku wakes up. His eyes dart back and forth in the unaccustomed light of darkness. Constancia sings to him softly and, in the singing, understands how completely the world is rigged with afflictions. On her grandson's heel is a red birthmark. It is the shape of the gash on Isabel's left foot, where Constancia bit out an inch of flesh.

The axis suddenly shifts. Fierce and hissing, no longer buried, the knowledge comes to Constancia whole. She would kill to save him, kill to save them all.

THE ANDARAZ

❈

Blanca and I were married at City Hall the day after her graduation. It was only the two of us, the one-armed judge, and a listless witness from the state. Blanca wore a fitted carmine suit and a broad-brimmed hat with a spray of fresh violets. I found her ravishing.

For our honeymoon, we traveled to the Isle of Pines, where I had seen the great leatherback so many years before. Blanca wanted to sit on the same beach and wait for the she-turtle, convinced that it would return. We lingered night after night under a waxing moon, but the leatherback never came.

Those nights on the beach are still vivid to me, yet remote as a diorama. Our love was sheltered by the coconut palms, serenaded by the low whine of insects. How slight Blanca was, ribbed like an underfed cat, but soft too, in unexpected places. Her scent was sharp and green then, like budding leaves, inextricable from our passion. I would lie beside her and *whisper:* Estoy contento, querida. *And for a moment, time seemed to stop its audible march in our small paradise.*

The Isle of Pines is scrubby, about two thousand square miles in all, and has a single languid river, Las Casas, that cuts through the capital city of Nueva Gerona. During the day, Blanca loved to wade in the river and drink from it, of questionable purity even then. I sat under the shade trees on the riverbank and watched as the water echoed off her body, overcome by the wonder of my possession.

One day, Blanca playfully coaxed me, fully dressed, into the river. When I was chest-high in the slow waters, she dove in beside me and tugged off my belt. Her boldness startled me, and I lost my footing. A force I could not fathom pulled me down and held me underwater. Just when I was certain I'd drown, I heard a child's voice imploring: Yield to the river! Yield to the river! *Instead I broke free into the morning air.*

Blanca emerged from the water simultaneously, sleek as a river goddess. She kissed me with a hard ardor, continuing her caresses until I surrendered to a violent pleasure. I am the river, *Blanca breathed in my ear.* I am the river. . . . *And around us, the waters murmured assent.*

That evening, Blanca showed me a wound on her left heel. She told me that something had bitten her while we were making love, a river rat or snake—she couldn't tell which from the size of the double puncture. Within hours, her foot swelled monstrously and the flesh around the wound turned yellow with suppurations. The doctor who came to examine her nervously advised an amputation.

The swelling subsided by morning, but by then a fever had taken hold of her body. Blanca lapsed in and out of consciousness for nearly a week. I appealed for help from a medical colleague in Havana, Dr. Eduardo Iriarte, a specialist in tropical diseases, who took the ferry to Nueva Gerona to treat my wife. By the time he began his administrations—an arsenal of foul-

smelling medicines and saltwater baths—Blanca emerged from the worst of the crisis.

We never learned what attacked Blanca in the river. The shape and depth of the wound were unlike anything I'd ever seen. I consulted countless reference books, queried experts on dangerous marine creatures. But nothing coincided with my wife's wound or subsequent symptoms.

When we returned to Havana, Blanca and I moved into a furnished apartment I had rented from an astronomy professor who took off to fight in the Spanish Civil War. The place was filled with thick tomes about the origin of the universe and all manner of celestial phenomena. I remember reading one book on the asteroids that hover in space between Mars and Jupiter, another on the varied trajectories of comets. There were many history books too, including one recounting how the first crate of peaches arrived in Venice from the New World, electrifying the city's richest inhabitants. Strip man of his curiosity, Dr. Forrest used to say, and you strip him of his appetite for life.

After our sojourn on the Isle of Pines, Blanca lost interest in carnal pleasures. She succumbed to my desire infrequently, and then only in fresh running water. This was a serious handicap in Havana, since its one river was terribly polluted and offered no privacy except in the wee hours of the morning. Perhaps I should have protested, stood firm against my wife's caprices, but at the time I would have indulged Blanca anything. It disturbs me now to think how passion ruled me like any ordinary man.

Later that year, I received a research grant to do a comprehensive study of the andaraz, a large native rodent that inhabits the remotest forests of Oriente. Once abundant in Cuba, the creatures were becoming increasingly scarce. Moreover, they were difficult to find because they confined themselves to the tops of the highest and densest trees. An international commis-

sion of wildlife conservation decided I should investigate its status.

Blanca and I headed for the Sierra Maestra, to the town of Jiguaní, where we slept on vacant cots in the rural-guard barracks. My wife had not seen the rodent before, and so I brought along an illustration of it that I'd found in the Proceedings *of the Zoological Society of London. The next morning, we set out on excellent horses furnished by the guard and rode far into the mountains to the village of Los Negros, which served as our base.*

Not surprisingly, it was Blanca who spotted the first andaraz, expertly bringing it down with a single shot from her custom-made rifle. Within a week, we'd collected enough of the creatures to make a series of skins, rough out several skeletons, and substantiate the precise point where its prehensile tail separates from its body.

On the last evening of our expedition, resting in hammocks inside a coffee bean warehouse provided by our local host, Blanca complained of severe nausea. She rejected her early-morning steak and eggs, and said that the sight of her daily mango made her ill. The obvious did not occur to us. Not until we returned to Havana and consulted Dr. Iriarte again did we learn that she was pregnant.

The day we returned from her medical examination, Blanca insisted that I pay her a salary. I had stopped remunerating her since our marriage because, frankly, I no longer saw the need. I admit I am not what one might call an emancipated man. Although it is true that my parents raised me with progressive ideas and Mamá taught music all her life, I had certain expectations for my wife. Not only did I refuse to pay Blanca; I prohibited her from seeking other employment.

Blanca disregarded my edict outright. In spite of her pregnancy, or perhaps because of it, she applied to various scientific institutes in Havana under the name B. Mestre Sejourné. I was prepared to disrupt her quest, but I found it unnecessary. No one would hire Blanca, even with her stellar qualifications. Each time she appeared for an interview, her stomach tightly bound to conceal her condition, the story was the same: If only you were a man . . . Our wives would not stand for it . . . Cuba, my dear, is not America.

When I finally relented and agreed to resume her modest stipend, Blanca accused me of insincere motives. How could I deny it? Our research was receiving international attention, and I did not wish to impede the momentum of our efforts.

Blanca began to speak of leaving for the United States, where professional women were treated marginally better than in Cuba. She developed a sudden interest in desert herpetology, wanted to visit the American Southwest, northern Mexico, the driest parts of Africa. Cuba, of course, has its savannas and plains but not the extreme dry conditions that warrant equally extreme modifications by desert fauna. I remember Blanca rhapsodizing about a certain horned lizard of Texas she'd read about, a prehistoric-looking creature that squirted blood from the corners of its eyes when alarmed.

Despite these distractions, Blanca and I intensified our fieldwork in Cuba. Her condition hardly slowed her progress as she led the way across rugged terrain, on horseback and on foot, climbed mountains, waded hip-deep in streams, and ventured into underground caves thick with the stink of bat guano. As her pregnancy progressed, Blanca took more aggressive risks, as if she were denying the baby's increasingly evident existence. She seemed happy only on the road, sleeping under the stars, with the soothing obstinacy of a stream nearby.

At our new apartment in Vedado, Blanca grew restless and cross, distressingly erratic. She slept fitfully, twisting the sheets around her swelling, disobedient body. She would wake up in the middle of the night, shivering with imagined fevers, and I would give her sponge baths to settle her nerves.

It was clear that she resented the unborn life inside her, resented what she considered the misery accumulating at her center. "If only I were oviparous," she repeated again and again. Blanca said she would infinitely prefer to lay eggs like her beloved lizards and snakes and be done with the entire maternal ordeal. Not even her little wristbone, which continued to dangle in its pouch from her belt, seemed to be of much help.

In her sixth month, Blanca decided to move all her belongings into the empty guest room. I tried to dissuade her, but she ignored my wishes. She furnished the room with discarded chairs she salvaged from garbage heaps, nineteen in all. A musty feather mattress on the floor completed the decor. There were days Blanca did not leave the room at all, sitting in one chair and then another, fretfully consulting her watch for a precise number of minutes only she could gauge.

"It's raining in my room," she stated calmly each time I knocked on the door. Then she would ask me to bring her another umbrella. She complained that the dozens of umbrellas already at her disposal did not shield her from the rain.

Toward the end of her pregnancy, I encouraged Blanca to visit her family in Camagüey. I had never met her father and brothers and was not even certain they knew of my existence. Each time I suggested she introduce me to them, Blanca clicked her tongue and looked away. This time, however, the prospect of returning to the ranch seemed to cheer her.

It was December, and it rained the entire journey. Her injured leg swelled with the humidity, and she insisted her teeth were receding to the back of her throat. I read to her from the newspapers, filled her in on the war in Spain. But nothing I said or did seemed to distract her.

No sooner did we arrive at the Mestre ranch than Blanca wanted to leave. She gave no explanation, nor did she seem angry, just emphatically matter-of-fact. Her family, brusque in *the manner of parrots, took her decision in stride. One by one, her brothers—Arístides, Ernesto, Virgílio, Fausto, Cirilio, and Dámaso—embraced her, nodded to each other in unspoken agreement.*

Blanca barely took notice of them except for Dámaso, with whom she whispered a few words. Her father, Ramón, kept an unnatural distance from Blanca, as if he feared receiving an electric shock. Not one of them mentioned her condition. I understood that something had transpired among them, but I could not fathom what.

I did not see the Mestre men again until three and a half years later, when I delivered Constancia, our firstborn, to them in Camagüey. I remember Ramón Mestre and his sons waiting for us at the train station. They'd arrived in their tumbledown truck and were uncomfortably dressed in new suits from another era. It occurred to me then that they'd most likely worn those suits only once before—for Eugenia Mestre's funeral in 1919.

Our daughter, Constancia, looked preternaturally old from her first breath. During labor, which lasted the better part of two days, Blanca would ask, her inflection rising: Will someone please tell me . . . ? Will someone please tell me . . . ? But she never completed her question. When I looked into my wife's eyes, I saw a woman who had drowned a thousand years before.

After the baby was born, Blanca rocked Constancia for hours in the nursery, a deceptively cheerful room with a border of leaping frogs. Round the clock, Blanca rocked, unaware of the hour, the day, of my physical presence.

In the mornings, the sun hit her face directly, but she did not seem to notice. Except for the baby, everything around her was dead, a sad contagion. Periodically, she loosened her night-gown to let Constancia nurse. Blanca made no other movement, no other sound. Her mouth was a pale, immovable gash.

Dr. Eduardo Iriarte said he alone could not save Blanca, and so he enlisted the help of physicians I did not fully trust. They prescribed vitamin shots for my wife, metallic medicines to stir her blood. One psychiatrist, freshly trained abroad, fastened electrodes to Blanca's temples and gave her intermittent shocks. But nothing broke the terrible spell. After the last doctor left, hopelessly shrugging his shoulders, there was no one I could confide in, no one I could turn to for help.

Five months after Constancia was born, Blanca disappeared. She left no note, no clue to where she would go, only our daughter shrieking blue in her crib.

A NATURAL HISTORY

❀

KEY BISCAYNE

AUGUST 1991

The doors of the restoration garage are open to the night, a balmy mingling of eucalyptus and acacia and warm axle grease. There's a trace of ocean in the wind, a hint of a coming squall. Reina wonders if the pull of death isn't stronger at night, when life is so much less distracting.

Lightning strikes a nearby cluster of palms. The tallest tree flares up in a plume of smoke. A black gash divides it in two. Then a slow blaze begins in the canopy of leaves. Birds flutter and screech, stirring the soot like pollen. Reina decides that this isn't an accident but an act of translation. Only she doesn't yet know the language.

Reina rolls under a 1959 Cadillac, an apple affixed to her mouth. The sweet juice seeps onto her tongue. The car is a big-finned baby with a white exterior and cherry-red seats. The owners told Reina that for years the automobile was sheltered in a Tampa garage by an agoraphobic Armenian who didn't drive.

This Cadillac could make someone rich back in Cuba, Reina thinks, finishing her twelfth apple of the day. Weddings, tourist rentals, *quinceañeros*, cameo appearances in foreign films. Reina knows an electrician in Havana, modestly talented at best, who built a house on the beach at Santa Teresa del Mar with money he earned chauffeuring his dead father's Chevrolet.

Reina makes a final adjustment to the carburetor. They're usually the weakest link in these antique cars. Reina likes to take the carburetors apart and soak the pieces overnight in a solution of her own devising. Then she leaves it all to ferment outside under fleecy evening skies. In the morning, she wipes each piece clean with her chamois rags and rebuilds the carburetors from scratch. She hasn't had one dissatisfied customer yet.

After quitting her sister's factory, Reina hadn't intended to find a job right away. But in fact, it's done her some good. Unlike her work as an electrician, fixing vintage cars is comfortingly predictable. There's no chance of electrocution or breaking her neck falling off the curve of a fantastic fin. And thankfully, no chance of attracting stray lightning. Reina keeps the hours she wants, no pressure whatsoever. Considering all her other adaptations lately, this new job suits her just fine.

Reina would much rather tinker with these aging cars than work at the Cuerpo de Cuba factory any day. Constancia's cosmetics business is expanding so rapidly (in her second month of operation, she's quadrupled output and secured fifty-four accounts nationwide) that she barely has a spare moment to herself, much less for poor Isabel and Raku. If *her* daughter were visiting with a newborn grandchild, Reina certainly wouldn't be wasting her time fussing with useless lotions and creams.

Her sister is launching yet another product—Décolletage de Cuba—which has her moodier than ever. Last week, Constancia was on a Miami cable TV show called *Mi Fortuna*, about Latino success stories like hers. She shared the stage with Fredi Torriente Díaz, a manufacturer of do-it-yourself liposuction kits, and Rosita Luz Roja, a perky peroxide blonde whose dating service, for the previously incarcerated (Rosita herself has served time for extortion and credit card fraud), is the most popular in Dade County.

Constancia's face recently appeared on the cover of a Florida financial magazine too. Inside, there were photographs of her sister in action: checking the temperature on a too-hot vat of Pies de Cuba; breaking up a fight between the ever-feuding Odio cousins on the factory floor; testing the freshness of bushels of lavender, daffodils, and peppermint. All the while, Constancia's signature royal-blue bottles (as always, pasted with Mami's face) continue to clink and rattle down the assembly line.

Reina skimmed through the article, picking out the English words she understood. As far as she could tell, there was no information whatsoever on sales figures or plans for international expansion, not a single conventional indicator of success. Constancia, it seemed, only wanted to talk about why customers loved her products. So much gibberish about nostalgia and femininity that it made Reina sick.

At least with a car, Reina thinks, you can fix it, paint it, or improve its performance. *Por favor*, mere creams and lotions won't make a woman desirable. The confidence in her walk is what gives birth to lust. A sense of humor. A look in the eye that says *Acércate, Papi*, come a little closer. Reina doesn't wear deodorant and never shaves her underarms. And she still feels disoriented without her pre-lightning scent. Why would any woman want to deliberately disguise her natural odor? Why would any woman want to smell of anything but herself?

At breakfast this morning, Constancia reprimanded Reina for the number of men she'd already "processed" at the yacht club.

" 'Processed'? Is that what you call it, Constancia?" Reina laughed so hard she succeeded in further infuriating her sister.

Isabel was sitting between them, eating a bowl of granola and nursing Raku. "Tía's right, Mom. At least you could call it 'fucking.' " It was the first thing Isabel had said to anyone in days.

"What kind of language is that for a new mother, *mi cielo*?" Constancia asked, her voice low and measured.

Then she faced Reina.

"And you! You have a rep-u-ta-tion already!" Constancia emphasized the syllables as if they were four separate words, whether out of outrage or lack of imagination, Reina didn't know.

Finally, Constancia wheeled around on her forties crocodile heels and stormed off to work.

Coño, Reina thought, her sister has slept with the same man for thirty years. What could she possibly still know of desire? And why are married women so stingy about other people's sex lives anyway?

"I don't think I'd want anyone making love to me right now," Isabel said, looking down at her month-old son.

Reina regarded her niece affectionately across the kitchen table. "Don't worry, *mi amor*, you're not supposed to. Now's the time most men rediscover they're polygamous."

Reina had heard the whole story about Austin and that hula dancer. The only thing that surprised her was that anyone should be shocked. Women expected too much from men, too little for themselves. Sexual fidelity—what an absurd concept! This younger generation was, if anything, more intransigent on the subject than her own.

Later that morning, Reina took her niece and great-nephew for another ride in Heberto's motorboat. They skimmed through the bay as they often do before noon. Isabel put the baby in a sling facing forward so he could get a full view. They glided around for an hour or two, past mangrove islands and the glistening waterfront of the city.

Sometimes Isabel steered the boat and Reina got a chance to hold Raku. A humming filled her then, enduring and pure. Reina dangled seaweed before Raku's eyes, dripped water on his wrists, rubbed sand between her fingers and let him take a whiff. He seemed to know her already, watched her expressions closely. When his face was opposite hers, Reina felt the warmth of his milky breath like a bit of lace at her lips.

Reina puts the final touches on the white Cadillac, then sets to work restoring a 1955 Thunderbird. For thirty-five years, the client said, he'd kept this sky-blue beauty in a climate-controlled garage as a tribute to his lost first love. But now his love is a widow in Pensacola and eagerly awaiting his return.

On the radio, there are reports of an impending hurricane gathering strength off the Bahamas. An evacuation of Key Biscayne may be necessary. Reina has been through so many hurricanes in Cuba, they no longer frighten her. The real danger, she knows, is not from the floods or the screaming winds but from the damn flying fruit—mangoes or plantains turned to deadly weapons at ninety miles per hour. A dear lover of hers from Santa Cruz del Sur, Hermán Duyós, was killed in 1986 by a high-velocity avocado to the back of his head. Poor Hermán. Reina cannot think of a more undignified way to die.

Somehow she can't imagine her current lover being killed by an avocado or some lesser vegetable. Russ Hicks is the closest thing she knows to a hero, a concept Reina resists in principle. The night he rescued her on Heberto's boat, Russ took her straight to his cabin (he didn't have to ask). His body was surprisingly light and silvered with hair. It was the first day of Reina's period, but Russ didn't mind. He covered her body again and again, then held her in place with his tongue until he found her true center.

They barely spoke after the first acknowledgments, flourished wildly without language. Russ stoked their love-making with Greek figs and dates, teas sweetened with honey, assorted cream cakes. Their days were metered by shadows, by heat and its absence, the famine of smooth, burning candles. Reina yearned to hold the world inside her again, to have the sky empty all its gifts in her lap. What, then, was holding back her pleasure?

"Where's my toolbox?" she demanded on their third day together. She searched Russ's plush cabin for a clue. He opened wide the portholes, and the sea was visible all around. Anchored a few yards away, Heberto's motorboat rocked modestly in the breeze. Russ held her hands, twice as large as his, and stared at Reina for another hour. Reluctantly, he returned her toolbox, then took her to his restoration garage.

"I'll pay you whatever you want," he said, and handed Reina an orange jumpsuit and a pair of workman's boots. "I need you close by."

Reina is learning English. A slow English with the flavor of the Southwest. She isn't sure she likes the way English feels in her mouth, the press of her tongue against her palate, the lackluster *r*'s. Russ is from Omaha—part Chippewa, part German, part French. He's writing a book in three parts, like himself. An autobiography that ends when he is born. He reads sections of it aloud to Reina, but she admits she hardly understands a word.

Russ told her he left Nebraska in 1959, intending to join the rebels after reading an article that glamorized El Comandante in *Life* magazine. But he made it only as far as Fort Lauderdale. His fortune came quickly, in stocks and real estate and antique cars, and so he decided to stay.

Reina is learning Russ's American songs, outsized music from this endless land. Reina sings them as they speed through the intercoastal waterways, as she works on her vintage cars and eats her lover's barbecued steaks.

> *Blue skies smiling at me,*
> *Nothing but blue skies do I see.*

Reina dismantles the Thunderbird's carburetor and drops the parts in a bucket of her special solution. She wipes her hands on a rag, then pulls a pack of loose tobacco from her jumper pocket. Carefully, she presses together a cigarette, drags the smoke hard into her lungs. Reina didn't smoke much before. In Cuba, she enjoyed the occasional cigar with a tumbler of rum. The two go so well together, they're a kind of *congrí*, a red-beans-and-rice stew. For her, fixing cars and smoking have much the same dual appeal.

Reina wonders if her English will serve her better here than her quotidian Spanish. In Miami, the Cuban Spanish is so different, florid with self-pity and longing and obstinate revenge. Reina speaks another language entirely, an explosive lexicon of hardship and bitter jokes at the government's expense. And her sister sounds like the past. A flash-frozen language, replete with outmoded words and fifties expressions. For Constancia, time has stood linguistically still. It's a wonder people can speak to each other!

Constancia rarely mentions their mother, despite the

thousands of royal-blue bottles she processes daily, despite Mami's face firmly cemented over hers. For her sister, it's always Papi this and Papi that, as if their mother had never existed. Constancia and her fretwork amnesia. Constancia and her worn, jarring lies. Papá also had lied. He'd lied to Constancia, and then she guarded his lie, a hideous jewel, for forty years. So why should Reina believe anything her sister says now?

Until Mami died, Reina accepted what Papá said without question. Her memories are rich with his pronouncements, looming and fixed, like faces in musty oil paintings. Reina breathed in his words and they clung to her, became tissue and sinew, live buckling cells. Once, Papá pointed to a ridge of mountains edged with pines and empty sky. "Pity the poor souls condemned to interpretation rather than enjoyment," he said, surveying the landscape as if he'd fashioned it himself. "Never trust anyone who cannot surrender himself to nature."

Reina used to help her father feed birds on the balcony of their Havana apartment. In the cool release of evening, they scattered bread crumbs and seeds, the city's colonial architecture blooming at their feet. He entertained her with old wives' tales about what happened to birds in cold climates, theories about hibernation or supposed flights to the moon. No less a luminary than Aristotle, he told Reina, fancied that redstarts turned into robins to survive the cold and that swallows buried themselves in the mud.

All the while, Papá never held her or stroked her hair. She suspected he didn't love her.

One day, Reina asked Papá whether he was her real father. He was in his study, hermited behind a book. She touched his elbow and waited. Papá ignored her. Reina waited because it was important, because she wanted to know something for certain beyond the soothing circumference of her mother's face. She waited all afternoon, until the faint arch of a new moon was visible through the window. Then she went to bed, emptied of all suspense.

Reina couldn't mourn her father's death. By the time he put the twelve-gauge shotgun to his heart, Reina was gangly with anguish from her mother's untimely death. She had spurted nearly a foot in two years. Reina remembers the cottony smell of Sundays, the stagnant contractions of weekly routines. She wishes her sister could have given her something vital then, something to ease her grief. But all that was essential collapsed between them in those years, collapsed but did not die.

It is ten o'clock. Reina turns the dial from the frenetic weather report to the late-night edition of Constancia's favorite radio show, *La Hora de los Milagros*. Over recent weeks, Reina, too, has gotten hooked on the program. Although she doesn't consider herself conventionally religious, she's intrigued by mystical phenomena, by occurrences her sister attributes to one obscure saint or another. Reina reaches inside a paper sack for another apple and listens.

Tonight a carpenter from Elizabeth, New Jersey, calls in, claiming that Saint Joseph appeared to him while he was sanding a nightstand and gave him valuable woodworking tips. Another caller, a manicurist from Hackensack, complains that her husband, Lázarus Delgado, disappeared three days after their marriage in Saint Hilary's Church. Last night, she dreamed that he was eating a *carne asada* at the Versailles restaurant in Little Havana. The show's hostess, the flamboyant Aurora Galán, announces that dreams about *carne asada* can mean only one thing: that the caller should devote her life to God.

A news bulletin interrupts the show. It seems a third-rate invasion of Cuba is under way: a hundred or so exiles in jungle gear are attacking Varadero Beach. Reina laughs at their preposterous effort. What could they possibly be thinking? That the Cuban people will welcome them with open arms? Roast suckling pigs in their honor? Start an impromptu carnival in the streets? No matter how dissatisfied her poor *compañeros* are in Cuba, these exiles are the last people on the planet they'd want taking over.

In recent years, small propeller planes buzzed over Havana like persistent insects, dropping leaflets urging a mass uprising. If these pilots were truly interested in building solidarity with their *hermanos* in Cuba (who, incidentally, were already gagging on propaganda), they would have dropped more useful items: sewing kits or instant soup, bars of soap, even decent novels, for that matter. The leaflets, Reina remembers, were barely suitable for toilet paper. They left tenacious exclamation points on her buttocks, which, despite vigorous scrubbing, took many days to fade.

It is nearly midnight when Reina returns to Constancia's apartment on Key Biscayne. Her niece is awake, nursing her baby in the living room. Raku's mouth works rapidly, gorging on the lighter foremilk, then settles into a slower rhythm for the rest of his meal. The television is on, with no sound. Two fat men—one bald, the other sporting a squarish haircut—are poking each other in the eyes. Outside, the wind is blaring, rattling the balcony screens. The first drops of rain quickly turn into a downpour.

Reina settles opposite her niece and watches her nurse her son. In 1971, repairing electrical lines in Puerto Manatí, Reina spotted an odd configuration of cats in the bushes. Upon closer scrutiny, she saw a calico cat nursing a litter of kittens while it suckled its own mother's teats. Reina's throat, then as now, went completely dry.

When Reina gave birth to Dulcita, the nurses insisted

she didn't have enough breast milk. Reina checked herself out of the hospital and began nursing Dulcita round the clock. She loved the luxuriousness of her swollen breasts, the frank relief when Dulcita drained them of milk. Reina's body would go lax with the pleasure, her thoughts drifting back to those endless hours in her own mother's arms.

Over the years, Reina made a hobby of studying the nursing habits of mammals. Only the guinea pig, she learned, is sufficiently well developed at birth to survive without milk. At the other extreme is the pilot whale calf, which may suckle its mother for up to seventeen years. Opossum mothers, she was dismayed to discover, always have too few teats for their young, inciting a brutal fight for survival among her offspring.

A strange clay pendant hangs on a choker around Isabel's neck. She told Reina that the day she shut off her kiln, it produced for her this last token of exquisite red. Her niece said that she'd been trying to concoct this precise shade for many months. She explained how color was what she had the least control over in pottery, how the heat of the kiln, the humidity in the air, a minute or two more or less, can make all the difference in how a piece turns out.

Isabel said that during her last month in Hawaii, her studio began to have an air of neglect about it, of quasi-extinction. In a year, she predicted, liana vines would push their way through the cracks and crevices. In two years, birds would feather their nests on the tin roof, lay creamy, speckled eggs. Nothing would be left to announce that she'd once worked there, that what she'd done ever mattered.

Raku falls asleep at his mother's breast, still sucking sporadically. Gently, Isabel slips her little finger into the corner of his mouth to break the suction.

"*¿Puedo probar un poquito?*" Reina's voice is thick with longing.

Isabel doesn't seem surprised by the request. She motions for Reina to come closer.

Reina kneels and stares at the calm landscape of her niece's breasts. The nipples are large and dark brown. A few pale hairs sprout in their orbits like a faint halo. Isabel lifts a breast toward her aunt. Reina closes her eyes and breathes in the distant scent of her mother, closes her eyes and settles her lips on her past.

Silvestre Cruz

*S*ilvestre Cruz gives no forewarning of his arrival in Miami. He simply goes to La Guardia Airport and buys a ticket with some of the penitent cash his mother sent over the years. He packed nothing. Only a paperback in his pocket of Spanish Civil War poems.

> *To take the wrong road*
> *is to arrive at the snow . . .*

Now he's taking the road back, to the palms and the heat and the father he avoided for so long.

Gonzalo Cruz is in the hospital. He has a degenerative liver ailment, his mother wrote, like what alcoholics get but not caused by alcohol. Silvestre has never met his father. Mamá protected him from Gonzalo. She said that he had no interest in his only son. And it was true. Gonzalo had lived up to her words all these years.

At times, Silvestre feels an error breeding inside him, stamping every living cell, and he wonders whether he inherited this from his father. Not that it matters. According to his mother, Gonzalo is completely immune to guilt, claims zero remorse for abandoning their son. These traits seem oddly appealing to Silvestre, something he finally decided required his personal investigation.

On the morning flight to Miami, Silvestre asks himself a familiar question: What might have changed if he'd ever heard his father's voice? It was a pointless game. Silvestre knows, if he knows anything, that conjecture is less necessary than the everyday answers. After a certain point in life, nothing aimless and purely happy can happen again. Perhaps only death After all, the dead have many advantages over the living. Like being infinitely more revered.

The blast of tropical heat reminds Silvestre of his first winter in the orphanage in Colorado, reminds him because all he could think of in Denver   a city of treacherous ice and mountains and strange, anemic light—was heat. Heat and Cuba's fragrant seas. Perhaps that is why he willed the fever within him, willed the fever that revived everything that the Denver cold threatened to extinguish. Even today, Silvestre can recall the first spiking of his temperature, the glow of Cuba remembered shimmering off his skin.

While the fever had relieved the numbing chill, it also rendered him stone cold deaf. Consolation, he discovered, came with a price. Silvestre desperately attempted to conquer the damage, to discipline his other senses to make up for the unyielding silence. He strengthened his eyesight, his senses of smell and touch and taste, to fatiguing degrees.

It is not difficult to find his father. The Good Samaritan

Hospital. Where his sister's baby was born. Raku Silvestre Cruz. There's never a shortage of irony in Silvestre's life. It's something he's learned to rely upon.

Silvestre has driven only a few times in his life, but he rents a car anyway. Who would believe that a thirty-three-year-old man, deaf or not, can barely drive? Silvestre shows his driver's license to the clerk, a young Cuban with an alarmingly patriotic jacket and tie. Silvestre pays cash in advance, with more of his mother's guilt money. He doesn't plan on staying in Miami very long.

It takes him an hour of maneuvering until he feels confident enough to take the car out of the airport parking lot. For now, Silvestre decides to avoid the highways. He drives for several miles north on Le Jeune Road before realizing he must go in the opposite direction. The faded clapboard and cement houses of Hialeah are vaguely comforting to him. Here and there, he spots an outdoor shrine to La Virgen de la Caridad del Cobre.

His mother told Silvestre that La Virgen was his patron saint because his birthday coincides with her feast day. One year, she took him to the evening mass at Saint Patrick's Cathedral on September 8. Hundreds of people crowded the pews, mostly Cuban and Puerto Rican blacks and mulattos, wearing amber beads and waving yellow handkerchiefs and flags. The altars were laden with oranges and honey and elaborate fans.

Silvestre turns the car around on a side street, grazing a tin mailbox with his sideview mirror. Then he drives south, past acres of flatness and whitewashed filth, past sporadic solitary palms and the layered promises of Mediterranean roofs. The bay quivers in the distance, a soft blue-gray. A few drops of rain fall on the windshield, and Silvestre overcompensates with hazard lights and wipers on the fastest possible setting. He fears the rain might distort some essential clue.

The hospital is a monstrosity, a nightmare of angles and haphazard wings. Silvestre abhors this proximity to death. In New York, it's become all too common, almost casual, a forced acquaintance. He's been celibate since the Christmas before last. It's much easier than living with the certainty of doom.

Gonzalo Cruz is on the eleventh floor, in the ward for the terminally ill. Silvestre's mother wrote that Gonzalo has occupied this bed longer than anyone in the hospital. *Your father is a river that refuses to dry.* Out of nowhere, a fat pigeon soars down the hallway, brushing Silvestre's cheek with a shiver of feathers. Two women give chase, but the bird disappears down a dumbwaiter chute. Silvestre is startled. He wonders whether the omen is good or bad. Neutrality, he can't afford.

His father is asleep, breathing hoarsely, his face cankered and closed. He looks deserted, a dusty, uninhabited town. There are machines in his room, multicolored wires, bottles with fluids suspended from circular racks. A fax machine whirs on the nightstand next to a stack of newspapers quietly fluttering disclosures.

Silvestre closes the door. He pulls down the sheet tucked under Gonzalo's armpits and stares at the bone heap of his father's body. The belly is hard and grotesquely swollen, the legs withered and rivered with veins. One leg is noticeably shorter than the other, the knee a welter of scars.

The hospital gown skims Gonzalo's spindly thighs. Silvestre raises the hem of his father's gown until everything is visible. So this is his origin, his inheritance. His first resurrection. These hairy orbs, so huge and sagging. This limp little snout, still pink as a boy's. So this, too, is his future.

Silvestre moves closer. His breath stirs the damp triangle of gray, bewildered hair. Gonzalo shifts in his sleep, releasing decay from every crevice. His hands move as if to protect his groin, but instead he absently strokes himself with stiff, intimate fingers.

A moment later, Gonzalo awakens. He looks up and stares straight into the face of his younger self, heedless and precipitate, looks up and stares straight into the face of his only son.

CORAL GABLES

Constancia sits in the waxy air of the church. The clicking of smoking, hand-swung censers quietly meters her grief. Men in berets and guerrilla attire line the pews, cellular phones hooked to their belts. Evidence of Gonzalo Cruz's excessive life is everywhere. Women of all sizes and shades, mostly his old lovers and previous wives, cry behind their veils of mourning black. Constancia scrutinizes his teary-eyed conquests, dozens of them, in various stages of disconsolation. One woman, a gruff, bottom-heavy redhead from the Florida Panhandle, wails hardest of all.

It is the ninth eulogy of Gonzalo's funeral mass. The speaker is a self-avowed man of action—an anti-Communist freedom fighter—a frail-looking *viejito* with disordered bones. As he tenderly remembers Gonzalo "El Gallo" Cruz (*He feared nothing . . . He made the best roast pork sandwiches at the training camp . . .*), his sorrow rises above the assemblage, orbits and burns like an inconsolable planet.

> *Just as a star long extinguished continues to grace us with light, so does El Gallo continue to bestow his fire upon us. It is our duty to share this fire, to pass it from torch to torch until the world is lit with his knowledge, until the world knows of what his courage was made . . .*

Constancia is seated in a pew next to Gonzalo's second wife, Nena Prendes, an abdominous *dominicana* with a floor-length cloak of glossy crow feathers. Gonzalo's fourth wife, an exotic dancer from Venezuela named Vilma Alabarán, slips Constancia a business card advertising her new fortune-telling kiosk. Chachi Osorio, the teenager from El Salvador whom Gonzalo married last year, kneels in a back pew, wiping her eyes with paper napkins from the fast-food chicken place where she still works.

None of these women ever bore Gonzalo a child. Over the years, Constancia had heard the rumors. That his seed had turned acidic. That he burned his lovers' wombs, rendering them sterile. That after him, no woman could ever feel pleasure again. Somehow despite his reputation, women still flocked to Gonzalo, glorying in the lavishness of his transient attentions.

When Constancia heard that Gonzalo had died, she sent Silvestre a telegram: *Your father is dead. Come to Miami at once. It's finally safe to see him.* As usual, her son did not respond.

> *Gonzalo Cruz, hero, earthly saint, godfather to freedom, was murdered as he slept. There were signs of a valiant struggle. We can only imagine El Gallo's disgust at finding a pillow pressed to his face. The cowardice of his*

*enemy, Communist scourge of the earth! But we who sur-
vive will not be conquered by history's mistakes!*

Constancia considers whether the reports about Gonzalo's demise might be true. The exile radio stations are
broadcasting her ex-husband's death as the work of El
Comandante's secret agents. It was no coincidence, Radio
Así announced, that Gonzalo died the day after his long-
planned invasion of Cuba was launched. It was sabotage,
Radio Pa'llá concluded, an attempt to cut off the head of the
hawk in flight. Just as in the Bay of Pigs, Gonzalo's soldiers
were left orphans in the midst of attack.

The reports are conflicting, but this much Constancia
knows to be true: that at Varadero Beach, forty-four men in
guerrilla fatigues died storming the Hotel Bellamar. That
two French-Canadian tourists and an Italian pop star who
were trysting together in a cabana also got caught in the
cross fire and killed. That seventeen other freedom fighters
were captured by the Cuban militia with the help of the bartender—a former middleweight boxing champion named
Enrique Capote—at the Siboney Lounge. That Heberto is
among the twenty-nine missing, presumably hiding or dead.

Reina told Constancia that she was familiar with that
stretch of Varadero Beach, that she'd threaded electricity
there in the early years of the revolution, brought light to
the new tourist hotels. The beaches were strewn with Russians then, she added, beefy sunburnt men with no aptitude
for love.

Constancia had asked Reina to accompany her to Gonzalo's funeral, but her sister refused. She said she was
restoring a '57 Bel Air convertible that she had to finish that
day. "*Mira*, Constancia, if I had to stop and attend the
funeral of every man I ever slept with, I'd never get anything
done." Constancia dropped her sister off at the restoration

garage where she works. Reina was wearing her uniform: a loose orange jumpsuit with a Model T embroidered on the back. Her hands, as always these days, were blackened with grease.

Constancia wants to shatter Reina's confidence, to tell her how their mother returned to Havana eight months pregnant, big with another man's child. How the apartment in Vedado became restless then, as if the world were licked senseless by a great wicked cow. Constancia wants to tell Reina that *she* was that unborn baby, that her surname should be not Agüero but God only knows what.

A fan of light refracts through the stained-glass windows of the church, disrupting the settled shadows. How easy it is to forget the sun in here, to forget that the world isn't all refuge and trembling flame. How easily the body grows accustomed to darkness, how smoothly it ultimately adjusts. Constancia wonders whether Heberto might still be alive. If he were dead, wouldn't he have given her a sign? She finds it hard to believe that her husband would simply go off and die.

If only Heberto could see their grandson, his small, perfect glory. If only he could watch the pink ferocity of Raku's mouth. If only Heberto could hold him, Constancia thinks, he'd know his immortality was intact.

Constancia worries about Isabel too. Her daughter is adrift in a dusk of days, worn out from the rapture of loss. Isabel smells damp and cloyingly sweet, like an armful of crumpled flowers, like Reina's fading roses. To keep up her milk supply, Isabel consumes gallons of pineapple juice every day. Constancia remembers how her own breasts went dry from the fright of crossing the Straits of Florida, how nothing eased her daughter's crying except sucking on grapefruit rinds.

Yesterday two letters arrived for Isabel. One was from Austin, postmarked Honolulu but with no return address. Inside was a money order for two hundred dollars and a request for a photograph of their son. Isabel tore up the check without a word. Her daughter's resoluteness frightens Constancia, reminds her of her own impractical stubbornness. *Por Dios*, what good has it done her all these years?

The other letter, postmarked Oaxaca and trimmed with colorful stamps, was from Silvestre. Constancia had been tempted to steam open the letter, but she decided, uncharacteristically, to refrain. What was her son doing in Mexico anyway? Why hadn't he even bothered to send her a postcard? Constancia suspected that another man was involved, some terrible ignominy of the flesh.

Constancia watched as Isabel read the letter, four onionskin pages scribbled with her half-brother's childish script. She asked Constancia for an ashtray and matches, brought the flame to a corner of the sheets, and stared at the extinguishing fringe. Then she settled down on the balcony to nurse Raku, to behold another ordinary day glide by.

The murmuring in the church grows louder as the mourners at Gonzalo's funeral recite the Lord's Prayer. It is a steady, choral dissonance. Tío Dámaso used to tell Constancia that prayer is nothing more than another form of lust, a rumor in the flesh impossible to quench. She remembers a story he told her once, about how Pope Urban VIII ordered all the songbirds in the Vatican garden killed because they disturbed his concentration.

Constancia picks up a beat-up Bible from its rack on the back of a pew. Its marker ribbons are badly frayed, the corners worn aslant. She opens the book randomly for a message meant for her.

And there appeared a great wonder in heaven; a woman clothed with the sun, and the moon under her feet, and upon her head a crown of twelve stars: and she being with child cried, travailing in birth, and pained to be delivered. And there appeared another wonder in heaven; and behold a great red dragon, having seven heads and ten horns, and seven crowns upon his heads. And his tail drew the third part of the stars to heaven, and did cast them to the earth: and the dragon stood before the woman which was ready to be delivered, for her to devour her child as soon as it was born.

The procession past Gonzalo's corpse is slow and staggered with anguish. A squadron of furtive saints crowds the altarpiece. The organ music is more of a military march than a funereal hymn, but no one seems to notice. A rumbling begins near the front of the line, and Constancia soon observes why. It is starkly apparent that at the moment of his death, Gonzalo Cruz, out of great dread or desire—she supposes no one will ever know which—was fully roused for love.

Constancia stands for a moment before the body of her ex-husband. His cheeks are rouged to a false robustness. A stubble of gray hair covers his skull. Gonzalo gives off a diseased, alkaline scent, as if he'd been rescued from many leagues under the sea. In the crook of his arm is the hospital pillow the nurses found smashed against his face. Constancia considers this a macabre touch, but Gonzalo's compatriots insisted that the murder weapon be on display.

Constancia steadies herself against the coffin, leans over to better examine Gonzalo, when the world begins splintering, whirling out of place. She sags to the floor. Gonzalo's ex-wives surround her, support her by the waist. They carry her outside in a cloud of competing perfumes to the tidal heat of the church's courtyard. One by one, they splash her with holy water they bring from the baptismal font.

"So you were his first," Nena Prendes mumbles tenderly to Constancia amidst a fuss of crow feathers. "He told me he never forgot you."

It is one-thirty in the afternoon. Constancia listens as the bell in the church tower inexplicably rings nine times, listens as it echoes incessantly against the leaden sky.

Several days later, a stooped *guajiro* with a thick Camagüey accent appears at Constancia's door. His name is Evaristo Leal, and he claims to have worked on the Mestres' pig ranch before the revolution of 1933. Humbly formal, he presents Constancia with an envelope smudged with black ink. Inside is a letter from Tío Dámaso, written in 1984.

"On the day he died, your uncle sat up in bed and demanded something sweet to eat," recounts Evaristo Leal, who'd spent four years caring for Dámaso. "I brought him my month's ration of sugar and watched him eat sixty-two *cucharadas'* worth. Then he gave me this letter to deliver to you personally. He told me he didn't trust anyone else."

Evaristo Leal explained that he'd been planning to leave the country that same winter, but his departure papers were inexplicably delayed for six years.

Constancia wants to read her uncle's letter immediately, but too many images assault her at once: Tío Dámaso at the stove, stirring his plantain soup; galloping with her across fields of radiant grass; devouring guayaba paste beneath a ceiba tree (her diabetic uncle insisting all the while that his blood was safe under the sacred leaves); accompanying Constancia to her mother's funeral in 1948. Tío Dámaso lingered for hours after the ceremony, waiting for the evening star. When it appeared, a violet circle amidst the darkening blue, he pointed it out to Constancia and told her, *Don't worry, lindita, I will always watch over you.*

For the next two years, Tío Dámaso wrote to Constancia every week at her boarding school. He sent her wildflowers to press into collections and bags of freshly baked meringues. Constancia enjoyed receiving his packages, the solace of his stale scent imprinted on all his gifts. But after her father shot himself, her uncle's letters abruptly stopped. She wrote to him another year more, then concluded bleakly that he, too, must be dead.

Constancia invites Evaristo Leal in for a *cafesito*, but he declines, bowing more deeply than necessary. It is nearly ten o'clock. His daughter is waiting for him in a car down the street.

"Did you know my grandmother?" Constancia asks hurriedly.

"Doña Eugenia was a fine woman."

"Is it true how they say she died?"

"I was only a boy then." Evaristo Leal looks up at the ceiling, as if in celestial consultation. Then he tilts his head methodically from side to side. "Forgive me, señora, but my father liked to say that the Jews were right about one thing. Pigs bring bad luck."

Then he bows again and bids Constancia a good night.

Constancia carries her uncle's letter to the guest room and sits opposite the photograph of her mother. Tío Dámaso used to tell Constancia that she reminded him of his sister, Blanca. Constancia didn't want to hurt Tío Dámaso's feelings, and so she never told him how much she hated Mamá.

Mi querida Constancia,
The news is old and sad . . .

Her uncle wrote that he continued to live on the ranch after 1950, when his normally docile horse threw him against a baobab tree and left him paralyzed below the waist. After his father and brothers died, he donated the family property to the revolution, with the agreement that he'd always have a place to stay.

Tío Dámaso buried Papi's last papers there, near the site of the sarcophagus where Eugenia Mestre's remains were laid to rest. *"I could not trust myself to stay silent, as your father asked, and so I no longer wrote to you . . . Perdóname, Constancita . . ."* Her uncle spent his remaining years at the decaying ranch house, studying Latin until he could puzzle out Pliny's *Historia Naturalis*, which Ignacio Agüero had bequeathed to him with his penultimate missive.

Her father, Constancia remembers, used to expound on the incredible feats of memory Pliny recorded. How Cyrus, king of the Persians, knew the name of every one of his thousands of soldiers. Or how Mithridates Eupator ruled his kingdom in the twenty-two languages of his subjects. *Ut nihil non iisdem verbis redderetur auditum.*

Constancia turns on every light in her apartment and waits for her sister to return home. The floor lamps in the living room make huge shadow crosses on the walls. Constancia senses something arching inside her, like the time she was pregnant with Silvestre. But she took four-hour naps then, slept through the night, a baby herself. Now Constancia isn't tired in the least.

At precisely 4:22 a.m., the lights flare brightly, before blinking off. The refrigerator moans from the kitchen, starts another round of coughing. The front locks tick with keys. Reina is finally home.

"What are you doing here, sitting in the dark?" Reina sets her toolbox down in the foyer.

"I was waiting to tell you something." Constancia

studies her sister, the triangular flush of red skin strangely glowing at her throat.

"What's up?" Reina comes closer, curious.

"He wasn't your father."

"Who?"

"Papi. Papi wasn't." Constancia moves her gaze up from Reina's throat. Her sister's eyes are gentle and sad. It is not what she expected.

"You didn't think I knew?" Reina looks at Constancia a long time. Then she shakes her head and slowly walks off to bed.

The next day, Constancia, dressed in a brocaded yellow suit, meets Oscar Piñango for lunch in South Beach. He's been wanting to try out the food at La Conga's, a trendy restaurant bankrolled by a Cuban pop singer.

"The beans are too watery," he pronounces as he spoons them over his rice. "And the portions are small, ridiculous. American portions!"

Constancia orders the vegetarian plate: *yuca* in garlic sauce, sweet plantains, and the requisite black beans and rice. Everything is lukewarm, as if the management didn't want to delay table turnover by serving the food steaming hot.

"I feel envy ruling here," Oscar Piñango continues, between mouthfuls of fried pork. "Envy and greed." He lowers his sunglasses as a bevy of high school girls in neon miniskirts saunters by.

Constancia stares past the parade of tourists and cruising convertibles to the glinting expanse of sand. A brisk wind rattles the fronds of the palm trees, lifts modest curls of waves. Constancia pulls her uncle's letter from her purse and slides it across the glass tabletop.

The santero exchanges his sunglasses for a pair of bifocals he extracts from a fold of his guayabera. He reads the letter straight through, twice.

"How much time do you have?"

"Not much," Constancia says. "I'm launching Caderas de Cuba tomorrow at the Coconut Promenade. I've got two thousand bottles, but I don't think it'll be nearly enough. You know how much women hate their hips."

"Give me an hour," Oscar Piñango insists. "Follow me home. Do you think we can get a rice pudding to go?"

Constancia trails the santero's yellow Buick across the MacArthur Causeway, past the port of Miami, and onto the highway toward Hialeah. She calls the factory from her new cellular phone, checks in with her manager, Félix Borrega, on the day's progress of Caderas. "Double the output!" she shouts over the roar of traffic. "Pay overtime if you have to! I have a good feeling about this one!"

It's the last day of August, a week before the Catholic feast day of La Virgen de la Caridad del Cobre, twelve days before Oshún's Yoruban celebration. Already, Oscar Piñango has collected hundreds of pumpkins, sweet-scented candles, and a vat of orange blossom honey for his beloved saint. In a few days, his godchildren will bring him so many gifts that the room will be every inch a shrine for Oshún.

"I think I ate too fast," the santero says, after a series of resonant belches.

He accepts Constancia's impromptu offerings—her braided gold bracelet and a sampling of Cuerpo de Cuba creams she happened to have in her trunk. He smears a bit of honey on Constancia's lips and ears, on her nostrils and eyelids, the better to receive the *orisha*'s intentions.

"Time to get serious now," Oscar Piñango says as he disappears into another room. He returns with a pitcher of fresh water and a plump guinea hen. He rinses its beak and feet, then passes the bird over Constancia as she slowly turns in place.

"*Ñaquiña, ñaquiña loro,*" he chants, plucking the guinea hen's feathers. He instructs Constancia to tug the bird's throat in respect for its life sacrifice.

Constancia feels the hen's pulse against her thumb, its last quivering violence before Oscar Piñango tears off its head. He directs the blood in widening circles over the *orisha*'s sacred stones. Then he traces the pattern of blood with a thin stream of honey and sprays it all with a mouthful of rum. After the final candles are lit, he stuffs the guinea hen's carcass to bulging with candies, coconut, and toasted corn, fashioning a small nest of death.

"You will return home, disguised as night." Oscar Piñango wraps the dead hen in brown paper and lays it at Constancia's feet. "As the river flows to the sea, so does Oshún flow to her sister, Yemayá."

Then he rubs Constancia's temples with river fern and whispers a story of the gods:

> *Long ago, the sun married the moon, and they had many children. Their daughters were stars and stayed close to their mother's side. But their sons followed their father across the morning sky. Soon the father became cross and ordered his children home. The sons, small suns themselves, fell into the ocean and drowned. That is why the sun burns alone but the moon shares the sky.*

Oscar Piñango gathers his cowrie shells for the final part of the ritual. Constancia notices how the veins in his forefingers are straight and slightly raised, like perfectly sewn seams. Her father's fingers had been like that. Why hadn't she realized this before?

"How strong are the dead?" Constancia is appalled by the tenacity the deceased have for the living, by their ferocious tribal need for reunions.

"Dead is not death. It's merely a transition. Nobody is ever truly dead."

Oscar Piñango blesses the sixteen cowries, then shakes them in his cupped hands before throwing them on the mat. The shells seem to stop in midair before falling facedown. *"Se me fué el caracol de la mano."* A bad omen.

Constancia is uneasy with the implications. Oscar Piñango brings his hands together, doubles over to pray. Constancia tries to breathe with him, to find comfort in the forced rhythm of his back. She touches Tío Dámaso's letter in her jacket pocket, stares at the top of the santero's starched cap. Its whiteness seems to leak into the air like a poison.

A breeze flutters through the low-ceilinged room. The forest of candle flames stutters. Constancia stands up and begins circling in place. The breeze turns to a strong wind, dry and funneling and scented with death. It thrusts open Constancia's mouth, scorches every passageway, blasts her dry lungs hot. Her tongue shrivels in place, unhooks from her life like a dead desert lizard. Her ears roar with a harsh internal storm.

Constancia falls to the floor and grabs a nearby pumpkin, smashes it at the santero's feet. Then she aims another at the ill-omened shells, yet another at the fetish of dead guinea hen. Pulp and seeds splatter across the room, stain the hem of Oshún's gold lamé gown. Oscar Piñango is motionless. He watches as Constancia lifts a hunk of pumpkin and smears it against her face. When she tries to do the unthinkable — eat a piece of Oshún's sacred gourd — he wrestles her to the ground and ties her up with a length of electrical cord.

Quickly, he throws the cowries again to determine what to do. The pattern falls in *ofún*, where the curse was first born. He throws the shells twice more to refine the message. It doesn't waver: *oddi*, where the grave was first dug, where the grave was first dug.

The santero tells Constancia that she must go with her sister to the sacred trees by the river before returning to Cuba. That in Cuba, the secrets will lie buried in their original grave. That long ago, a streak of fire, supple as evil, had altered their lives. Then he gives her precise instructions that she must not change. "We die many times," he reminds her, "but never forever."

And when he is satisfied that Constancia is listening and adequately subdued, Oscar Piñango finally unties her and orders her from the room.

OWLS OF ORIENTE

❄

During the two and a half years that Blanca disappeared, I tried everything possible to find her. I pasted her picture in town squares, enlisted the help of the rural police, persuaded every newspaper from Havana to Guantánamo to run her photograph. In my grief, I also hired an American detective, a Mr. Frederick Noose from Tallahassee, Florida, who specialized in retrieving fugitive spouses.

After all my efforts failed, I consulted a famous santera in East Havana, a thin, mulish woman with a mild case of scrofula. Her name was Estér Salvet Llagunto, and her blue-black skin hung in folds from her skeletal frame. The santera told me that there was nothing I could do to bring my wife back, that Blanca would ultimately return of her own accord, bearing a child for the god Changó.

For a man of science, I became shamelessly superstitious. I lit candles according to Estér's instructions, brought her young

hens and a gelded goat to behead. Estér gave me a beaded neck-
lace to wear surreptitiously beneath my starched shirts. How
can I explain my weakness? When logic fails, when reason
betrays, there is only the tenuous solace of magic, of ritual and
lamentation.

I taught my university classes as usual, frequented the
requisite departmental meetings, gave lectures at conferences
that were well attended largely on account of my presence. But
I was not myself. Blanca continued to live inside me like a rest-
less river. I would have gladly chosen blindness over this
sorrow.

After Blanca left, I doted on our baby, spent hours gazing
at her as she slept. I hired a nanny, Beatriz Ureña, a cousin of
Estér's, to take charge of my daughter's daily needs. Over time,
it seemed to me that Constancia grew healthy and reasonably
happy, although she was somewhat slow to speak. My daughter
was skinny, with abundant black hair like her mother's. Her
voice had a tinge of wistfulness to it, as if she were always
wanting something.

In the second year of Blanca's absence, a marine biologist
from California came to teach in our department. Her name was
Leticia Greene, and she spoke Spanish with a Mexican inflec-
tion. I yielded to this gringa *with the short, flaming hair.*
Guiltily. Insatiably. With an acute sense of treason. I cannot
say I loved Leticia, but I am grateful to her. I believe she saved
my life, saved it longer, perhaps, than was necessary.

On May 10, 1942, in the midst of a terrible thunderstorm,
Blanca returned to our apartment in Vedado, nearly eight
months pregnant (just as the santera had prophesied). One eye
was bruised shut, and her clothes were torn and dirty, missing
buttons. She wore a single high-heeled shoe and a strand of
onyx beads that fell past her massive stomach.

I carried Blanquita, sneezing and shivering and soaked

to the bone, into the bathroom. Carefully, I washed her in a tub of warm water, perfumed every lovely swell of her body, the puzzling scar on her heel from our honeymoon. I slipped one of my dressing gowns over her head, then put her to bed in my room.

Blanca stayed there for the next month, eating red grapes and cashews and knitting a blanket with a pattern of mallards. In June, she gave birth to another man's baby, twelve pounds strong, nutmeg brown, with huge hands, and eyes that devoured the world.

Although Blanca's black spells ceased, she never again became my wife. This was difficult for me, because everything about Blanca continued to mesmerize me: The disturbing slide of her bare legs. The wealth of her loose black hair. The way her skin hoarded the morning light. And her voice. Blanca's voice left me hungry for more than I could articulate.

It is my conviction that to our dying breath we have a will, diminished though our range of possibilities may be. Even a man condemned to death can shout one last obscenity. This is our grandeur, what separates us from the lesser creatures of the planet. What, then, could be more wretched than its voluntary surrender?

I admit there were many forsaken nights when I wondered why I'd spent my heart on Blanca, why I'd let her pillage it like a common corsair. Then I simply stopped questioning. Even now, two years after her death, I love Blanca. A rich, blind, orphaned love.

After the baby was born, Blanca installed herself in the guest room again and redecorated it to suit her taste. She had the walls painted a thick flaxen yellow and draped a changing array of textured fabrics over her nineteen mongrel chairs. Then she set up a parrot named Pío on a trestle and ordered Constancia and her nanny from the house.

Beatriz Ureña left the next day, but I insisted that Constancia remain. Blanca was not pleased. She barely acknowledged our daughter, refused to address her directly. Constancia threw tantrums, tore the fabric on her mother's chairs, called her names she'd learned from the departed nanny. One day, Blanca found Constancia trying to force-feed the baby mud from a tin cup. She'd dropped spiders in the crib too, venomous ones that stung Reinita's face.

The following Saturday, my daughter and I boarded a train for Camagüey. I tried to console Constancia about spending the summer at her grandfather's ranch, but she did not care to listen. She said nothing during the trip, and in the rhythm of her silence I understood the harm I was inflicting on her.

Constancia kept to herself on the ranch, hiding in the tangled bushes to look at the storybooks I gave her. That first summer stretched into fall, then to winter and to the spring after that. I argued frequently with Blanca, but she refused to accept our daughter back. I asked Dámaso, my wife's favorite brother, to look after Constancia. And I believe, over the years, they grew close. When I visited her (always unbeknownst to Blanca), Constancia begged me to take her home. She promised to behave herself, to not hurt Reinita anymore. Soon, I would tell her. Soon. But soon did not come.

As she grew older, I began enlisting Constancia on my field trips. She proved to be an exceptional companion, watchful and adept, as her mother used to be, at catching anything with her hands.

In Havana, Blanca devoted herself to Reina's care, nursing the girl until she was ready for school. I heard the neighbors' whispering, noticed their eyes on her nutmeg skin. Reina used to climb the tulip tree in our backyard to escape their surveillance, happy amidst the shimmer of leaves and the boisterous song-birds. I cared for the girl in my way, but I never considered her mine.

One summer, when Blanca was vacationing with her daughter at a rented beach house in Guanabo, a giant mulatto, tall as a lamppost and with incalculable heft, loitered at the end of our street. He had a broad, smooth face and eyes that sug-gested a touch of Oriental blood. He was impeccably dressed, every inch tailored, and he wore a Panama hat with a broad red band. His resemblance to Reina was unmistakable.

Day after day the goliath waited, unhurried, as if time held no consequence for him. It was a blistering day in August when I finally approached him. The street wavered in the heat. I offered him an envelope stuffed with the last of my savings, nearly eight hundred dollars. He reached for the money, care-fully counted it, handed it back to me. It was then I noticed the beaded bracelet on his wrist, the unmistakable red-and-white pattern. Por favor, no vuelvas más, I beseeched him. Don't ever come back. I desperately wanted to believe that he would heed my request.

Somehow I managed to work productively during those lonely, straitened years. I published numerous books. One, on the mat-ing habits of tropical bats, is considered the definitive study on these most maligned of beasts. Another, entitled Owls of Ori-ente, analyzes the diminishing habitats of native owls in our easternmost province. To my surprise, the latter became some-thing of an academic best-seller. It was translated into English, German, and French, and acclaimed by prominent ornitholo-gists in Cuba and overseas.

Despite the Second World War and the privations, both material and moral, it imposed on our island, I received a great number of visitors in Havana, naturalists from Europe and *the United States who came to investigate Cuba's unique zoo-geography. Several herpetologists claimed that their research had been influenced by the seminal studies Blanca and I had done on our island's rare lizards and snakes. But my wife dismissed her earlier work as if it had been no more than the silly enthusiasms of an adolescent girl.*

By then, Blanca exhibited only a vestigial interest in the natural world. At dusk, she and Reina might climb a nearby belfry to watch the city's bats take flight, or stroll along the river to count centipedes. I encouraged my wife to join me on my collecting trips, but she always demurred. How I longed to offer myself to her: Take my brain, my steady hands. See with my eyes the pattern of your life. But I knew I was only being presumptuous, a self-righteous man who'd done nothing but fuss with the captivating insentience of nature when, near me, Blanquita was dying like the rarest of birds.

Occasionally, my wife consented to an excursion in our 1934 Packard, an automobile so temperamental that I decided, eventually, to trade it in for a pair of reliable horses. One Sunday, we visited the sponge markets of Batabanó, where long ago I'd taken the steamer to the Isle of Pines and where, years later, Blanquita and I had set sail for our ill-fated honeymoon. My wife bought armloads of sponges on the wharf, then suspended them with wire ("sponge clouds," she called them) from the ceiling of our living room, adding to the incomprehensible decor of our home.

Often, I drove to Pinar del Río alone. The landscape of my childhood never failed to move me: The blue rock mountains clinging with mist. The fertile earth dark with vegetation. The cheesecloth tents sheltering my father's beloved tobacco. I toured Papá's old cigar factory, but the place had lost its luster. The deafening blare of the radio and the clamorous cigar machines had replaced the rapt, papery hush of a hundred cigar rollers listening to my father as he read them a poem.

• • •

In 1948, Blanca decided unexpectedly to throw a carnival party. She invited our neighbors for blocks around. My wife, who rarely cooked, made enough arroz con mariscos to regale a hundred guests. She decorated our apartment in festive anarchy: with jasmine garlands, Japanese cranes, and intricate ornaments she fashioned herself from colored paper and foil.

On the night of the party, Blanca transformed herself into a dazzling bird. She wore a filmy pink bodice, a long swirling skirt, and a diadem of artificial jewels. Reinita was outfitted in a dragonfly costume that Blanca had sewn together from crepe de chine scarves. And I, rather too sensibly, dressed up as if for one of my cave expeditions, complete with rubber boots, a flashlight, and my fine-mesh net.

The evening got off to a riotous start as the bartender, whom Blanca hired from an establishment called Happy Pete's, served his drinks—presidentes, daiquiris, Cuba libres, and the deadly Sazarac cocktails—at thrice their usual strength. I dusted off our prehistoric turntable and played my modest collection of big-band music and Cuban dance songs from an earlier era. But the potent libations scrambled everyone's rhythms. Rumbas and guarachas were danced to Tommy Dorsey's "Boogie-Woogie," improbable jitterbugs to the most romantic danzón.

Blanca disappeared from our apartment about eleven o'clock, but returned at midnight with a crowd of gaudy revelers from the street. The party stopped, and the newcomers were assessed with suspicion. They were from Regla, perhaps, judging by the darkness of their skin.

Blanca coaxed a huge, near-naked man onto the dance floor. He was dressed in a sequined loincloth, a red velvet cape, and a towering headdress with a red stone fastened to the crown. He and Blanquita danced close, not an inch of space between them, so close they seemed an erosion, and before the song ended he pulled Blanca down the hallway without a word.

Later that night, after the last guests had trickled away, I forced open Blanca's bedroom door. The shutters in her room were flung open. Her parrot was gone from its perch. Blanca sat alone on the window ledge, as if in private discourse with the moon. She was wrapped in nothing but an unraveling mantilla.

I closed the door behind me, disentangled myself from my clothes. Then I led her to the bed. Blanca did not resist. I felt my desire striking like a slowly tolling bell. "Au pays des aveugles, les borgnes sont rois," Blanca whispered. Then she merely received me, forlorn in her dimming flesh, concealed by a thousand invisible veils.

Our last months together were relatively peaceful. It was as if my dreadful assertion the night of the masquerade ball had altered Blanca's view of me. My wife addressed me kindly again, questioned me about my work, reassessed me, it seemed, with her stark green eyes. We spoke of touring America's deserts, of searching for the blood-spurting toad. We went so far as to obtain passports, secured our visas for the United States.

Late that summer, when I told Blanca about my commission to hunt ruddy ducks for the natural history museum in Boston, she surprised me by wanting to come along.

FLOWERS OF EXILE

❀

MIAMI
SEPTEMBER 1991

The river is hardly a river at all, so still and black, its banks mostly concrete. But there's a sacred spot in its southernmost bend, a conjunction of trees, one ceiba and one palm, whose leaves and roots and surrounding ground are replete with prophecies. Reina follows Constancia, walking along the river. They're both dressed in white to deflect interferences. Reina is carrying a wooden bucket for her sister, who is balancing a platter of broken coconut on her arm. A white paste, stiff and vaguely sweet, coats Constancia's hair. She wears a knotted cloth over it for extra protection.

There are weeds in their path and half-starved bushes, foul with absorptions. Factories grind the night downriver, marking time. The air around them is slow and solid, thickening all motion. Insects Reina cannot identify hover near her face, colossal with blood. The river itself has no margins or tides, no submarine life. All fishermen extinct.

The sisters stop before the sacred zone of trees. Constancia kneels on the ground next to Reina, strokes the fallen fronds and the five-pointed leaves. There are warm spots and cold, others too hot to touch, unnecessary blanched stones. Maybe the ground is the true river, Constancia thinks, alive, pulsing with currents and destinations. She longs to scratch the dirt with her fingertips, harvest one distinct thing.

"Let's go by the river, Reina." Constancia appears taller under the moon, an elongated priestess. Her face, her mother's face, is a balcony flooded with light. Constancia begins reciting the prayers she learned at their boarding school, recites every set note of their intonations until she is crowded with grief.

> *The Lord is my shepherd; I shall not want. He maketh me to lie down in green pastures: he leadeth me beside the still waters . . .*

Reina hated those prayers, the canticles they were forced to sing at Sunday mass. She senses an electricity swilling within her, giving off random sparks. A stench like something freshly singed emanates from her skin. Reina wonders why she agreed to help Constancia, why she isn't at home with her boyfriend instead. She's grown accustomed to Russ's hands, to the steaks he barbecues for her, bleeding rare. Better yet, she should be with her niece and great-nephew, skimming the bay in Heberto's motorboat.

Here by the river, Reina thinks, she has no name. And there is only this persistent, velvety fear.

The water is remarkably clean. Reina lowers the bucket into the river with a long loop of rope. Then she unknots the white cloth from Constancia's head, and they kneel together by the river's edge.

"We travel in the family," Constancia says.

"We travel in the family," Reina echoes, as the santero directed them. Then she swings the bucket in an arc through the air and pours the languid river over both their heads.

It is four in the morning by the time Reina and Constancia set out in Heberto's motorboat from Key Biscayne. Their first stop is Key West. Constancia plans to charter a fishing boat there that will take her to Cuba.

A storm of pelicans is driving fish into shallow waters, the better to catch their prey. The birds drift and turn in tightening circles, drop to the water like fired shots. To the west, the city is a smoky exhalation of yellow, the air still turbulent from the hurricane that nearly came ashore last week.

Reina maneuvers the boat along the coast. The chronic churning of the engine is oddly bolstering to her, like a radio played for company after a lover's uncertain departure. The wind shifts this way and that, turning the sleeping sea. The exhaust from the motorboat's engine trails the sisters like a billowy spirit.

Reina is still annoyed with her sister for painting Heberto's motorboat in a garishly floral motif to promote her new perfume: Flower of Exile. Its name is immodestly trumpeted on either side of the little boat; in English on the left, and in Spanish—*Flor del Destierro*—on the right. Constancia even imbued her fragrance with a citrusy scent so that it would match the José Martí poem:

> *Que en blanca fuente una niñuela cara,*
> *Flor del destierro, cándida me brinda,*
> *Naranja es, y vino de naranjo.*

Reina feels ridiculous in this gliding advertisement for her sister. She protested the paint job *and* the historical appropriation, but Constancia remained nonplussed. "A little extra publicity can't hurt," she retorted. Reina considered repainting the boat to its former blood-orange glory, but Constancia would only accuse her of undermining her business plans.

Despite her misgivings, Constancia agreed to follow the santero's instructions and have her sister come along on the initial leg of her journey. Reina donated one of her regulation jumpsuits so that Constancia could travel incognito in Cuba, borrowed a top-of-the-line wet suit from a diver she knew, even assisted in preparing and packing the cargo Oscar Piñango specified: one large fresh shrimp-and-watercress omelet, to appease Oshún; five six-packs of orange soda; a silk Spanish fan with a copper handle, which had to remain in constant motion until they reached Key West.

On the first morning of their voyage, the santero also advised, Constancia must swim naked in the ocean for an hour, straight into the horizon. She must empty her mind as she swims, imagine herself unnamed as the sea around her, organic and anonymous. Only her arms and legs must twitch with exertion, consume the present like a fugitive. The sun, Piñango warned, might burn Constancia's skin, lift blisters on her back. But still she must swim, fixed on the distance before her.

The boat is less than a mile from the Florida coast, but to Reina it seems to have no relation whatsoever to land. The current is strong beneath them, presses them darkly through the waves. Underneath her life jacket, Constancia's white dressing gown clings to her thinly pleated ribs. Even through the padding, Reina can see that her sister's back is soft and curved as an invertebrate's.

"What do you think we're supposed to remember?" The wind nearly swallows Constancia's words.

Reina notices the tiny cleft of their mother's dispirited chin, the familiar ravaged expression. How drawn she is to it, how tempted by its promised tenderness. How easy it is to believe that their mother might still exist.

"We're supposed to remember what happened," she says irritably. It occurs to Reina that even the worst of lies, if sustained, devolve into hard, bright facts.

At the prow of the motorboat, Constancia wanly flutters the Spanish fan. The wind lifts her hair until it looks like a quivering nimbus about her head. She senses an absence in the breeze, the metallic taste of an old emptiness.

She recalls her father's face when he first told her about Mamá, his forgone eyes. Then, a year later, he confessed how she'd really died. Constancia knew for certain then that she couldn't save Papi, wonders now whether she can save herself.

"Could you ever kill yourself?" Constancia asks loudly, cutting through a swell of wind.

Reina pops open a can of orange soda, floods her mouth with its acidic sweetness. Even the most humdrum of days had a hint of a surprise, of possibility. Reina would miss that if she died. "I'd probably sooner kill someone else than myself."

"Have you ever . . . ?" Constancia wants to know what her sister is capable of, where her empathies lie.

"What?" Reina is distracted by a school of flying fish, by the unrestrained optimism of their leaping. She wonders if all their jumping serves any biological function.

"Killed someone. Have you ever killed someone?" Constancia insists.

"*Casi, casi.*" Reina recounts how she nearly murdered the mayor of San Germán once, a hirsute fellow with a mouthful of baby teeth. It was 1964. Reina didn't consider herself severe by nature, but she never said no unless she really meant it. The mayor was exceedingly lucky that she only broke his nose.

The boat pitches to the left, disrupting the ocean's tread. Constancia notices that the strip of Dulcita's skin on Reina's forearm has dulled to the color of butter. There is light enough from the half-moon to catch a flash of her own reflection. Nothing in focus, just a vague ocean promise of her presence.

Constancia leans over the side of the boat, seeking a better view of herself. She yearns for her own face, for the precise pink hue of her skin. What separates her from her mother's resemblance? What ultimately divides their blood? And to whom does she owe allegiance? All these years, Constancia thought it was to her father. She's no longer so certain.

"Animals are blind to sin," Reina says. "Mami told me that once." It was the thick of spring, and she and her mother were in the Havana woods, watching a pair of crinkly lizards mate. The male turned from green to deep purple before scurrying off into the leaves. Why is it that people rarely perceive the underlying violence of nature? Its quiet, sensational dramas? Since when, Reina thinks, has there ever been a trusting species?

"Mamá didn't drown," Constancia says flatly, bouncing hard as the boat slaps against the roughening waters.

"*¡Claro que no!*" Reina snaps. "I told you what I saw in the funeral home! You never believed me!" Reina remembers that morning, the bloody disorder of Mami's throat. Worst of all, their father offered no apology, no repentance, only his sorry, self-indulgent end. That was the darker crime. To pay his debt of flesh, and nothing more.

"Mamá shot herself. Papi told me not to tell you, Reina, that it would only make things worse." Constancia lurches backward in the tossing boat. She twists her wrist, clinging to the Spanish fan, suddenly raises her voice. "She used her own gun. She held it to her throat."

The outboard motor catches fire without warning. Smoke belches heavenward, voluminous and black. The sight inexplicably appeases Reina. Then the wind dismisses the scarring smoke. The motor dies with a last sputter. The little boat is covered with soot. It creaks and complains in the rocking vastness.

Reina calmly lifts an oar from the hull of the boat, holds it perpendicular to her neck. With both arms outstretched, she strains for the blade of the oar, tries to aim it at her own brown throat. "Mami couldn't have done it. She couldn't have reached the trigger."

Reina nestles the narrow end of the oar into her right shoulder. Points the blade straight at Constancia. Around them, the waves spangle like autumn foliage. Reina approaches her sister slowly, refines her sight to the center of Constancia's throat. Her sister's eyes are green and wary. Their mother's eyes.

"You think the dead just lie still, Constancia? *Coño*, just look at yourself."

Constancia is motionless, studies the convex edge of the oar. She'd welcome its relief, the blackmail of total peace. Then she looks up at Reina and sees something she's never noticed before. A dark mistake in the set of her face.

"Papá killed her." Reina fixes the oar on her sister, doesn't shift it an inch. "He shot her like one of his birds, and then he watched her die. Mami fell into the swamp, and he watched her die."

Constancia senses a quick alertness in her flesh. She lunges forward, sick and trembling with her father's claims. She falls, tears her dressing gown. Tries to stand again. Loses her balance. Fights to wrest away the menacing oar. Then she blindly claws at Reina's arms, leaves streaks of blood down her sister's mismatched skin.

Reina breaks the oar in two with her foot and discards the splintering halves. With one hand, she lifts her sister by the throat. To choke out the final lies. Papá's lies. Constancia's willful, stone-blind lies. Reina is sweating profusely, rivers of salt laving her face and back. A wild blood storms up from her heart. She smells the wet earth, Mami's freshly dug grave.

The sight of her sister's pale breast stops Reina cold. She loosens her grip on Constancia, drops her to the deck.

Constancia scrambles to retrieve the broken oar. She lifts the paddle end and, with all the force she can muster, brings it crashing against her sister's head. Reina falls into the ocean. Tumbles underwater for an immortal moment. Constancia tries to calculate how long it would take for her sister's body to disintegrate. To become one with the enveloping blue.

A moment later, Reina resurfaces among the silvering waves. She is shaking hard. Her head is forced back, her temple split and bleeding from the impact of the oar. The constellations seem jumbled and overburdened above, as if tired of the same senseless repetitions.

"It's all a mock history," Reina whispers. The wind oddly amplifies her words, transports a gust of her harsh scent.

Constancia grabs the silk Spanish fan. Urgently flutters it in the air, trying to dispel the smell. She fights the urge to push Reina's head underwater again. To shatter her sister's skull with the oar and call it home.

"I needed to believe him!" Constancia plants one foot on the rim of the boat. She wants a megaphone. No. Some rumbling thunder to back her up. *"¿Me oyes?"*

Above her, the sky rotates forward a degree. The half-moon presses down, robust and stained blue.

Reina is drifting away from the boat. In a few weeks, she remembers, the sun will cross the equator, and day and night everywhere will be of equal length. Then a buzzing begins inside her head, as if minute stars were vibrating in place. There's a pressure in her lungs too, like milk or mercury.

A slow warmth encircles Reina, laps at her thighs, her hips, the soft swell of her stomach. She closes her eyes. *"Así. Así mismo."* Her mouth opens and shuts of its own accord, gradually fills with sea water, with anxious moonlight.

Knowledge is a kind of mirage, Constancia decides, watching her sister drown. What could the truth subdue now that regret already hasn't?

The horizon is crimson with sunrise. Constancia drops the fan, sinks the blade of the broken oar into the ocean, paddles hard toward her sister. She hooks Reina by the collar of her sodden jacket and, with more unexpected strength, drags her back aboard. Constancia bends over, seals her sister's mouth with an open kiss. Forces in breath until Reina's chest rises and falls of its own accord.

Constancia leans back and reaches into their hamper of food. She serves her sister a hunk of the shrimp-and-watercress omelet. Then she cuts a piece for herself. It tastes good cold, she thinks, like something just fished from the sea.

CODA

A Root in the Dark

Constancia

he squall is condensing in the southern sky, querulous with an almond moon and a million stars. Constancia senses the ferment of every dying thing, the liturgy of the vast green salt. There is lightning in the distance, a radiation of clouds. The air scrawls its moist messages on her breath. Constancia touches her uncle's letter in her sweater pocket. Its damp presence reassures her.

After Reina dropped her off in Key West, Constancia hired another fishing boat and a geomancer captain she met at the Blue Cockatoo Bar. "I could've been a water diviner," he said, his only joke, before lapsing taciturn. Constancia is grateful for his silence at the helm. The journey to Cuba is long, and there's so much else to listen for.

Heberto is dead. Constancia heard this yesterday on Radio Así. She's not surprised, although the odds against his dying within a week of Gonzalo must be high. She consoles

like mother

herself with the knowledge that matter never expires, only takes unforeseen new disguises. Heberto, Constancia expects, soon will send her a sign.

The storm gets closer, unleashing a warm-colored rain. The horizon is a confusion of light and fog. Constancia feels a dry gnawing at her center. She's eaten very little in the past two days, since she and her sister uneasily took leave of one another at the Mallory Wharf. Each time Constancia thinks of that night, of Reina collapsed to mere flesh in the ocean, it takes away her appetite.

But suddenly Constancia's hunger is enormous, like a beast's crude need for a mate. There are ham sandwiches in the cooler and a six-pack of Mexican beer. Constancia unscrews the cap of a gold-labeled bottle, puts it to her lips, tilts back her head. Then she eats four of the sandwiches in quick succession and a bunch of overripe grapes. She'll need all her strength, she decides, for the landing ahead.

The boat is aimed at Varadero Beach. Constancia is convinced, and the captain agrees, that the Cuban militia won't expect invaders twice in the same place. Yet another one of Reina's lovers, a politically savvy buildings inspector named Calixto Peón, has agreed to be Constancia's guide in Cuba for a day or two. She wants to claim Heberto's body first, have his bones burnt to a portable ash. How can anyone refuse her that?

Constancia considers what rites she needs to perform with her husband's remains, what prayers to offer to Oshún. But no ordinary dispersal seems right. Perhaps she'll simply carry Heberto from town to town until she reaches Camagüey.

Papi's papers are buried there, under the Mestre farmhouse. The house in which her mother was born, the house of the grandmother who'd been pig-trampled to death. Tío Dámaso wrote that he'd concealed Papi's memoirs in a copper chest lined with yellow felt. Every few years, he would dig up the chest and read them again. Her uncle claimed he didn't know why Constancia's father had sent him this last testament.

Constancia balances on the deck of the rolling boat. She tries to stand without support, but she's thrown face forward when a wave slams aft. It would be so easy to offer herself to this wind, to become one with the ocean, surrender herself to each harsh element. No mission but existence and cycle. Laws greater than any one sad thing.

Constancia checks the boat's location on the captain's nautical map. They could veer sharply left and miss Cuba altogether. Past the Santaren Channel and the Great Bahama Bank, through the Mayaguana Passage to the wide open ocean. But the earth, she thinks, is too small to contain the escape she wants to make.

The captain announces that they're near the Tropic of Cancer, that there's often good bonefishing here. Constancia wants to ride the imaginary tropic around the planet, compulsive as a satellite, ride it and ride it until there's no longer any reason to stop.

The Sabana Archipelago is visible in the distance, guarding the hazy lights of Cárdenas Bay. The captain confirms her pickup for exactly one week from today. She can't risk being away from the factory any more than that. If she doesn't show up, for whatever reason, Constancia insists, he must return every Sunday until she reappears.

Constancia prepares herself, squeezes into her slick black diving suit. In a waterproof satchel, she's packed Reina's old Cuban jumpsuit, retailored to fit her, a pair of rubber-soled boots, two thousand dollars in cash, her makeup kit, a cellular phone, and a canteen of fresh pomegranate juice. The captain assists her with her flippers, then holds the ladder steady as she descends into the sea. Constancia is exactly three miles from the Cuban coast. Three miles from all the answers she desires most.

Dulce

MIAMI

It was hell to get here. I needed seven hundred dollars for the flight, and so for three endless days, I resorted to my old Havana tricks. I try to tell myself it doesn't matter, that it's always a means, not an end. But when the hell will I ever stop needing the means?

I never worked so hard for so little. I tried to think of each bed as a desk, a place of calculation, each body as a collection of unrelated parts. Here a hideous metatarsal, there a trapezius rippling with knots. Anything to provide the necessary distance. Again and again, I soldered myself into those deadening men, approximating lust.

One *madrileño*, with a sword tattooed on his chest, insisted I impersonate saints. He told me that I was the spitting image of Saint Elmo, patron saint of sailors. Hardly a compliment, I thought. In stormy weather, Saint Elmo's fire can sometimes be seen from airplanes and ships. It's a

flaming phenomenon, he explained, resembling a brush discharge of electricity. Strangely enough, my next two clients
complained that I gave them electric shocks. Each time they
touched me, I sparked.

It's chaotic in Miami, and that's saying a lot after what
I've been through. My Tía Constancia took off for Cuba last
week, so I haven't met her yet. Meanwhile, Mamá is threatening to paint my aunt's apartment black. Everything black
but the wide ocean view. She wants to paint Abuelo
Ignacio's dead birds too. All she says by way of explanation
is that the time for mourning is long overdue.

I tell Mamá I'm tired of doing the contrary, the
everyday outlawed things. In the end, I say, it's the worst
kind of predictability. But I don't think she understands.
Lately, all she wants to do is comb my hair, two tight braids
down my back, like when I was a kid. Mamá winds flowers
through my hair, violets she snips on the sly from clay pots
at the supermarket. And she sings American songs nonstop.
I don't understand the words, but her voice sounds off to
me, like the discontented peacocks I saw once at the Barce-
lona zoo.

"I want you to have a baby," she announces at
breakfast. Mamá fries three eggs for me, heats up a slab of
honeyed ham. She claims she's trying to build up my energy
for the pregnancy ahead.

"Por favor," I sneer, "I'd rather be struck by lightning."

Mamá gives me a wounded look. I know I'm being
insensitive, but if I don't exaggerate, she never gets the
point. Fuck it, I don't want my body permanently entangled
with another's. I don't tell her, either, that I've been bleeding in between periods for months. Enough blood to fill a
small sink.

I dip a piece of ham into the egg yolk. It's delicious.

After my starving in Spain, everything here tastes so good. I've gained six pounds this week alone. I have to lie flat on my back to zip up my jeans.

"I'd take care of your baby, *mi amor.*" Mamá stops, fixes her eyes on mine. "I'd pamper him to death."

Yesterday Mamá bought me leather cowboy boots at a place called Parrot Jungle, where the birds walk tightropes and eat seeds from your hand. My boots, tooled with canaries at the ankles, are a size larger than the ones Mamá bought for herself. She's convinced that if we sleep every night in our identical boots, we'll finally know what to do. I tell Mamá, as nicely as I can, to stop wasting her dreams on me.

My cousin Isabel is here with her baby, Raku. They float through the rooms together like a pair of anemic ghosts. The little boy bleats as if he were part goat. Isabel hardly speaks. She drinks pineapple juice all day from a plastic cup with a built-in spiral straw. Mamá tells me that my cousin is heartbroken, her anguish only barely interruptible, that it kicked in after the baby was born. There's something incurable in Isabel's eyes. I wonder sometimes, looking at her, which might be worse: to know her misery, or to never know it at all.

Last week, I checked out Tía Constancia's factory to see if I could work there, do something legitimate for a change. My aunt makes weird lotions for cellulite and sagging everything. The air was so dense with perfume that it gave me an instant headache. The manager, a Cuban guy with a Beny Moré–style mustache, seriously looked me over, then invited me out for lunch. For about a day, I harbored plans of taking over the factory, of making a million dollars in no time flat. I'd buy one of those oceanfront fortresses, build a tennis court and a helipad, have a foot massage every night. What is it about this city that fosters such empty delusions?

Then Mamá suggested that I help her rebuild carburetors at her restoration garage. She says that my hands are talented, underutilized (if she only knew). But working with her is the last thing I'd want to do.

Today I found a job at a sandwich shop. It's on Crandon Boulevard, a few blocks from Tía Constancia's condominium on the beach. I think it'll be okay for now. The owner, Nestor Vallín, was a famous Cuban volleyball player in the fifties. When I recognized him, he hired me on the spot. "The Cubans own everything in Miami," he told me proudly, working the silver meat slicer. Nestor is teaching me how to make a *medianoche*—the precise proportion of pork to ham to cheese, quick smears of mayo and mustard, three slivers of sour pickle, all grilled to melting perfection on a hunk of crusty bread.

I ate a sandwich like that once in Cuba, years ago, before the hard times hit. It made me realize how close we are to forgetting everything, how close we are to not existing at all.

Constancia

Constancia hitches a ride on the back of a military truck just outside Sancti-Spíritus. The transportation was arranged for her by Reina's old flame Calixto Peón. The truck is empty except for a metal cabinet secured with a rusting lock. There could be anything inside, rifles or auto parts or butchered hens on their way to the black market. Four days in Cuba, and nothing surprises Constancia anymore. Four days in Cuba, and, thanks to the burly Calixto's assistance, half her mission is done.

The central highway cuts through an arid plain dotted with royal palms. Constancia searches the skies and the trees for the rare birds she remembers, but she spots only vultures and doves, a family of finches in a lone coral tree. The truck jumps violently with every bump and pothole. Constancia squats in place to cushion the jolts.

Soon they cross two rivers toward vast fields of sugarcane. The soldiers stop for a *guarapo* by the roadside, and Constancia treats them all to the treacly cane juice. Everywhere she looks, the green stalks sway, crowned with ripening flowers. Here and there, a clump of shacks breaks the waving monotony. In a month, when the harvest begins, the fields and sugar mills will exhale a sweet black smoke.

It's late afternoon by the time the soldiers drop Constancia off in Camagüey, in front of the colonial cathedral near Agramonte Park. She's glad to stretch the journey from her legs. Enormous *tinajones* filled with rainwater occupy several street corners. Constancia buys a warm soda from a roving vendor and hunts for the hotel Calixto recommended.

Her supply of dollars is getting dangerously low. Constancia has spent nearly all her money to get her this far. From the moment she emerged shivering from the sea at Varadero Beach, it seems there's been nothing but bartering and bribes.

Mostly, she's let Calixto do the talking. She feared that her accent, her obsolete language, would betray them both. What she didn't realize was that her appearance would give her away time and again. Her skin is too smooth by local standards, too protected from the sun. Her makeup is flawless, her nails manicured. When El Comandante kicks the bucket, Constancia speculates, just imagine all the lotions and creams she could sell!

It's a mark of the island's privation, she thinks, that not a single person has turned her down. Even Constancia's most outlandish requests have been met, like exchanging her wet suit and flippers for her husband's rigid corpse. The coroner told her that Heberto arrived at the morgue dead but not wounded. Most likely, he'd died of a hemorrhage or heart attack. She thanked the coroner, then paid him six hundred dollars to cremate her husband clandestinely.

The only thing Constancia hasn't managed to do is get

through to home. Her cellular phone doesn't work from Cuba. And there isn't a fax machine for miles. Even the ordinary telephone lines are either busy or irreparably dead. She hopes Isabel and Raku are holding up, with Reina in charge. That the factory doesn't fall apart, with her gone.

Constancia pats her waterproof satchel to make certain Heberto is still inside. His remains, a half pound of irregular gravel, are stored in her emptied cold cream jar. Constancia is disconcerted by Heberto's final condition. She'd expected him to look softer, pinker, like a high-grade face powder. Not this handful of gritty shards, this irreducible bone.

Constancia wanders down Maceo Street and checks into the Gran Hotel. The clerk tells her that the pipes are broken, so there won't be any water tonight. And his phone, unsurprisingly, hasn't worked for weeks. But the dining room is open, he says, with a tremor of Saint Vitus' dance, and for a change, there is plenty of *malanga* and pork chops to eat.

"Calixto sent me," Constancia says quietly. She pays the clerk ten dollars for his torn map of the province and makes of him an instant friend. "I need a reliable car and a workman's shovel at dawn," she continues. "A hundred dollars for the day. *Sin preguntas y sin compañía.*" Then she climbs the stairs to her room.

The sun is just setting, and Constancia pulls a chair to the window to watch. The colors disrupt the sky like something merciless spilled. It occurs to her that night and day are nothing more than a pair of alternating thieves. It's impossible for her to recall her life before this trip. It all seems a perishing dream. Is she really a grandmother now? Is her son lost in Mexico? How did she spend her evenings? What did she used to eat?

Constancia loosens her clothing and settles into the flat-mattressed bed. She wants to be rational, map out the morning's plan. But the closer she gets to her strange inheritance, the more it feels unreal. It's as if every moment in Cuba is absorbing many times its weight.

She opens her cold cream jar and shakes Heberto loose on the sheets. She takes an opaque shard and holds it up to the light. Then she places the piece on the tip of her tongue and slips it in her mouth. Constancia wishes it would dissolve completely, reveal to her something significant. But stubbornly, just like when he was alive, Heberto remains maddeningly inert.

Reina

There is a lazy curve of Key Biscayne saturated with pines and papaya trees. The
fruit is in season, fat and lush, garlanded
with open-mouthed flowers. Reina plucks several papayas
from a female tree and splits the skins with her teeth. She
offers the meat to her lover, Russ, and licks the juice from his
unshaven chin. Then she pulls on the swinging stalks of a
nearby male tree. Its fruit is small and contains no seeds but
tastes just as intensely sweet. Reina settles into the back of
Russ's '56 Nash, the one with the fold-down seat.

Around them, the night vibrates its tropical din. The
moon is high, just shy of full, coaxing the ocean in its
monotony dance. A soft wind stirs the pines, carries the passions of insects on its back. Reina sees a three-legged rac-
coon peering down at her from a tree. Its paws daintily clean
its spectator face. Behind it, the stars are distant pinpoints, a

useless map of light. The city seems farther still, crouched low against the horizon.

Hip-to-hip against Russ's hold, Reina sears his skin electric. She is fastened to this immediate love, but her malaise persists. Reina closes her eyes and loses herself in a reverie. She is naked and willful and four times her normal size. She's gorging on fruit—massive pineapples and mangoes, breadfruit, star apples, and soursops—trapped and glistening on raw platters of light. One by one, Reina tears off their monstrous rinds, swallows each whole as a century. Russ is motionless beneath her, his head dropped back from the heat and release.

Reina opens the back door of the car and walks toward the ocean. The moon is a shadow on her spine, unloosed from its slot in the sky. As she wades waist-deep into the sea, it slides across her naked shoulders, down her slow brown throat. She is a river of sinew and muscle now, forcing the moon toward her will. Finally, Reina senses the moon sinking within her, lowering itself in her womb. She arches her back, and a tiny clot quickens in the storm of moist lightning, quickens until the first fragile tendril takes root. It shatters the dense heavens within, brings Reina a wave of contracting, immaculate pleasure.

She lifts her eyes and finds the moon fully restored in the sky. It is midnight. The tent of stars, unmoved, stares on. Tonight, Reina knows, she will sleep deeply, a complete, satisfied sleep. In another month, the bit of flesh at her center will grow to a delicate skeleton, to the size of a hummingbird. Already, Reina feels it fluttering in its net of blood, fluttering its steady work toward eternity.

Constancia

CAMAGÜEY

Twenty-nine *vintage automobiles* are double- and triple-parked before the Gran Hotel at dawn. Word has spread of the crazy exile lady's request. All the men shout to Constancia at once, praising their outmoded cars. She is furious at the clerk's indiscretion, but she must seize this chance nonetheless. Constancia only hopes the local police don't get wind of her presence. Rapidly, Constancia surveys the Chevys and Plymouths, the Fords and the Oldsmobiles. Then she spots the black Packard from the thirties, like the one her father used to drive, and decides at once to rent it.

The old Mestre ranch is fifteen miles outside Camagüey. Constancia lurches along a dusty road, upsetting chickens and meandering goats. Above her, the sky is rubbed a preternatural blue, so blue it seems impossible that clouds exist. Children scamper in the dirt, whistling for a ride as she passes. Cattle snort in the fields. *Guajiros* in pointed straw hats amble along on mules. This is a world preserved, Constancia thinks, a landscape where every origin shows. For the first time in her life, she's grateful it's a part of her past.

Tío Dámaso wrote to her that the Mestre farmhouse is easy to miss these days. It's a broken sketch of a place. No porch or roof to speak of, weather-beaten and worm-eaten, with shutters hanging loose. The best way to find it, her uncle advised, was to search for the cloud of bees that always hovers over the place. Long ago, he said, Eugenia Mestre's sarcophagus was taken apart by pilgrims and miracle seekers. A piece here, a piece there, until nothing was left of her tomb. He couldn't stop the thefts. Worst of all, no one knows what became of his mother's remains.

Constancia slows through a village of thatch-roofed homes. A procession is under way. All the girls wear yellow dresses, have flowers braided through their hair. The boys, also in yellow, carry a statue of their beloved patron saint. Others offer pumpkins and strands of amber beads to La Virgen de la Caridad del Cobre. Constancia is surprised by the celebration. She didn't know public displays of devotion were still permitted in Cuba. She waits quietly as the feast day parade winds its way down the road. Suddenly, she remembers that it's her son's thirty-fourth birthday.

Although it's only early morning, the heat is a steady pressure against her skin. Constancia idles in her Packard along a stretch of deserted dirt road. She keeps imagining she sees her uncle's mirage of whirling bees, but each time she stops, the vision mysteriously disappears. Constancia rolls down her window and decides to listen for the bees without any visual distractions. The road is straight and empty ahead, and so she creeps along with her eyes shut tight.

At first, Constancia hears nothing, only her temples pulsing with blood. It is soothing to rest her eyes in their

sockets, to dismiss all this blinding light. Then a droning filters toward her from the south. The Packard strays off the
road and hits a stone fence, crumpling its front fender.

Constancia is startled by the sudden curtain of light. She
shields her eyes and spots what looks like a heap of bleached
bones in the distance. The past is a wilderness, she thinks, as
she approaches the abandoned farmhouse. High above it, a
wreath of bees furiously rotates. Faster and faster the bees
spin, until they're no more than a wheel of dark yellow. Then,
as abruptly as they appeared, the bees reel out of sight.

Inside the farmhouse, the wood gives way under Constancia's feet. The floor is so weak, in fact, she fears she'll be
absorbed in its rotting undertow. Constancia dislodges the
crumbling floorboards with her sturdy farmer's spade,
methodically at first, then wildly as her impatience grows.
The heat strangles from all sides, until Constancia is salt
damp and exhausted with purpose.

She stops for a moment and leans on her shovel. Scraps
of colored satin flutter in through the window, sustained by
an imperceptible breeze. Then, like a sinuous rumor, she
senses where she must search. Constancia digs outside in the
dictated spot, tunnels a wound in the earth until she hits
the copper box.

Her uncle left it unlocked for her. Inside, nestled in felt,
is a paring knife, a box of matches, a faded flannel pouch
containing a worn bit of bone, and the stack of her father's
last papers. Constancia slips the little bone from its pouch,
fingers its knotted end as she begins to read. Papi's writing is
neat, legible, crisply formal—intended, it seems, for no one
in particular.

My name is Ignacio Agüero, and I was born in the
late afternoon of October 4, 1904, the same day, my
mother informed me later, that the first President of

the Republic, Estrada Palma, arrived in Pinar del
Río for a parade and a banquet and a long night of
speeches at the governor's mansion. . . .

Constancia reads Papi's words carefully, reads and reads them again, until only the stars are left to clarify the sky. The little bone, she decides, she will take home to her sister.

THE HUMMINGBIRD

I did not plan what happened in the Zapata Swamp. You must understand this. One moment, my wife was standing at the edge of the morass, wiping a wisp of hair from her cheek. The next, a most extraordinary bird hovered into view. It trembled in the air above Blanca's helmet, between the limbs of a hammock tree. A glittering jewel, no bigger than the tip of my thumb.

I do not recall taking aim, only the fierce recklessness of my desire, the press of the twelve-gauge shotgun against my shoulder, the invitation from the bird itself. I moved my sight from the hummingbird to Blanca, as if pulled by a necessity of nature.

It was noon, and the sun was unsparing. The air shuddered with the sound of my shot. Our horses, tethered to a tangle of mangroves, snapped their restraints and sank into the swamp without a trace. In an instant, the future spread before me, a thin permanent season.

The day stole past in an hour. Clouds scrolled by, dragging their shadows across the watery land. I heard Blanca's voice in the stirring of grasses and reeds, in the crisscrossing cranes overhead, in the swaying clumps of cow-lily leaves. All afternoon the Zapata clicked and rustled, clicked and rustled its fatal chorus, until a lone red-tailed hawk soared above us.

I held my Blanquita. I held her. A mournful, bitter pleasure. Then, in the broken violet light of dusk, I carried her seventeen miles to the nearest village and reluctantly began to tell my lies.

ACKNOWLEDGMENTS

My profound thanks to Richard Gilbert and Ana
Sanchez-Granados for their kind and unwavering
sustenance. To my friends Wendy Calloway, Mona
Simpson, Mary Morris, Eric Wilson, and Bob An-
toni for their generous insights and enthusiasm.
And to Laura García, Norma Quintana, and especially to José Garriga for all the precious rest.

Special thanks, too, to Ellen Levine, Sonny
Mehta, Jenny Minton, and Louise Quayle for their
exquisite and myriad attentions. And, finally, to the
John Simon Guggenheim Memorial Foundation,
the Mrs. Giles Whiting Foundation, the Council of
Humanities at Princeton University, and the Cintas
Foundation for invaluable support.

The Agüero Sisters

CRISTINA GARCÍA

A Reader's Guide

A Conversation with Cristina García

Q: **What served as the inspiration for this story?**

A: One event that served as an inspiration was a visit, many years ago, by my Cuban aunt to my mother in Miami. It was supposed to be a six-month honeymoon reunion for the two of them but it ended after only a month with much acrimony on both sides. I didn't witness the reunion, but for years afterward I heard each sister complaining about the other. That got me thinking about what happens to siblings and family when they've been apart for a long time and how they go about reconciling what divided them in the past and in the present. I also became interested in Cuba's natural history. Studying it became another way to explore loss, extinction, and the nature of memory.

Q: **How would you describe the themes of your latest novel?**

A: It is a story that explores how family myth evolves and how history is made. This is a subject that has always fascinated me—particularly when it comes to Cuba—because there are always so many different versions of the truth. In *The Agüero Sisters*, I tried to develop a narrative where there were many conflicting realities that had to be reconciled. I wanted to see what survived from this while also considering the ongoing dialogue between memory and loss. This story also gave me an opportunity to explore the extent to which the past continues to inhabit the present and how we transform the past to accommodate it with our current sense of self. How do we live with the past? How do we tailor it so we can go about living our daily lives?

Q: **You were born in Havana but moved with your family to New York when you were two. Do you have any memories that survive from those early years in Cuba?**

A: None whatsoever.

Q: **You first began traveling to Cuba when you were in your mid-twenties. How did that change you?**

A: Going back to Cuba was instrumental in the resurgence of my own Cuban identity, which really didn't take hold until I began writing fiction. There's something in the excavation process that one goes through in creating a book that allowed me to reach areas that I didn't even know existed within myself. The Cuban aspect of my identity has, to my surprise, become my wellspring. It is now an indelible, strong, and very visceral part of my identity.

Q: **The theme of mystical religion—in this case santería—plays a large part in this novel. Has it played a large part in your own life as well?**

A: It didn't when I was growing up, but in recent years—particularly during my trips to Cuba—it is something I have explored. I happen to have a cousin in Cuba who is a santera. Through her I've had the privilege of access to santería ceremonies and to an intimate discussion about the daily living of that religion. Santería was publicly disdained for a long time in Cuba and dismissed as a form of African mysticism. It is, in fact, a very powerful force in the daily lives of millions of Cubans.

Q: **Many reviewers have described you as a "magical realist." How would you define magical realism?**

A: To be a magical realist, from my point of view, is to use reality as a departure point for the imagination. It means having a lack of imaginative inhibition and taking reality to its furthest possible extreme—and then some. In many ways it's harder to do than realism. You have to be that much more specific if you're going to have your readers suspend their disbelief. The specificity, texture, and detail that you need in order to pull it off is much more demanding than that needed for a book that merely records daily events.

Q: **Do you consider yourself a magical realist?**

A: There are definitely surrealistic elements in my books, and I'm definitely influenced by magical realism as it exists in contemporary Latin America fiction and elsewhere. My first encounter with magical realism, however, was with Kafka's *Metamorphosis*. There are stories with magical and mystical events from many cultures and traditions. And although all traditions contain some elements of mysticism, I find those of South America to be particularly baroque and lush.

Q: **In exploring the reasons Ignacio Agüero murdered his wife, one reviewer has written, "Blanca betrays her husband...but he is so much under her spell that only by killing her can he break free." Do you agree with this interpretation?**

A: I won't dispute that interpretation any more than I would dispute fourteen other interpretations that I've read. I wanted to leave readers to draw their own conclusions when it came to deciding why Ignacio murdered his wife. I'm not really sure myself as to what ultimately pushed him to pull the trigger. It was a confluence of many events at that precise moment that made the murder inevitable. If the moment had come five minutes later, maybe he wouldn't have pulled the trigger.

Q: **Various chapters of this novel are written from various perspectives. Was it difficult moving from one "voice" to the next?**

A: I like using different voices to tell a story because I find it creates a varying texture for the narration that you don't get if you use a monolithic omniscient voice. A multiplicity of voices is also a more effective way to surround what I'm trying to get at in my stories.

Q: Does the sisters' eventual reconciliation, and the unraveling of the mystery surrounding their mother's death, imply the possibility of a national reconciliation?

A: That wasn't my intention but I certainly see how one could interpret it that way. I personally would love a national reconciliation, but that wasn't the aim of this book.

Q: There was a lot of media attention paid to the Pope's visit to Cuba in 1998. What are your impressions of that visit and what do you think it accomplished?

A: I think the Pope highlighted the societal downside of the revolution and what the revolution has done to families and to people's priorities in Cuba. When I visited Cuba, I was dismayed at the utilitarian nature of many relationships. It's almost as if leaps of faith, true romance, even basic optimism, are in short supply there. Cuba can be a rigid, closed off country. That's been changing a lot because of tourism. But the kind of access or exposure provided by tourism is not necessarily the best thing for a developing society. I hope the Pope's visit will create a bridge that will ultimately reconnect Cuba to the rest of the world.

Q: Your debut novel received much critical attention including a National Book Award nomination. One reviewer recently characterized you as "a new star in the American literary firmament." What sort of pressure comes with that kind of success?

A: I never realized how successful my first book was. I was pregnant when *Dreaming in Cuban* was published and gave birth six months after it first hit the bookstores. As a result, I was rather preoccupied. It wasn't until *The Agüero Sisters* came out that I did a real book tour, met a number of my readers, and began to fathom the impact of my work. Having said that, however, I must admit that I did feel quite a bit of pressure to follow up with a strong second novel. My efforts in that direction became a struggle. In fact, *The Agüero Sisters* is my third book. I worked for two years on another novel that I eventually decided to shelve.

Q: **How does the writing process work for you?**

A: I work in a small office outside my home that has no telephone or means of communication with the outside world. Ideally I try to put in six hours of writing per day but I rarely accomplish that. Usually I end up getting four or five hours of writing time per day. The key, for me, is that I make my time and space inviolate. I allow no visitors and no one knows where I am. It's only when I know I won't be disturbed for several hours on end that things begin to coalesce. At home I get too distracted. There are too many interruptions. I need that inviolate time and space to work.

Q: **Do you ever suffer from writer's block?**

A: I did with that moribund second novel. At one point, I was stuck for months. That's because the book wasn't viable. I knew it, but it took me a long time to admit it. *Dreaming in Cuban* had been percolating inside me since the early 1980s. I gave it all I had. But I didn't realize how depleted I was after it was finished—a depletion that was compounded by having a child. When I began *The Agüero Sisters*, after taking time off and struggling with the second novel, I feared that *Dreaming in Cuban* was the only book I had in me. So I decided to write *The Agüero Sisters* as a book for myself. I let it develop organically. I didn't invest it with all the anxiety and pressure that I had felt while working on the follow-up to my debut novel. As a result, the writing became pleasurable once more and created its own momentum.

Q: **What advice do you offer for the young writer who is just starting out?**

A: You need to carve out, and protect, uninterrupted time for yourself on a daily basis. Getting in the habit of taking time seriously is important because time is the ultimate factory for these novels. They don't get written without it. And you have to be comfortable with solitude because novel writing is not a collaborative process. Party animals need not apply when it comes to being a novelist.

Reading Group Questions and Topics for Discussion

1. Why do you think García chose to write this book using several voices and perspectives? With which characters do you most closely identify? Do you think this use of multiple narrators interrupts the flow of the story or enriches it?

2. How do you think the Agüero sisters' feelings about their own childhood and their parents have affected their relationships with their husbands, their own children, and each other? What things do the sisters have in common? What sets them apart from each other?

3. How would you compare and contrast the different styles of femininity displayed by the two sisters in this story?

4. Why do you think Ignacio Agüero killed his wife? How do his lies about that event affect his children?

5. When they were children, Reina tried to tell Constancia what she had learned about the death of their mother but Constancia steadfastly refused to listen. Why do you think she so desperately needed to believe her father's version of that event?

6. One reviewer wrote, "Blanca betrays her husband, but he is so much under her spell that only by killing her can he break free." Do you agree with this interpretation of the events that led to Blanca's death?

7. Each sister seemed to be loyal to only one parent. Why do you think this was the case? How were allegiances formed within the Agüero family? What allegiances exist within your own family? Are you closer to one parent or another? How about your own siblings? Are they closer to one parent or another?

8. Which of the two sisters do you see as more dominant—Reina or Constancia? Does that change after their final, physical confrontation?

9. Why do you think Reina has made herself the keeper of her father's books and specimens? Her lover has asked her to clear these relics from their love nest but she has refused. Why?

10. Why do you think Constancia wakes up looking exactly like her own mother? What affect does this have on her and, later, on Reina?

11. Much of this story focuses on family themes and the bitter schism that exists between members of the same family. Have you ever experienced similar divisiveness in your own family or observed it in other families? If so, how have you dealt with those divisions?

12. What surprised you most about García's depiction of life in Cuba and among the exile community in Florida?

13. *The Agüero Sisters* focuses on the difficulties that arise when confronting the truth. Have you ever found yourself in a situation where you've had to confront a difficult truth? How do you go about letting go of an old reality in favor of a newer truth?

14. What's the difference between García's presentation of male versus female characters? Do you see García's male characters as fully developed individuals?

15. What role does mysticism play in the lives of both Constancia and Reina?

16. Why do you think Reina takes her father's twelve-gauge shotgun and tosses it into the sea? Reina walked away from an opportunity to defect from Cuba in the mid-1980s. Why do you think she changed her mind and decided to leave the country in the early '90s?

17. Why do you think Heberto decided to join a revolutionary group planning another invasion of Cuba? What does Constancia think of his decision?

18. What motivates Silvestre to kill Gonzalo?

19. What do you think goes through Constancia's mind as she finally reads her father's diary and receives confirmation of Reina's story about the death of their mother?

ABOUT THE AUTHOR

CRISTINA GARCÍA was born in Havana and grew up in New York City. Her first novel, *Dreaming in Cuban*, was nominated for a National Book Award and has been widely translated. Ms. García has been a Guggenheim Fellow, a Hodder Fellow at Princeton University, and the recipient of a Whiting Writers' Award. She lives in California with her daughter, Pilar.

Excerpts from reviews of Cristina García's
The Agüero Sisters

"An extraordinary new novel does justice to the Cuba of history as well as the Cuba of imagination....García has crafted a beautifully rounded work of art, as warm and wry and sensuous as the island she so clearly loves."

—*Time*

"In 1992, Cristina García's *Dreaming in Cuban* announced the presence of a new star in the American literary firmament.... García's remarkable second novel, *The Agüero Sisters*, is even better, a deeper, more profound plunge into the mysteries of loyalty, love and identity (national, familial and otherwise)....Cristina García again proves herself a gifted chronicler of exile's promise and peril."

—*Newsday*

"Five years after her debut, the former journalist has made good on her early promise with a superb second novel, *The Agüero Sisters*....With sensual prose and a plot that captures the angst of the Cuban diaspora...García seductively draws us in and refuses to let go."

—*Newsweek*

"The conventions of magic realism can either amplify the story and give it resonance or fragment the narrative, draining it of clarity. García's beautifully written second novel...seems to embody both extremes....Her prose is lush and rhythmic, so that the novel has an almost feverish air."

—*Booklist*

"A bold and very richly detailed portrait...Fluid, graceful, and extremely rewarding: a work of high seriousness and rich detail."

—*Kirkus Reviews*

The Agüero Sisters

"Cristina García neatly sidesteps the curse of the much-feted first novel...with the assured *The Agüero Sisters*, a vibrant tale of a repressed Manhattan cosmetics saleswomen and her sexy, Havana-based sister that blends family, culture, and García's shapely prose into a rich, velvety world one is loath to leave."

—*Elle*

"This is no paint-by-numbers allegory. García's characters are three-dimensional and her novel is filled with rich and compelling detail."

—*San Francisco Chronicle*